I'll Be Slaying You

I'll Be Slaying You

CYNTHIA EDEN

B
BRAVA

KENSINGTON PUBLISHING CORP.
www.kensingtonbooks.com

BRAVA BOOKS are published by

Kensington Publishing Corp.
119 West 40th Street
New York, NY 10018

All Kensington titles, imprints and distributed lines are available at special quantity discounts for bulk purchases for sales promotion, premiums, fund-raising, educational or institutional use.

Special book excerpts or customized printings can also be created to fit specific needs. For details, write or phone the office of the Kensington Special Sales Manager: Kensington Publishing Corp., 119 West 40th Street, New York, NY 10018. Attn. Special Sales Department. Phone: 1-800-221-2647.

Brava and the B logo are Reg. U.S. Pat. & TM Off.

ISBN-13: 978-0-7582-3430-8
ISBN-10: 0-7582-3430-9

First Kensington Trade Paperback Printing: July 2010

10 9 8 7 6 5 4 3 2 1

Printed in the United States of America

3 9082 11435 9535

This one is for Nick.

Promises, promises . . .

Chapter 1

As far as Dee Daniels was concerned, too many idiots with death wishes filled the world.

She stared into the darkness of the night, caught the whispers on the wind, and saw the shadow of the two lovers as they ducked behind the side of the beat-up building. Shaking her head, she reached for her weapon and followed.

They didn't see her when she rounded the corner. The guy had the woman pinned up against the wall, his hands shoved under her skirt, and his face buried between her very, very ample breasts. He groaned and grunted and she moaned and twisted against him.

Dee blew out a hard breath as she waited. Not for them to finish, but for the monster to show itself.

Probably in about ten more seconds, maybe less, cause they were getting pretty hot over there and—

The woman, a long-legged redhead, opened her mouth wide. Thanks to the spill of lights from the building's second story windows, Dee got a great view of that mouth.

And of the woman's two-inch long fangs.

Got you.

Fangs that were currently heading right for the idiot's neck as the vamp prepared to rip open his throat and guzzle his blood like a frat boy enjoying the cheapest beer in town.

Death wishes. Would people never learn?

Dee cleared her throat. "Ah, excuse me?"

The shiny white fangs froze over the guy's neck.

"*What the fuck?*" From the idiot. The man still didn't know how close death was to him. Judging from what Dee could see, it looked like death was about, oh, an inch away.

He swung around to face her. Early twenties, preppy, with a face that she judged as handsome, if kind of bland.

Dee smiled at him. "Hi, there."

His gaze raked her and the vamp hissed.

Vamps always got pissy when their food was taken away.

"I'm afraid I'm going to have to ask you to leave," Dee murmured. The fangs were too close to his carotid artery. The vamp might get twitchy and decide to take a bite, and, well, Dee's shirt was white and when she snatched the dude free, she'd ruin her shirt with that dark red splash. Not that it was anything fancy, but . . .

She really hated doing laundry.

"Get. The. Fuck. Away." Bland/handsome snarled at her.

Ah, now some people could almost deserve a bite from a vamp, but—no, she was being paid for this gig.

The vamp smiled at her. "You heard him. Leave, bitch."

Dee lifted her weapon. Not her gun, that was still holstered at her side, but the wooden stake was an easy and familiar weight in her hand. "Just how long do you think it's gonna take me to shove this into your heart? A minute? Less?"

"*Jesus Christ!*" The guy's eyes bulged. "You're crazy!"

Debatable.

"Come on, Karen, let's get the hell out of—"

The vamp grabbed him and twisted the man around. *Using him as a shield.* Why did the vampires always do that with their prey? Like a human shield was ever going to stop her. Dee just shook her head.

"You take so much as a step, and I break his neck."

She could do it. Vampire strength. She'd snap him in half a second, but . . . "I'll be on you before his body hits the ground."

The man whimpered.

The vamp's eyes flashed to black. "*Who are you?*"

"Just a woman who was hired to do a job." This wasn't a

kill mission, but if there was no choice, she'd bring her prey down any way she could.

Besides, vamps were already *dead*, so it wasn't like she was really breaking the old bring-'em-in-alive rule, anyway. Not that the Night Watch Agency really followed that rule. Not when the bounty hunters were after dangerous supernaturals.

"I'm getting bored," Dee said, "let him go and come with me."

The guy was crying now. Sobbing. Hell.

The vamp's gaze darted from Dee back to the edge of the street. Desperation there. Fear.

Time for the takedown. "Let him go," she repeated, voice lashing out, and then, Dee heard the faintest sound.

A soft rustle. A footstep?

Behind her.

She tensed.

The fear faded from the vamp's eyes and a smile tilted her lips.

Uh, oh.

"Take the bitch out!" The vampire screamed and Dee knew that the person behind her wasn't just some innocent bystander drawn in by morbid curiosity. Not innocent at all. Shit.

She spun around, ready to face another vampire, ready to—

He lunged at her, hitting her hard and fast and slamming her ass right down to the ground. At that same instant, she heard the shot. A crack of fire that would have taken her out.

Had her ass not been on the ground.

A hard cry broke the night. Pain. Fear. Not her cry, because she'd learned long ago not to cry out.

Dee stared up at the man before her. *Darkness.*

Black hair, hair much longer than her own. Sharp-edged, hard features. Cold, gray eyes, thin lips. Cheekbones that jutted too sharply.

And his body . . . his weight pinned her to the ground. His body was tight with muscle, heavy with strength.

He felt hot against her. His flesh so warm and—

Ah, fuck it.

Dee rammed up with her elbow, catching him hard and fast in the chin, sending his head snapping back as she scrambled beneath him, twisting, jerking, and punching.

"Stop it! Shit—I just saved your ass!" He clamped down harder on her, freezing her movements. "Woman, someone just tried to shoot you!"

And some big and thick asshole had tackled her.

But the crack she'd heard had registered in her mind now and the cry of pain—

If it hadn't been hers, then it had been . . .

Damn. Her neck craned and she glanced back. The idiot lay on the ground, moaning. Not with passion anymore. Pain. Blood soaked his shirt and pooled around him.

The vamp was gone.

But was the shooter? Only one way to find out. "Get off," she gritted.

His jaw clenched but he rolled to the side. "Your funeral, babe."

She'd lost her stake. Whatever. She had plenty more in the car. Dee jerked her gun free of the holster. She scanned the buildings, the darkness.

It was at times like these when being a human was a real vulnerability for her. The shifter hunters who worked for Night Watch would never have been caught off guard like this. They would have caught the shooter's scent on the wind, heard him creeping up for the shot.

Even the demons would have gotten more warning than she had.

But when you played with the big boys, you didn't get to piss and moan about the extra senses you didn't possess.

So she scanned every building. Every shadow. Then, staying as low and keeping as much cover as she could, she went to the idiot.

"Help me! I'm dying! You've got to—"

Her gaze darted over him. A lot of blood. Huh. And the

vamp had run away from that? Who ran when the buffet was free?

"*Help me!* I can't die like this, I can't—"

"You're not dying." Jeez. She yanked out her phone, then pressed the button that would send an SOS to the surveillance team at Night Watch. "It's a flesh wound, moron." She'd sure had her share of them.

"Dispatch." A soft, modulated voice flowed over the line.

"Need an ambulance." She didn't identify herself. Why bother? Stella would recognize her voice. "Four fifteen Brantley. Human down and—"

Sirens wailed in the night. Of damn course. The shot would have attracted attention.

Her fingers tightened around the phone. "Never mind."

Hell.

Time for explanations.

Or, okay, lies.

"What do we say?"

The deep, rumbling voice came from the left. From Mr. Tall, Dark, and, yeah, Sexy, who'd tailed her over to the victim. She spared him a glance. "You can get out of here. I'll handle the cops." She'd had lots of experience with the Baton Rouge PD. Most of the uniforms owed her, anyway.

One black brow shot up. "It's okay, you don't have to thank me." A grin flashed, one that showed a lot of strong, white teeth. "I was happy to save your life. Really. Think nothing of it. Yeah, I nearly got shot, but I'm okay. No need for concern." His right hand lifted and gingerly rubbed his chin.

A patrol car rounded the corner, screeched to a stop, and Dee clenched her teeth. "Thank you," she managed.

"Not very gracious, are you?" he murmured, and he knelt, his hands going toward the moaning guy's wounds. "You should work on that."

Her eyes slit. "I didn't need saving." Cops were approaching. She could see them from the corner of her eye. Their guns were up, their steps slow.

"Yeah, you did."

She almost growled at him. Any minute now, the cops would be saying—

"Put your hands up! Nice and slow and—"

Ah, good. She recognized that voice. "Harry, we've got a gunshot vic here. He needs to be routed to Mercy General."

"*Dee?*" Not real surprise. More like horror.

"Yeah. Be careful, the shooter could still be around."

Harry and his partner immediately crouched. Harry jerked out his radio and barked some commands.

"Why am I not surprised that the cops know you?" Dark and Sexy murmured.

She spared him a withering glance. Then she leaned in close to the victim and whispered, "If you want to stay out of the psych ward, don't say a word about the vampire."

He blinked once, then gave a quick, jerky nod.

Good. Because the cops on scene didn't understand the paranormal score in this town, and if the vic started rambling about Dee trying to take down an undead bloodsucker, things could get tricky.

She eased back into her crouch. So much for an easy bag. The guys at Night Watch would be giving her hell about this one for days.

And who'd been out there with the gun? Why had the shooter been aiming for her?

She'd find out. As soon as damn possible.

Because no one took a free shot at her and got away. No one.

Sandra "Dee" Daniels was small, grubby, and she really, really shouldn't have been attractive.

Her blond hair barely skimmed her chin and it looked like the woman had taken scissors to it herself—leaving the hair in short, twisted layers. Her nose was a little off center, her bottom lip a little too big, her chin a little too pointed.

No, she shouldn't have been attractive.

The jeans she wore were ripped and faded. Her white T-shirt

clung too tightly to her small breasts, and her black boots were scuffed pretty much to hell and back.

But—

But she was damn sexy. Maybe it was the eyes. So big and dark. Chocolate. Once upon a time, he'd loved the stuff.

And that mouth. The lips were lush, soft, so red. Okay, so maybe he liked her mouth.

A lot.

She had her hands balled into fists on her hips. Cops were everywhere, running like ants as they searched the scene. He'd already been questioned three times, and both he and Dee had been given the all clear to leave.

But the woman wasn't moving, and if she wasn't moving, neither was he.

After five minutes of silence from her, she finally deigned to glance his way. "Harry said you could leave, buddy."

"Simon. Simon Chase." She knew his name. She'd been right there when he spelled it for the uniforms. Each time.

She grunted.

He almost smiled. Almost. "Ah, I can't help but notice, Sandra—"

"*Dee.*" Her voice snapped like a whip.

He'd been there when she had to spell her name, too. He'd rather enjoyed her gruff, "*Harry, you know this shit, S-A-N-D-R-A . . . oh, fuck off.*"

"Dee," he allowed. But he'd be calling her Sandra again soon. He liked that. Liked the way her cheeks flushed so red when she heard the name. "You don't seem too upset that someone tried to kill you tonight."

The victim had been hauled away in an ambulance. Blood still soaked the ground, but Simon didn't glance at it. His nostrils twitched, just a bit, but the scent was starting to fade.

She rolled her shoulders in a little shrug. "Not like it's the first time."

He let his eyes widen. "Really."

A grunt from her. She seemed to like that sound.

"And you have no idea why folks want you dead?"

A furrow peaked between her golden brows. "No clue."

Right.

Her hands lifted, then fell in a vague little gesture. "Well, it's been fun, Chase, but I've got work to do."

He pulled the wooden stake from his back pocket. "Just what kind of work is it that you do, Sandra?"

Red flush. She lunged for him and locked her fingers around the stake, but he didn't let go. She was close now, close enough that he could see light flecks of gold in her dark gaze. Close enough that he could see the pulse pounding at the base of her throat. Close enough that he could almost taste those lips.

He tightened his hold on the stake. The wood was smooth and hard. The woman had obviously spent some time honing her weapon.

"Give it to me." She glanced back over her shoulder. "I don't want to have to explain this shit to all of them right now, not with the last silver shooting still hanging over me."

Silver shooting? Sounded like an interesting story.

Slowly, he released his hold and she jerked the weapon from him. Kneeling, she shoved the weapon into some kind of custom holster near her ankle.

When she lifted the ragged hem of her jeans, he caught sight of her leg. Nice. Smooth and pale and—

She shot back up, nearly clipping him in the chin. Again.

Simon shook his head. She was so not what he'd been expecting. "You didn't answer me," he said and tried to ignore her scent. A heady scent, rich and dark. A woman's sensual flavor.

She licked her lips. A quick swipe of her tongue that had his cock jerking.

Definitely *not* what he'd been expecting, but he wasn't going to complain. No way.

"Trust me on this, you don't want to know." She shuffled back a few steps and tossed him a careless smile. "Thanks for watching my ass tonight, Chase."

Then she was gone. Turning away and marching through

the cops still on scene, and he kept watching that ass. Nice and firm, round enough to hold tight.

Yeah, he kept watching that ass, right until the moment she disappeared around the corner.

He waited a beat. Two.

Then he stalked after her because he wasn't about to let his prey escape that quickly. There'd be no fun in such an easy exit.

He followed her, giving brief, polite nods to the cops as he made his way past their vehicles.

It only took a moment to realize that Dee wasn't headed back to the main street. His eyes tracked her. No, the woman wasn't retreating to the safety of her car. She was snaking through the back alleys, going even deeper into the under-belly of the city.

And she wasn't even glancing back.

Because she was hunting, too.

What the hell? The woman had almost been shot, shouldn't she be hesitating a bit? His hands fisted as he followed her. The night closed around him, her, and they both hunted.

The minutes ticked past. Another tight corner. Another alley. He kept her in his sights. His nostrils stung because these streets *reeked*. Garbage. Shit. Who knew what the hell he was stepping in as he trailed her?

The woman had better be worth this effort. She'd better—

He rounded another turn, one that led him between two thick buildings.

Dee had vanished.

He froze and stared straight ahead.

A soft footfall sounded behind him. Could have been a whisper, could have been—

Simon spun around and came face to face with Dee. She was armed, not with a stake this time, but with her gun, and the lady had it pointed dead center between his eyes.

He probably should have acted scared. Should have mum-bled some kind of half-assed apology for following her.

Instead, he just stared at her.

"There a particular reason why you're tailing me?"

The gun didn't waver. Those sexy-as-sin lips pressed into a thick line.

"Yeah." He allowed himself a glance down her body. He'd have to be careful with her. He kept forgetting how small and fragile she was.

Maybe because of the gun. Maybe that was making him forgetful.

She acted tough. But that body—soft curves and sweet, tender flesh.

"Eyes up, asshole."

Apparently the lady didn't like him ogling her breasts. Fair enough. "You left before I could get your number."

Her jaw dropped. *"What?"*

He shrugged. "Your number. I mean, I saved your life. Shouldn't I at least be able to get your number for that?"

She growled and finally lowered the gun. "Look, buddy—"

"Simon Chase."

"Whatever. I don't have time for this shit. I'm not going to screw you because you shoved me into the pavement. And, just so you know, I didn't need you to save me. Not like it's my first ball game, okay?"

I'm not going to screw you. Hmmm. "Don't remember asking for a screw." Though he wouldn't refuse one with her. "Just your number."

She barred her teeth. Pretty teeth. White and straight. Not too sharp, though, but then, she was human.

His tongue scraped across his own teeth. A bit sharper than hers.

"I'm working now, I don't have time for this—"

"Yeah, you never did answer my question." Simon cocked his head to the side. "Just what kind of work do you do?"

She holstered the gun. "The kind you wouldn't understand."

Doubtful. "Let's see . . . you had a wooden stake and you were about ten feet away from a vampire the first time I saw you." He paused. "I'd say that makes you a hunter."

Her gaze raked over him. "So what? You know about vampires? Good for you."

"Oh, I know about vampires." Too much about them. "I also know about the demons and the charmers and the shifters that are running this city." He even knew her boss, Jason Pak. Pak *was* the Night Watch Agency. He'd started the bounty hunting business almost twenty years ago, and Dee was one of his top hunters.

But she didn't need to know that he'd already researched her.

His hands were loose at his sides now. "I know all about the *Other.*" The humidity from the hot July night had his shirt sticking against his flesh. "And I stopped being afraid of the monsters in the dark one hell of a long time ago."

Her lips parted.

"Fucking hunter." A snarl, high-pitched with fury.

Shit.

Simon's stare shot over Dee's shoulder. The vamp was there, blood dripping down her arm, her fangs bared and her eyes glazed black.

"I'm going to rip your throat open and drain you dry, bitch, I'm going to—"

Dee shifted her stance slightly. Simon's gaze jerked back to her. "Sure you're not afraid?" She whispered.

He gave a curt nod.

"I'll slice your lover open! He'll beg for death. He'll—"

Dee spun around. The stake was in her hand. Wow—he hadn't even seen her grab it and now the wood was in her hand, no—it was in the air. Flying end over end in a deadly arc.

Then sinking into the vampire's chest.

The vamp gave a muffled scream and dropped to her knees.

"I wanted to take you in alive," Dee murmured. "But you just couldn't make this night easy, could you?"

The black faded from the vampire's eyes.

Dee squared her shoulders and stalked toward the vamp. "And he's not my lover."

"Not yet," Simon said and realized that he was impressed.

Sandra Dee had taken down her prey. She hadn't let him distract her. She hadn't given up and faded away when the cops appeared.

And when given a chance for the kill, she hadn't hesitated. Interesting.

Finally, *exactly* what he'd expected.

A team from Night Watch came to clear the alley. The vamp's body was taken away, hell if he knew where. But, then, he didn't really care.

Tonight's exercise had been very fruitful. In all, Simon was pleased with the progress that had been made.

Of course, if he'd gotten Dee's number, he would have been more pleased.

Next time.

Simon stepped into the shadows and rapped against the black door that waited in the darkness. It opened instantly and he crossed the threshold, already pulling out his money.

The man inside was small, squat, and he had his gun cradled in his hand. Greasy black hair was slicked back from his forehead and his beady eyes gleamed when he caught sight of the cash in Simon's hand.

The guy reached for the bills—

Simon snatched his fingers back. "You hurt the human."

Sweat trickled down the man's cheek. It was hot as fuck in there. But, hell, it was summer in Baton Rouge, it was hot as fuck everywhere. "D-didn't mean to, when you took the woman down, the bullet clipped him—"

Clipped him, hadn't killed him, and that was why the shooter was still alive. "I want you out of town, tonight." Simon kept the money out of the guy's reach. "If I ever see you again, you're dead."

A gulp.

Simon leaned in close, close enough for the shooter to see the intent in his eyes. "And it won't be an easy death." Those he delivered rarely were. "Do you understand?"

The man managed a quick nod.

Simon tossed the money to him. The bastard had done his job. He'd taken the shot at Dee. Given Simon the perfect opportunity that he'd needed.

The human's injury just hadn't been part of the plan.

Simon turned away from him and headed for the door. There was more work to do. Always more.

The bullet slammed into his back, a hard punch of fire that burned through skin and muscle, and tore right through the bone.

He hit the floor hard, his face slamming down and the blood pouring from his body. *Dammit.*

Should have seen that one coming. You just couldn't trust killers these days.

He heard the creak of footsteps and caught the whisper of excited breath. "N-nobody threatens Frankie Lee." Another shot. This one fired into the back of his right leg.

Simon didn't cry out. He locked his jaw and battled the pain.

"You're the one who won't get an easy death, asshole." Another shot. Left thigh this time.

Sonofabitch.

Frankie grabbed the back of Simon's head and wrenched his face up. The gun barrel stared back at Simon and the scent of burning metal filled his nostrils. "Nobody threatens—"

Simon lunged off the floor. One jerk of his hand and he broke Frankie's wrist.

"*Fuck!*" Frankie's face bleached of color.

The gun clattered to the floor. Simon didn't even glance at it. He wouldn't need the weapon. The gun really would be too easy, and so not his style.

Simon grabbed the squirrelly bastard, wrapped his hand around Frankie's throat, and pinned him up against the wall. Frankie's fat legs dangled a good two feet off the ground.

"*How the hell—*"

Simon smiled.

Frankie started to shake.

"Don't say I didn't warn you," Simon whispered, the scent of his own blood clogging his nostrils. "You had your chance."

Now, it was his turn.

Chapter 2

"**R**eady for a new case?"

Dee glanced up when Jason Pak strolled into her office. The guy had on one of his fancy suits—always, the fancy suits—and he was smiling.

A smile from Pak was never a good thing.

Dee slowly eased her feet off the desk. "What kind of case?" She'd been thinking about taking a break. Maybe heading over to Biloxi and staying at one of the casinos and enjoying the beach.

He shut the door. No sound. Pak was good at not making any noise. He'd told her once that he'd learned to hunt and track with his Choctaw grandfather.

And that he'd learned to kill by trailing his Korean mother.

He crossed the room and tossed a file onto her desk. "We've got word that a Born Master is in town."

Her blood froze. The ice thickened inside of her, then rose to coat her skin as the chill enveloped her.

Born Master. She licked dry lips. Okay, not a lot scared her, but those bastards did. "What's a BM doing in this city?" Born Masters were rare, thank Christ. Only a handful were in the United States. Most of them preferred to stay in Europe or Africa.

Born Masters were the vamps who were born bloodsuckers. Well, okay, technically, they were born looking human, acting human, but they weren't.

Eventually their bodies stopped tolerating human food. The hunger for blood consumed them. Their teeth sharpened. Their senses kicked up to super level, along with their strength. And then you knew, those freaks weren't human. They were pretty much immortal.

Pak gave a shrug and his dark eyes never left her face. "I'd guess he's looking to build a beautiful little vamp army."

Her back teeth locked. The disease of vampirism had come from the genetic jokes that were the BMs. The Born Masters had gone out, bitten their prey, exchanged blood, and what should have been a few DNA freaks way back when—well, they'd multiplied. Nearly swept away a whole country back in the Middle Ages.

Black Plague, her ass.

It was so easy to rewrite history sometimes. Especially when you were trying to stop the humans from panicking.

Dee pressed her palms against her jean-clad thighs. The better to wipe the sweat away. Because, yeah, she was sweating. Taking down a Born Master wasn't an easy task. BMs were too strong. All the ones she'd ever heard of were close to a millennia old.

In the vamp world, age brought strength. Especially to the Borns.

"The streets can't be flooded with Taken," Pak said, crossing his arms over his chest and watching her with the cold stare that always saw too much.

She rolled her shoulders and tried to look like her heart wasn't about to break out of her chest. "Maybe the bastard isn't planning to change folks." The Taken were the vamps who were killed, then reborn to a life of blood and fury. Not everyone could survive the transformation. "Maybe he's just looking for some kills." Her voice was cool, expressionless. "Could be he just wants a bloodbath."

Sandra Dee! Run, baby, run—

The scream pierced her mind and her hands pressed harder against her thighs. *No, can't think about that now.*

Not with Pak watching her like she was some kind of lab rat.

"Been a long time since the city saw a vampire rampage." Her face had been ice cold, now her cheeks burned with pinpricks of heat. "Yeah. About sixteen years." Could have been yesterday though. Because those blood-soaked memories weren't ever gonna fade.

Mama? Not sleeping. No, she wasn't sleeping in her bed.

Pak's head cocked to the right. "I need you to be straight with me, Dee."

Now that snapped her out of the past. She sat up, fast, eyes narrowing. "I've *always* been upfront with you, Pak. Always." There wasn't a shadow in her life he didn't know about. Without Pak, she would have been on the streets.

No, she would have been dead.

She'd been eighteen and he'd given her a place to stay. He'd taken shit for it, too. A forty-year-old man bringing in a stray from the streets.

Sex hadn't been an issue with them, though most folks didn't buy that. Course, Dee didn't give a shit what most folks thought. Pak hadn't been a father figure. She'd *had* a father. Pak had just been someone to keep the monsters at bay.

Then someone to teach her how to kick the monsters' asses.

And he'd been someone who understood loss.

"This is different. This *case* is going to be different." The man was so still. She'd never understood how the guy could be so motionless. She was always moving. Twitching. Tapping.

"It's just another vamp," she said, and tried to believe the words. "Born Master or Taken, they can all die." Just getting them to die was the tricky part.

Getting them to die *again*.

"If you can't handle this, I'll put Zane on point. He can go after the bastard."

"Zane doesn't know vamps like I do." Zane Wynter was a

good hunter, no denying it. But the demon didn't understand the undead like she did.

A pause from Pak. "Zane also isn't human. He won't have your . . . weaknesses."

Oh, now, that was just hitting below the belt. So Zane was half-demon. Dee shot to her feet. "Charmers don't have any damn strengths that put them above humans, either." So the charmers could talk to animals—yeah, like that was an advantage when you were hunting paranormal predators. Over a dozen agents at Night Watch were charmers and they had no advantage over her.

She stared down the lead charmer. "I'm not weak."

"Never said you were." Another pause. Jeez but the guy was always working the silences. That tactic used to drive her crazy. Okay. Still did. "Never said I was going to put a charmer on point, either."

No, just a demon.

"Zane would be a lot harder to kill than you," Pak said flatly.

"Maybe." Yes, dammit. Freaking demon strength. He wouldn't have been caught unaware last night. "But I'm one hell of a better vampire killer than he is." True and so what if she sounded bitchy?

His nod had her breath easing out. "Yes, you are." He pointed a finger toward her. "But you're going to need help on this one. I want Zane watching your back."

Not going to argue. She could always use the demon's powers.

"And I'll get Jude to come in for cover, if we need him."

Ah, Jude. The tiger shifter who was currently blissed out with his new mate. Dee gave a nod. No way would she turn down a shifter's nose when she was tracking a vamp.

Her pounding heartbeat still shook her chest, but her palms were dry now, and she asked, "So what's the target's name? Which badass thinks he's taking over our city?"

Pak smiled then, his gator grin, and Dee's muscles locked. "Don't know who is he. Just *what* he is." He inclined his head toward the file. "Intel says word is ripping through the city about the BM. No name. No face. Just the knowledge from every witch and psychic in the area that power is coming through—and it's coming through hard."

Her brows shot up. No name? "Then who's the client on this one?" There was always a client with Night Watch. The agents didn't hunt for pleasure. They weren't supposed to, anyway. They hunted the *Other* because the cops couldn't track those killers. When a supernatural went on a killing spree, the higher ups at the Baton Rouge PD called in Night Watch.

Sure, the Night Watch team brought down some humans every now and then, just for the sake of keeping their cover in place as a legit bounty hunting agency, but the paranormals were the real targets.

Pak straightened his already straight suit. "On this case, I'm the client."

Damn. He must think this threat was serious because Pak *never* let the cases get personal. His rule number one.

"And Dee—I want this bastard taken down, got me? Because I don't want to see blood pouring in my streets, not again."

With a Born Master, that could happen. Hell on earth *could* happen with one.

"Consider him staked." Easy words, hard job. But she'd do it, because no way was she going to stand by and watch innocents get slaughtered by vamps gorging on blood.

As Pak had said, *not again.*

Time to sharpen up her stakes and hit the hunting grounds.

The music was terrible, the food was shit, and the crowd of dancers were all but screwing on the floor.

Dee leaned against the bar, trying to ignore the throbbing in her temples and letting her gaze sweep past the throng inside Onyx.

This was the eighth club she'd been in since she'd hit the streets. Humans only. Well, mostly humans. Onyx catered to the unaware, and that made the place perfect for vamps. So much easier to pick up prey when the humans didn't realize the danger they faced.

They didn't realize it, not until their dates stopped seducing them and started feeding from them.

By then, it was too late to scream.

Her nails drummed on the bar. Zane lounged in the back corner, his emerald gaze sweeping over the room. Some big-breasted blonde was at his side. Typical.

Jude hadn't made an appearance yet. But he would soon. She'd use his nose to sniff out the place. See if he could detect the rot of the undead and—

"Let me buy you a drink."

She'd ignored the men beside her. Greeted the few come-ons she'd gotten with silence. But that voice—

Dee glanced to the left. Tall, Dark, and Sexy was back.

And he was smiling down at her. A big, wide grin that showed off a weird little dint in his right cheek. Not a dimple, too hard for that. She hadn't noticed that curve last night, not with the hunt and kill distracting her.

Shit, but he was hot.

Thanks to the spotlights over the bar, she could see him so much better tonight. No shadows to hide behind now.

Hard angles, strong jaw, sexy man.

She licked her lips. "Already got one." Dee held up her glass.

"Babe, that's water." He motioned to the bartender. "Let me get you something with bite."

She'd spent the night looking for a bite. Hadn't found it yet. Her fingers snagged his. "I'm working." Booze couldn't slow her down. Not with the one she hunted.

Black brows shot up. Then he leaned in close. So close that she caught the scent of his aftershave. "You gonna kill another woman tonight?" A whisper that blew against her.

Her lips tightened. "Vampire," she said quietly and dropped his hand.

He blinked. Those eyes of his were eerie. Like a smoky fog staring back at her.

"I hunted a vampire last night," Dee told him, keeping her voice hushed because in a place like this, you never knew who was listening. "And, technically, she'd already been killed once before I got to her."

His fingers locked around her upper arm. She'd yanked on a black T-shirt before heading out, and his fingertips skimmed her flesh. "Guess you're right," he murmured and leaned in even closer.

His lips were about two inches—maybe just one—away from hers.

What would he taste like?

It'd been too long since she'd had a lover, and this guy fit all of her criteria. Big, strong, sexy, and aware of the score in the city.

"Wanna dance with me?" Such dark words. No accent at all underlined the whisper. Just a rich purr of sex.

Oh but she bet the guy was fantastic in the sack.

Find out. A not-so-weak challenge in her mind. Why not? She wasn't seeing anyone. He seemed up for it and—

Dee brought her left hand up between them and pushed against his chest. "I don't dance." Especially not to that too fast, pounding music that made her head ache.

He didn't retreat. His eyes bored into hers. "Pity." His fingers skated down her arm and caught her wrist. He took her glass away and placed it on the bar top with a clink.

She cocked her head and studied him. "Are you following me?" Two nights. First one, sure, that could have been coincidence. A coincidence she was grudgingly grateful for, but tonight—

The faintest curl hinted on his lips. "What if I am?"

His thighs brushed against her. Big, strong thighs. Thick with muscle.

Dee swallowed. So not the time.

But the man was tempting.

She couldn't afford a distraction. Not then. "Then you'd better be very, very careful." Dee shoved against him. Hard.

He stumbled back a step and his smile widened. "You keep

playing hard to get, and I'm gonna start thinking you're not interested in me, Sandra Dee."

Who was this guy? Dee jumped off the bar stool. "You'd be thinking right, buddy."

He took her wrist again with strong, roughened fingers. The guy towered over her. Always the way of it. When you couldn't even skim five foot six with big-ass heels, most men towered over you. And since Dee had never worn heels in her life . . .

The guy bent toward her when he said, "I see the way you look at me."

What did that mean?

"Curious . . . but more. Like maybe you got a wild side lurking in you. A side that wants out."

Maybe she did. The guy sure looked like he could play. *After the case.*

"I don't know you, Chase," she finally told him, too aware of his touch on her skin. Too aware that her nipples were tightening and she was leaning toward him as her nostrils flared and she tried to suck up more of his scent. "I don't know—"

"I saved your life." A fallen angel's smile. "Doesn't that count for something?"

Maybe.

"Dee!"

Jude's hard snarl.

Chase's hold tightened on her.

Maybe not.

The white tiger shifter stormed through the crowd. People jumped out of his path because they were semi-smart. In seconds, he was at her side, nostrils flaring, lips curling back, blue eyes . . . watering?

"Uh, Jude? What's going on?"

"Problem," he growled and the man was good at growling. His eyes—and, they were most definitely watering—zeroed in on Chase. The two men were about the same height, and had the same rough, strong build. But Jude was light, his skin fair, his hair blond, and Chase . . .

Darkness. The thought came to her once more.

Jude's gaze dropped to the hand that still bound her wrist. "Man, you'd better *not* be bothering Dee."

Great. Because she needed him to act like an overprotective jerk right then. "Got it covered." More than covered. So what if Chase's thumb was sliding back and forth over her wrist and the movement had her heart jumping? No big deal.

Jude's stare turned back to her. "We've got a situation."

One that shouldn't be discussed in front of an outsider. She got that. She tossed a careless smile Chase's way, and tried really hard not to care. Her life wasn't like other women's. She couldn't go out, find a great guy, and forget the world while they had sex.

Not when killers were waiting.

If the people in this bar had half a clue what was hunting them . . .

"See you around," she told him, keeping her voice bland and tugging her hand free. His fingers had been rough against her, lightly callused, warm, and strong.

Too easy to imagine those fingers sliding over her flesh. Cupping her breasts. Spreading her thighs.

Dee swallowed. Okay. So maybe it had been too long since she'd been laid.

"I can help you." His cool words had her hesitating, glancing back, dammit.

He stared at her, unblinking.

"Not amateur night, buddy," Jude murmured and his nostrils twitched. "Dee and I have a job to do, we don't—"

"Maybe you need prey to draw out the vampire," Chase continued, never taking his eyes off her. "Maybe I'm the man you need."

Only one way to find out.

"Hell, what have you been telling him?" Jude demanded, swiping his hand across his forehead. "Low profile, woman, *low profile.*"

Dee ignored him. Pretty easy to do most days. "We've got this one covered."

Chase's jaw worked but he shoved his hand into his back pocket and pulled out a card. "You change your mind, you call me."

Don't take it, don't take it, don't, ah . . . hell. Dee's fingers curled around the card.

She didn't even see his hand move. But in the next instant, his fingers were around hers and he brought her hand to his mouth. His lips pressed against her flesh, his tongue tasted her.

Two seconds, maybe three. Then he dropped his hold and flashed that bad boy grin. "I wanted a little taste."

So did she.

"*Dee . . .*"

She knew that tone. Jude would be having a fit any second—or as close to a fit as a tiger could have.

Chase brushed past her and disappeared into the crowd.

"Shop for a new lover later, we've got problems now." He bent his head toward her and whispered right against her ear, "Kymine."

Dee sucked in a sharp pull of air.

"They're pumping it in the place. And if the kymine is here . . ."

Then the vamps were, too.

Kymine. A sweet little concoction the vamps had created about ten years ago, a brew that they pumped into the air in order to screw with a shifter's sense of smell.

With about 95 percent accuracy, shifters could pick up the stench of a vamp in a crowded room. Jude had told her once that, to him, vamps smelled like corpses. Yeah, that made sense, considering that vampires were dead. Kinda anyway.

To be reborn as a vampire, a human had to die. The heart stopped. The brain ceased to function. The lungs didn't rise.

Dead. Cold. Hello, afterlife.

Almost hello. Because if the exchange was successful, a few moments of true death were all the person would have. The heart would beat again, the lungs would fill, and the brain would kick-start to life again.

Alive once more, with a few new extra features.

Like fangs, super strength, and a nearly insatiable lust for blood.

Because the vampires knew that the shifters could smell them—and have one hell of a hunting advantage—they'd researched like crazy and finally produced kymine.

Kymine could only be used in a closed, restricted area. Once it was pumped into the ventilation system, it dispersed. A shifter unlucky enough to be in the area would temporarily lose his sense of smell.

And feel as if fire were burning the inside of his nostrils.

"I can't smell a damn thing," Jude said, still close, his breath whispering against her ear. To others, they'd look like lovers.

The best way to hunt. Deceive. Mislead.

"The bastards could be right next to me," he said, "and I still wouldn't know."

So much for the shifter being her secret weapon tonight.

But there were too many lights in that place. Too many people, too many eyes. If a vampire was there, he'd only be scouting for food. The feast would come later.

When he had his prey alone.

Time to switch up plans. "Let's go outside. You take the front, I'll take the back." They'd leave Zane inside, he could keep a careful watch on the bar.

The bar owners had to know about the vampires. No other reason they'd pump in the kymine.

"We need to tell Zane. He'll need to—"

"Already did." He eased back and she caught the glimpse of fang. "You armed?"

Her brow shot up. "Seriously? You're asking *me* that?"

A ghost of a smile tugged at his lips. "Let's get the bastards."

Good plan.

She reached into her bag and curled her fingers around her stake.

Showtime.

*   *   *

The night was too quiet. Especially for this part of town. There should have been laughter on the wind. Drunken voices. Car horns or the fading beat of music.

Dee paced about twenty feet behind Onyx. No stragglers waited outside. No lovers looked for a quick screw.

Alone.

With the thick silence.

So not natural.

She rocked back on her heels and tried to ignore the fact that Chase lounged somewhere in that bar. He'd probably moved on to a more agreeable partner. One of those women who could laugh and smile and mean it, and not someone who couldn't stop glancing over her shoulder because she knew there were monsters out there, waiting.

Be afraid of the dark. A lesson she'd learned when she'd been fifteen.

So very afraid.

The faintest pad of footsteps reached her ears. Dee didn't tense, that would alert her prey. She exhaled, nice and slow and—

"You're dead, Dee."

A woman's voice, soft and mellow.

Slowly, Dee turned toward her. Tall, thin, with a long mane of midnight black hair, the woman stood near the exit of the back parking lot. She was alone, unarmed, and smiling.

Dee kept the stake hidden. No way to tell yet if she was staring at a vamp, a demon, a human—or hell knew what. *Come on, Jude, get your ass back here.* But if the kymine hadn't worn off, he wouldn't be much help, either.

"Are you afraid?" the woman asked.

Dee decided she hated the bitch. "No. Are you?"

The woman glided closer. One of those annoying graceful moves that dancers seemed to make.

Dee marched toward her, more than ready to meet the chick head on.

"No one will mourn, Dee. No one will even miss you when you're rotting in the ground."

Ah, so she was little Miss Sunshine and Light. Dee grunted. "And what? You think you're the one whose gonna take me out?" She shook her head. "Sorry, sister, it's been tried more than a few times and the assholes who come for me are the ones who wind up in the graves."

The woman's lips tightened. Good. It was always better to get under their skin, to rattle them, to—

"You should have died with your family."

Dee's vision flashed red. Blood red. Like the blood that had stained her hands, covered her body, and pooled on the floor when she'd found them.

No.

"But it doesn't matter." The bitch's chin lifted. "You're dead now."

So Sunshine had gotten under her skin. "I seem to be breathing just fine." She didn't hear any other sounds. That could mean it was just her and Sunshine, or it could mean others waited silently and patiently in the darkness, ready for the perfect moment to attack and kill.

Uh, Jude?

Sunshine had on jeans, strappy sandals, and some kind of light, lacy top. Her smile was broad and flashed lots of teeth.

No fangs, not yet. A vamp's fangs grew right before they got ready to feed. Just like a vamp's eye color changed to black when they hunted.

Or when they fucked.

One way to find out what she was dealing with here.

Dee lunged forward, the stake gripped tight in her hand. She struck out, grabbing Sunshine and tossing her ass to the ground. Then she went in for the kill.

The woman never even flinched.

That same vacant smile was on her lips when Dee brought the stake down over her heart. "Dead," she whispered again.

No fangs. No black eyes. If the woman were a vamp, she'd be fighting for her life. She would have gone into hunting mode instinctively. Not just lay there like a lamb at a slaughter.

Dee froze. The tip of the stake pressed into the lace of Sunshine's shirt. "Who the hell are you?"

Laughter. Low. In-freaking-sane.

Dee lifted the weapon. Staking a human was not part of her agenda for the night. She rose, never taking her eyes off the nutjob. "You're playing a dangerous game."

"No, you are." The woman climbed slowly to her feet. "All alone. Poor little hunter. Will you beg at the end?"

What the—

"She's not alone." Hard, deep.

Not Jude.

Chase.

Sunshine's lips parted.

"Get out of here," Dee told her, fighting back the impulse to ram one fist into that thin little nose. "And stop screwing around in shit that you don't understand." The woman was obviously some kind of messenger. Most of the hunters at Night Watch had a standing policy of not hurting innocents. Well, Zane wasn't part of that "most" group. But she didn't like to hurt humans.

The *Other* knew the safest way to send their warnings to the hunters was to employ puppets. Humans who thought playing in the dark was fun.

When it was more like suicide.

Yeah, she didn't normally hurt innocents. But this time, oh, talk about temptation.

"You don't even have a week," the woman said and when she tilted her head, Dee caught sight of the bruises on her neck.

Bite marks.

Figured. "Neither do you," she told her, sadly, still not glancing back at Chase. Not yet. "You need to run from them, as fast as you can and never look back."

A blink. "Why? They can give me everything."

Or nothing. "You can't trust vamps."

Her smile dimmed. "You can't trust anyone." Her hand rose

to her neck. Covered the wounds. "But when you can live forever, does it matter?"

Yes.

Fingertips brushed her shoulder. Dee spun around, the weapon up.

Chase stared back at her.

"What? Christ, man, how the hell did you move so fast?" And so *quietly.*

"Where's your partner?"

Thudding footsteps. Dee glanced back in time to see Sunshine make a break for the line of cars. She lunged forward—

He jerked her back. "Your. Partner."

"She's getting away!" If she could trail her, they could find out where the vamps were hiding and—

"Good. The bitch just threatened you. If she didn't get her ass out of here, I might have killed her."

What?

An engine kicked to life. No time to argue. Dee elbowed him, twisted, shimmied, then kicked out with her foot.

He flew back, and she shot forward.

"Dee!"

Her legs pumped as fast and hard as they could. *Go, go.* A car lurched forward, a small, red Ford. Exhaust burned her nostrils and the squeal of tires grated in her ears. *Tag, get the*—

Damn. Her shoulders slumped.

Gravel crunched behind her. "That hurt, Dee."

Doubtful. If she'd wanted him hurt, he would have been hurt. "You should have let me go." She stared at the disappearing taillights. No tag. Sunshine had planned for their meeting. Turning back to Chase, she glared. "She got away."

He rubbed his side. "Where. Is. Your. Partner."

Dee tried to brush by him. He caught her shoulders, trapping her against him.

His eyes glittered down at her. "You know, the blond bastard who was licking your ear inside. Where is he?"

Ah, what was that? Jealousy? Men. Take away the jeans and designer labels and you had cavemen beating their chests. "Jude isn't my partner."

"Is he your lover?"

Her breath rushed out. "None of your business, okay? I'm on a case, you just let my lead get away and—"

He kissed her. Chase crushed that too hard mouth down on hers and drove his tongue past her lips.

She could have broken free. Could have given him another hard punch but—

Screw it.

She wanted to taste him.

So for a few wild seconds, she forgot the vamps and the death and she locked her arms tight around him and she opened her mouth wide.

Yes.

Her tongue met his. She wasn't the kind of woman who liked to be taken. She liked to take.

His hands caught her waist, pulled her closer, and the rising ridge of his cock thrust against her.

His lips caressed. Savored. His tongue swept into her mouth. Slid against hers and had her wanting more. So much more.

A quiver began in the pit of her belly. A stir of hunger that she hadn't felt in so long.

This man could make her feel. Make her want, and—the sex—it would be fantastic.

His fingers cupped her ass. Squeezed.

Then he lifted her, hauling her high in the air and holding her close so that her nipples, already tight, aching peaks, pushed against his chest.

Yes.

She liked her men strong. Liked her sex hot.

He sure fit the bill and—

"Dammit, Dee, I thought you were working the case, not screwing around with—"

He stiffened against her. Chase's head rose and his lips, red and shining from her mouth, hovered over hers. "Not your lover," he repeated and it took her a half-dazed moment to realize he was talking about Jude.

The guy who'd *finally* decided to make an appearance. "No."

He put her down, nice and slow. "Then you won't mind when I kick his ass."

Um, nah, generally she wouldn't mind but—

But this wasn't a fair fight. No way would Chase be able to take down a shifter, unless—unless he was much more than human.

"Come and try," Jude invited and she didn't have to look at him to know he'd be sporting his come-get-some grin.

She grabbed Chase's hands. "What are you?"

His eyes narrowed. "What the hell kind of question is that?"

"One that needs an answer." In this city, you couldn't take risks.

But he didn't answer and his jaw locked.

She glanced over at Jude. "Kymine gone yet?"

"Mostly." He sniffed a bit. "He doesn't smell like death." A grimace. "Just some fancy ass cologne."

Her shoulders relaxed. Not a vamp. Okay. Everything else was pretty much doable.

Chase stepped back from her and Dee dropped her hands. He slanted Jude a seriously pissed glare. "Don't come sniffing around me again, tiger."

Tiger? He knew about Jude?

Not a flicker of surprise crossed the shifter's face. "You gonna piss and moan all night or are you gonna answer the lady's question?"

What are you?

Chance stared back at her. Gazed too deeply with those smoky eyes. "I'm the man who had her back, twice, when you weren't anywhere around."

"Dee doesn't need anyone to watch her. The woman's a freaking machine—"

"Everyone needs backup." His fingers brushed over her cheek. Her breath caught.

"Aw, Dee . . . shit," Jude muttered.

Her shoulders snapped up. She wouldn't be weak. Not in front of Jude. He'd trained her. Walked with her on the first mission.

Not in front of him. "We had a visitor." Now she was the one to back away. Because that soft touch wasn't something she could handle.

Hard, wild, and rough—yeah, that was more her style.

Chase's fingers fisted, then fell.

"And you noticed the . . . ah . . . visitor with your tongue down this guy's—"

"I've got a name. It's Simon Chase."

"—throat?"

She stared at Jude. Long and hard and waited until his blue gaze dropped. That was better. "The visit came first. Some sweet little ball of fluff sporting bite marks on her neck."

Jude sucked in a sharp breath. "A lure?"

"No." Well, maybe. Vamps were known to use sexy women to draw in other prey. Worked wonders for them. Most folks were always attracted to a pretty package. You followed the package, and found hell waiting with open fangs. "She was sent to deliver a message to me."

"Huh."

Chase glanced between them. "Why send the woman? I mean, if you think a vampire sent her—"

She held up her unused stake. "They knew I wouldn't hurt her." Much.

"What did she say?" Jude asked.

Dee hesitated.

Chase didn't. "The bitch told Dee she was going to die."

Well, so much for subtle.

"Sonofabitch."

That pretty much summed things up nicely.

"And you let her get away?" Jude growled. A very deep, rumbling growl. His beast had to be close.

"I got distracted." The six foot three, two-hundred-pound distraction shifted beside her. "It won't happen again."

"Don't count on it," Chase murmured.

Her gaze jerked to his.

And the bastard *smiled* at her.

Trouble. Why, *why* did trouble always find her? And why did this trouble have to be so sexy?

Chapter 3

Dee awoke screaming, her skin slickened with sweat and her drumming heartbeat rattling her chest.

It took her a minute to banish the blood. To choke back the fear.

So long ago, but the dreams still came.

Dee jumped out of bed. The neon digits of her clock glowed too brightly. Four-oh-eight. She'd slept for an hour.

Shit.

Her T-shirt clung to her body, damp and too confining. Every muscle in her body quivered. Her skin burned and her belly knotted.

Damn dreams.

Why tonight? Why? It had been over three months since the last bout, and just when she'd thought she was finally mastering the demons, they'd come sneaking back.

She paced across the room. No way would she be going back to sleep. She couldn't.

Adrenaline had her walking faster, faster.

Get out.

The apartment was too small. Too hot in the summer. Dee shoved open the balcony doors, but the air outside was even thicker, even hotter.

Her air conditioner droned with a low hum. Not doing her a damn bit of good.

Love you, Sandra Dee.

Her eyes squeezed shut. Hell, no. She wasn't doing this. Not again.

Sirens wailed in the distance. There was always trouble somewhere in this city. Human killers. Supernatural monsters. Never any peace. Not for her, not anywhere.

No peace, but, maybe—

Maybe there was something else she could have. For just a little while.

Her eyes opened. She turned around, fumbled for the card she'd tossed on her nightstand. Her fingers trembled when she touched the edge.

The minute she'd come home, she'd balled up the card and tossed it into the garbage can.

Then she'd dug it out. Stupid. But—

But her heart wasn't slowing down. Her skin was burning hot, and when she thought of Simon, she pictured *him* and stopped seeing the blood.

Dee was so tired of the blood.

A name and a number were typed in black letters across the white card. No address.

She couldn't call him now. No way. Only one reason a woman called a man at this hour.

Yeah, one reason.

A hard breath shook her chest. Dee realized she could still taste him. Still feel the press of his lips against hers. The brush of his tongue.

He might not be alone. He probably wasn't. A guy like him, oozing sex, he'd probably snapped his fingers and—

She put the card down. For an instant, she thought she saw red staining her fingers.

No, no, just a memory.

Wasn't it?

Shaking her head, she walked toward the shower. A nice, cold shower, that was what she needed.

Or him.

Fuck. Dee grabbed the phone. Dialed before she could stop herself. One ring. *Stupid. You can't do this.* Two. *Are you crazy? You can't.* Three.

"Night Watch." The private security line for the team. The one they called when they needed Intel, twenty-four-seven.

"Grace? It's Dee. Did you—did you run that check for me?" Because she was a suspicious bitch, always would be.

A faint hum on the line, then . . . "Finished it earlier tonight. You want me to fax over the file?"

"Go ahead and give me a quick and dirty rundown." Because she had to know, *right now,* before she made a deadly mistake. "And then send over the paperwork." She'd want to know every detail later. That was her way.

"Simon Lawrence Chase." Dee's fingers tightened around the phone when Grace began. So she ran background checks on all her potential lovers, what was wrong with that? A woman had to be safe. These days, you never knew what you were dragging home.

"Age thirty-four." Really? It'd been so hard to judge his age, he could have been younger or— "Born in New Orleans, he left when he decided to be all he could be." Military? With that long hair?

"He's not still serving." Dee was definite on that.

"No. Looks like he went Merc for a while," Grace said.

Merc. Mercenary. Yeah, she could see that. A brief hesitation, then she asked the most important question, "Any sign he's more than human?"

"Negative."

Her shoulders relaxed. She'd had a demon lover once or twice. They weren't anything to complain about, for sure, they'd been phenomenal in the sack, but a human—

I can control him.

"There's . . . something else, though, Dee. Something you should know."

Aw, hell. Always something to spoil her party. "What is it?"

"The records show his parents were killed a few years back. It went down as a B and E gone bad, but . . ."

"But you're telling me it wasn't a breaking and entering? It was more?" Often was.

"Jewelry was snatched, the TVs and a computer were missing, and the parents, Janice and Ned Chase had their throats slit."

A slit throat. The easiest way to cover a vamp attack.

"I made a call to a coroner I know down in New Orleans." One of the reasons Grace was so good at Intel—the woman had connections everywhere. "Seems there wasn't enough blood at the scene to match the severity of the wounds."

Because the parasites had drained them dry. Huh. No wonder the guy knew so much about vampires.

Personal experience.

Just like me. "Thanks, Grace. I owe you."

Silence, then very softly, "No, you don't."

The call ended and Dee clenched the phone tight. He'd passed the screen, and his past was as screwed up as her own.

She swallowed. He was safe.

Or as safe as a lover could be for her.

Her fingers dialed quickly. There was no hesitation this time. No stupid voice whispering in her mind, no—

"Dee."

Just that, her name. Breathed with need. With the same lust that was tightening her nipples and making her sex clench.

Oh, boy. Her own breath came out in a hard rush. Course he would have known she was calling. In this techno crazy age, her name would have appeared instantly on his caller ID. No backing out now.

"Where are you?" He asked, a dark demand.

She pulled at her shirt, trying to break it away from her hot flesh. "My place."

"What do you want, Sandra Dee?"

Her sex quivered. Just that voice, whispering to her in the dark.

He knew what she wanted. Had to know. "Are you alone?" Probably not. Probably had some stacked bimbo crawling all over him.

"*What do you want?*" A sensual demand.

"You." She cleared her throat. "Apartment B-6, Groves Terrace."

His breath rushed over the line.

Then, *click.*

She knew he was coming.

Dee hung up the phone and paced to the edge of the bed. She lifted the mattress and checked to make sure her gun was close. She always kept her weapons close.

He was coming.

Her gaze darted to her hands. No blood. This time.

Fuck, fuck, fuck—talk about some serious bad timing. Simon jumped out of his Mustang and stared up at the apartment on the left, the one with the white terrace and the French doors open on the second floor balcony.

Dee.

She'd moved fast. Faster than he'd expected, but he wasn't about to turn away from her. If the lady wanted him, she'd get him.

Screw the dawn.

They had an hour. At least. He'd take more time later. Now, now he'd give her what she wanted.

And make her need him more. Because soon, she'd have to need him more than she'd ever needed anyone. Need him enough to turn away from everything and everyone she knew.

Simon bounded up the flight of stairs. He raised his hand to pound on the door.

Dee wrenched open the door. She stood there, clad in a thin T-shirt that cupped her breasts, a T-shirt that barely skimmed the tops of her pale thighs, and she stared at him with those dark, wide eyes.

Simon tried to jerk his tongue back inside his mouth. "Uh, Sandra—"

"*Dee.*" She grabbed him. Her fingers fisted around the front of his shirt, and she jerked him inside.

"Ah, what's the rush—"

"Don't want the neighbors to see."

What? She had neighbors who were awake at four thirty in the morning?

And since when was he the woman's dirty little secret?

"I don't want forever."

His eyes widened at that. Couldn't help it.

"I don't want you to tell me that you love me. I don't want lies or promises that you won't keep."

He kicked the door shut behind him. Stared down at her. No bra. Panties? His nostrils flared. Yeah, but they were wet.

Fuck.

She'd said she wanted him and she did, no denying her body's response, but even before her lips parted, he knew she was going to say—

"I just want to forget."

Yes, he'd known she would say that, because he knew her. *Know your enemy.*

But Dee wasn't his enemy. She was—

She stepped away. Caught the edge of her T-shirt and tossed it to the floor.

His cock jerked against the zipper of his jeans. *Damn.* Small breasts, but perfect. Round, with light brown nipples. Tight nipples, ready for his mouth and—

The couch was behind her. He caught her in his arms. Swept her back and dropped her onto the cushions. Then he followed and took a nipple into his mouth because he had to taste. To take.

Time was running out.

His lips closed around the peak and his tongue laved her. Her moan filled his ears and her hips thrust up against him. The woman's arousal flooded his nostrils. Rich, wet cream.

The edge of his teeth pressed against her flesh and she shivered. Not fear, no, not even close.

Damn her. *Damn her.*

He kissed his way across her chest. The faint ridges of scar tissue pressed against his mouth. Long, thin lines. Light white now because Sandra Dee was a fast healer.

She could have died.

He knew about the attack. He'd done his research, too.

He caught her other nipple. Sucked her with tongue and lips. Her fingers clenched against his shirt, jerked it up, and then she touched his flesh. Hot, fast fingers that skated over him.

He rocked against her, driving the fully erect length of his cock against her sex. Dee's legs were open, spread, and when he'd lowered her onto the couch, he'd pushed between them.

The better to play.

The better to torture himself.

"Lose the jeans," she ordered, her voice a husky rasp, and her fingers were on his stomach, sliding down, aiming for the button of his jeans.

No.

He caught her hands. "You're not calling the shots here, babe."

Her eyes were wide, so brown and deep, but burning with a hungry fire. Her lips had parted—

He kissed her. Drove his tongue deep inside and tasted the wild honey and spice that was Dee. Sweet and wild—the perfect flavor for his little vampire slayer.

The dark hunger built within him. Feeding the lust that he chained back. Tempting, tempting so much . . .

Her tongue swiped against his. *Give her what she wants.*

No, no, she didn't even know what she wanted. Not really. Not yet.

He tore his mouth from hers and tried to ignore the spreading darkness within.

Dawn comes.

He licked her neck. Sweet flesh. Her pulse pounded against his mouth. Fast with excitement. Bursting with life.

Testing now, he let his teeth score her flesh.

She jerked, but didn't fight. He chained her hands over her head, caught her wrists and held them against the couch with his left hand.

Dee probably thought she could break away from him at any time.

The lady didn't know how wrong she was.

She should have known better than to invite him inside. Now he held the power and she didn't even realize it.

His teeth wanted to press harder into her skin. Part of him wanted her to know the danger.

His right hand trailed down her body. Soft flesh, covering a finely muscled body. Dee was a fighter, no denying it or the marks of the past that scarred her pale skin.

His fingers paused over her belly. Flat and smooth.

His mouth opened wider.

Her hands jerked free in an instant. *Hadn't expected that.* She shoved against him, once, hard.

Simon raised up and stared down at her. So many lights were on in her house. Lights against the dark.

Dawn was coming.

"Don't play the vamp game on me. That shit doesn't get me off."

Didn't it?

"And it sure as hell can't work for you."

Ah, so she'd already done her research on him. That meant he had to let Grace go free.

Pity.

He could have used her services again.

"If you can't deliver, get the hell out."

Cold. Hard. Just what he'd expect from a hunter like her.

But her eyes were wild. Not just with lust but with fear. Her lips trembled and he knew, better than others, what demons rode her.

"I'm not going any place." Not yet.

Fuck the dawn.

Forget.

He'd make her forget all right. And make her always re-member him and what he could give to her.

His fingers caught the edge of her panties. Plain white cotton. Serviceable. The panties shouldn't have been sexy. On her, they were.

He eased down, lowering his head, and kissed her through the fabric. Her hips shot up at the sensual touch.

"Easy." His eyes lifted to hers. "Trust me."

I can't. He could read the words on her face though she didn't speak a word.

"You'll have to," he said and meant it. Sooner or later, there would be no choice.

He licked his lips and knew he couldn't stop. Didn't want to stop. His cock was nearly bursting, so full he hurt, and the woman who'd crept into his mind and twisted his fantasies into nightmares quivered beneath him. His to pleasure.

His.

For the moment, anyway.

Her scent was so much richer now and the hunger inside had only grown stronger. His teeth caught the band of elastic. He jerked his head and the fabric tore.

"Chase!"

His head shot up. "*Simon.*" No distance here. No walls. He wouldn't allow them.

His fingers ripped away the torn panties and tossed them across the room. Then he touched her. Easing his fingers into the blond curls between her legs, he found her plump, wet, and hot.

Just the way he liked a woman.

Her breath hissed out when he touched her clit. A hard press with his thumb then a slow caress with his fingers. He'd learned long ago how to pleasure a woman. How to make her moan and beg. How to make her scream.

He wanted Dee to scream for him.

His index finger found her opening. Pushed inside. *Tight.* Sweat beaded on his brow. So tight.

The back of his zipper was going to be permanently indented on his dick at this rate.

Another finger thrust inside and stretched her. Dee's neck arched.

Don't tempt.

His fingers wrapped around her thighs, and he opened her even wider to his touch and his stare.

To his mouth.

Pink flesh, moist and waiting.

His lips touched her first. A light caress. Gentle and easy.

"Simon, more!" No gentle and easy command there.

His tongue swiped over her clit and she jolted. His fingers tightened around her thighs, clamping down harder and he pulled her flush against his mouth.

He took.

His tongue tasted, licked. His mouth worked the tight button of her desire. He felt her stiffen, felt the coil of her muscles, and he learned what she liked.

What she loved.

Her thighs shook. Her fingers latched onto his shoulders—the better to hold him tight. Not that he was going anywhere. No damn place right then.

His tongue stabbed into her sex. Her taste, that sweet and spicy blend, filled his mouth, and he knew he couldn't get enough. Not now.

Not even close.

The tremble began in her sex, a telling tightening that he knew came right before orgasm.

Scream for me.

He freed her thighs. His thumb pressed onto her clit. His tongue thrust into that tight slit—

Dee came against his mouth, her body bucking, her fingernails biting deep into his flesh.

But the woman didn't make a sound.

His gaze lifted and he saw her eyes go blind. The perfect lash of pleasure covered her face, but she bit her lip, holding back the cry of pleasure.

Screw that shit.

He rose, licking his lips, tasting her and wanting to fuck her so badly that he burned. A bead of blood appeared on her lip. Small, so red.

His mouth lowered toward her. *Easy.*

She turned her head away and his lips skated over her jaw. Dammit.

Her nails retreated and he missed the bite immediately. Her hands curved over him, hesitant now that the fire was slaked. "That was . . . ah . . . nice."

What?

His eyes narrowed as he lifted his upper body. Simon caught her chin and forced her to look at him. Her tongue slicked over her lower lip, taking away that drop of blood. "Nice?" He repeated.

No, the woman hadn't just said that to him.

Her smile came then, a slow curl that lit her face, then her eyes. "Maybe better than nice."

A tease. Should have known it.

Her bare legs shifted against his jean-clad thighs.

"A lot better," he told her definitely.

One blond brow rose.

"The best you ever had," he continued, keeping his lips flat when they wanted to lift in response to the furrow that appeared between the brows.

Dee blinked, a long, slow blink. "You don't know what I've had."

He bit back the sudden fury that rose in him. "Don't want to know," he gritted.

Her fingers slid between them and reached for the button on the jeans. "Let's see what happens when we have—"

His jaw clenched. Now this was the painful part. His balls would be blue all day long. "I've got to leave, babe."

"What?" Surprise there. Hurt?

Maybe. A good sign.

He rose from the couch and didn't bother dragging his gaze off her naked body as he straightened his own clothes.

She didn't bother to cover up. "Where are you going?"

"To take one very cold shower." Honesty, finally. Kind of felt good to be honest with her.

Her brows pulled low in confusion as she asked, "Why?"

Because sex right then wasn't the way to gain her trust. The way to gain some hard, fast pleasure, hell yeah, but not the way to get to his end goal. "Because we're going to be more than a fast fuck, Sandra Dee."

"*Dee.*" Her breasts heaved as she straightened. Gorgeous. Maybe he'd have one more taste.

He bent toward her and swiped his tongue over her nipple. *Yes.*

Could have been his sigh. Could have been hers.

Leave.

A hard suck on that nipple, then he pulled back. "The hours before dawn are hard, aren't they?"

Her breath came fast. "Wh-what are you doing to me?"

Everything he could.

"You needed me to fight the dark. You called, I came." Well, not quite the coming he would have liked. "Remember that. I gave but I didn't take a single thing from you."

Next time, he wouldn't be so nice. Especially since being nice wasn't really in his genetic makeup.

His gaze dropped to her sex. He could still taste her. His teeth snapped together.

She rose but didn't bother reaching for her clothes. What was she trying to do to him?

He could lift her up, shove into her, and take the woman right there. Dee was so light, he'd hold her and thrust and *make* her scream.

Pleasure, not pain.

Because he could do that, too, no matter what the whispers said.

"I don't understand you," she said.

"I think you understand me better than anyone else." He let the words fall between them and managed to drag his gaze up to hers. "I did my research, Dee, just like I know you did yours."

Not even a flicker of expression. But she reached for her shirt. Tugged it on with steady hands.

"We both know what it's like when the monsters come."
He wouldn't say anything else. Couldn't.

Simon turned away and marched for the door. Dee didn't
stop him. He didn't expect her to. That was, after all, part of
the plan.

When he yanked open her door, the first rays of sunlight
hit him.

Dawn.

He glanced back. "More than a fuck, Dee." So much more.
"When you need me, you know how to find me."

Squaring his shoulders, he headed into the light.

And not once did he glance back.

Chapter 4

When night fell, coming with its thick, hot darkness and moonless sky, Dee headed back to Onyx.

There'd been no sign of the woman since their last encounter, and she'd spent all day using every one of Night Watch's contacts in hope of finding Sunshine.

No luck.

So Dee figured she'd better let the woman find her again.

And that was why her butt was parked once again at the bar.

Her gaze scanned the crowd. Pretty light since it was only a little past nine. The heavy hitters would come in later.

Her stare tracked across the room, not lingering too long, looking for the tall, muscled length of—

"Hell." Dee ground her back teeth together as she caught herself. The object was to find the woman from last night, not Chase.

Not the man who'd given her a fast, hard ride straight into one of her better orgasms, then walked away.

Walked away.

What had been up with that?

More than a fuck. She spun toward the bartender. "A beer, Mike. The cheaper, the better." One drink, that was all she ever allowed herself when she hunted. A big, long glass mirror ran the length of the bar and Dee stared at her reflection. Wow—was that her hair? Maybe she should—

Her eyes locked on a man. Black hair. Broad shoulders. Tall, strong. Don't-give-a-damn swagger.

Chase.

Her breath eased out.

The man was double-timing it to the exit.

Running from her?

Or chasing something? Someone?

"Hold the beer." She shoved away from the bar. "Be back in five." The exit door had already swung shut, but Dee rushed forward. If there was a hunt, she'd be in on the action. And if there wasn't . . .

Well, she had a few things to say to Mr. More Than A Fuck.

Her fingers clamped around the door knob. Just in case, she went out silently, armed, ready.

But no one was there. Just an empty back lot.

What the hell?

"You did well." The vampire stared into the human female's eyes, enjoying the soft ebb and flow of her blood. Her heart raced as he crossed to her. With every step, the blood flowed faster.

She smiled at him. "She was right where you said she'd be. All alone." A quick swipe of her tongue across those ripe red lips. "I-I could have killed her for you. I would have."

Such an eager little helper. "I know." He trailed his fingertip down her cheek. Lisa. He didn't remember her last name. Didn't care.

"I'd do anything for you," she whispered and her eyes were so wide and blue. *"Anything."*

Because she wanted to live forever. Because Lisa, with her thin thighs and her big breasts and her perfect face, was aging. Slowly. One faint line at a time.

"I'm not afraid to kill." Her chin lifted even as she swayed toward him.

His fangs lengthened. He'd love to have one more taste of her. Fresh blood was always the best. "No, you've proven that." She'd brought prey to him that very first night. His fingers trailed down her throat and curled over that frantic pulse. "But are you afraid to die?"

Hope lit her eyes. "You're going to do it? You're going to change me?" Her smile stretched her face. "I'm not afraid, I want—"

"Good." Then he lifted the weapon he'd kept hidden and stabbed her. Right in that laboring heart.

She choked at first, probably on her own blood because he saw the trickle of red slide from the corner of her mouth. Those wide eyes filled with pain and shock because this wasn't the death she'd expected.

Because he hated for all that good blood to go to waste, he bent toward her, and licked those sweet drops away from her lips.

Then he let her body fall.

Time to get the other bitch.

Now this was just . . . weird. Dee shoved the stake back into her ankle holster. She tilted her head, straining to pick up some sound to indicate movement, but she just caught the muted beat of music.

"Chase?"

Maybe he'd circled back around to the front of the building. Possible. But that fast?

Her gaze darted to the row of cars nestled on the left. She didn't see anyone over there, but . . .

Dee stalked to the vehicles, aware of a growing tension in her body. Last night, a woman had told her she'd die here.

Being back now, okay, that would make anyone nervous.

Narrowing her eyes, she caught sight of a small, red vehicle. Wait—that was—

A rush of wind behind her.

Oh, damn. Dee froze. She didn't need to look back to know she wasn't alone anymore. "I was wondering when you'd show up," she muttered. Her fingers were just a few inches away from her gun holster. So if she was right and a vamp had just closed in on her—damn but they were almost as quiet as shifters these days—then a gunshot wouldn't kill him.

But it would still hurt. A lot. And it would give her the precious minutes she needed to stake the asshole.

"I have been watching you," he said, his voice clipping a bit with an English accent.

"Have you?" She turned, slowly, to face the vampire. Her fingers brushed the holster. "And I've been waiting on you." Dee shook her head. "Didn't your mother ever tell you it's wrong to make a woman wait?"

His fangs were out. Long and sharp. As she watched, his blue eyes faded to black. Great. Dee swallowed. A vamp in full hunting mode.

"I'm not here to play with you." That black stare raked her.

"Oh?" This was it. "Then I guess we better skip the foreplay, huh?" No way to tell if this was the Born Master or one of his minions because the Borns, they *always* had freaking minions. "Maybe we should just get around to the death part." Dee jerked out her gun and fired, six times, dead center in his chest.

Flesh and bone torn away, blood splattered around them. Dee stood so close that the bastard's blood rained on her.

But he didn't flinch. Didn't fall to his knees. Didn't stumble. Just stared at her, and smiled. "You'll wish I killed you, before it's over."

She still had more bullets. This time, Dee aimed for the head. "Promises, promises." Her finger tightened around the trigger—and they attacked.

Five, no, six vamps jumped from the darkness, teeth and claws out and ready to kill. Dee didn't waste breath on a scream. She fired, fired until the trigger just clicked. They took her down and her body hit the ground, hard. But, twisting like a snake beneath the fists and bodies, she managed to grab her stake—new weapon, new fight. Dee swiped out at them, too aware that she'd made a fatal mistake and walked right into their trap.

You're dead, Dee. Sunshine's voice rang in her head. *No one will mourn. No one will even miss you when you're rotting in the ground.*

Simon had just walked into Onyx when he heard the distinct thunder of gunfire. Hell.

His gaze scanned the big room. *Dee, be here.*

A curvy redhead walked by him, a wide smile on her lips. "Hi there, handsome, I'm—"

"Not interested." He brushed by her and cut a quick path to the bar. He slammed his hands down on the counter. "I'm looking for a woman."

The bartender didn't glance up. "Try looking behind you."

Growling, Simon leaned over the counter and grabbed the idiot's shirt. Whiskey spilled over his hand. "You remember the woman I was with last night." Not a question.

The guy's eyes bulged. "You kidding me? Do you know how many chicks come in here every night? No way do I—"

"Small. Blond hair she'd hacked to pieces. Tight ass and lips that—"

"*Her.*"

"Where is she?"

The bartender pointed one hand to the left. Exit.

Simon thrust him back. He spun around—

And came face to face with a demon.

Not just any demon. *Her* demon. Another Night Watch hunter. Zane Wynter. The guy looked like a human, but Simon knew he was far more monster than man. Simon snarled, "You're supposed to be watching her ass."

"Thought that was what you were doing last night."

The music had kicked up. The band blasted some screaming shit and—was that another shot? "Out of my way," Simon ordered.

The demon didn't move. Fine.

Simon shoved the bastard back, a good three feet, and ran for the exit even as the demon shattered a table before he hit the floor.

A kick sent the door flying open. *"Dee!"* He could smell her, that wild scent drifting in the air.

Simon rushed forward and saw the gun tossed on the ground. Her gun. *"Dee!"*

But he couldn't see his little hunter.

Gone.

Maybe dead.

Sonofabitch.

Growling, he took off into the night, following the scent of the blood trail as fast as he could. Dee had made her attackers bleed and that sweet scent would take him right to her.

If he could get there in time.

The wail of sirens woke her. A loud, hard scream she'd heard too many times before. Dee fought to open her eyes. A groan tore from her lips as pain wracked her body.

Vampires.

The breath she'd tried to suck in now choked out as realization crashed into her.

Had she taken them down? Or had they *Taken* her?

Please, no.

The stench hit her then. The coppery odor she'd first caught long ago and had never forgotten. Couldn't.

No, not again.

Her lashes fluttered open. She squinted, trying to see. But it was so dark. Pitch black.

She shoved up and a blast of agony burned through her head at the move. *Shit that hurt.* Her hands slapped down as she struggled for balance, and something sticky and wet coated her fingertips.

No.

The scent hit her again, stronger now that she was aware, striking like a hard punch in the face. Bile rose and she choked, scared, sick.

Not again.

She scrambled back, but hit something. Something soft and still.

Her eyes narrowed as she strained to see but the darkness was too perfect. Her hands fumbled, reaching out.

Flesh.

An arm. Cold to the touch.

A hip.

Stomach.

Then—oh, God, no—

A loud boom blasted to her right and light exploded on her as—what? A door?—flew open.

"Dee!"

Her head jerked at the sound and the move sent fire burning through the base of her skull.

"Oh, damn, what the hell happened?"

That voice . . . *Simon.*

A crack of light shot in behind him, illuminating the sparse interior of her hell. She glanced away from him, following the horror in his eyes to see the body.

High-end clothes, soaked red. Long, tangled black hair covered half of the woman's face. A face she knew. Little Miss Sunshine lay dead beneath her hands. Not a pretty death. Too brutal.

Dee's fingertips fluttered around the wooden stake that had been driven into the other woman's heart.

Her breath rasped out. "I-I didn't—" Her hands flew back. A human. Sunshine had been a human. In life, and in death.

Dee tried to scramble up, but she slipped and fell in the blood that coated the floor.

Just like before. "Mom? Mom! Help me!"

But no one had helped her.

"Dee? Dee?" Simon grabbed her and lifted her into his arms. "Are you hurt?"

Yeah, but the other woman was dead.

Did I kill her?

Please, God, no. She couldn't remember anything. Not since the alley, when all those vamps jumped her—

Her hand flew to her neck. Had she been bitten? Christ. If

they'd bitten her, they'd be able to get into her head. Sick, twisted freaks.

Simon turned away from the body. "We've got to get the hell out of here!" His hold bruised her.

"No, no, we can't leave her. The cops—"

"Are about to storm the place any minute." The sirens screamed, so close now. So close.

Dee heaved against him, but he just clamped his hands tighter around her and ran from the pit. No, not a pit, she realized as more light spilled onto her. Some kind of warehouse?

Simon raced outside, holding her tight.

Yeah, a warehouse. With some boarded-up windows, a condemned sign on the side, and a few streetlights spilling light on her hell.

"The cops find you here, your ass will be headed for jail." He all but shoved her into his car. The smell of leather flooded her nostrils but it couldn't block the stench of blood. So much blood.

Sunshine's blood had stained her skin.

A car door slammed. Dee glanced up just as Simon cranked the engine, then he gunned the Mustang and they flew forward with a snarl of the motor.

"We can't . . . leave the scene." Her mind wasn't working right. She knew it. Everything seemed slow. The streetlights too bright. Dee squinted as she ran a hand over the back of her head.

When Dee touched the fist-sized knot at the base of her skull, her breath rasped out. *What did they do to me?*

Simon jerked the wheel to the right and turned down a street. Then another. Another. The mustang snaked through alleys and back roads, taking so many turns that Dee felt dizzy.

She'd thought she knew the city.

She'd thought wrong.

Her eyes squeezed shut and she saw—

A stake, driven deep into the woman's chest. Blood.

"Why?" The word broke from her lips as her eyes cracked open. "She was a . . . lure. She shouldn't have been—"

"Dee." Simon spared her a glance. "Focus for me. How much of the blood is yours? Did the bastards bite you?"

Don't know. Her hands started to tremble. The steady pounding in her head had nausea rolling through her. "Not sure." Okay, that sounded normal. Didn't it? Her tongue seemed so thick in her mouth. "The woman . . ."

"Fuck, Dee! She's dead! She was part of a setup! The vamps left you there, with a stake—probably one of yours—in that woman's heart, and they sent the police to find you."

The sirens—how had the police known to come?

He took another corner and the tires squealed. "What do you think would have happened when the cops found you crouched over a dead human?"

The throbbing was worse. She could actually *hear* the pulses. That couldn't be good. "Got . . . friends who are cops." They would've listened to her. Tony—she could count on him. "T-Tony . . ." Okay, that had been slurred.

"Hell! You're about to pass out, aren't you?"

Maybe.

Um, yeah.

"Dee? *Dee!*" He hit the brakes and she fell forward. The seat belt she didn't remember buckling—maybe he had?—cut across her chest. "Stay with me. I've got to know . . . it's important. Did they bite you?"

The street lights didn't seem so bright anymore. Or maybe her eyes were just closed. Hard to tell for sure.

"Dee?"

"Maybe," she whispered and the last thing she heard was—

"Fuck."

Yeah.

Death had a way of making the beautiful . . . ugly.

Baton Rouge Police Captain Antonio "Tony" Young stared down at the body before him. He was used to the blood, so the stench and the sight didn't bother him. This wasn't his first time to find a horror/freak show crime scene. Wouldn't be his last either.

He crouched beside the body and a soundless whistle passed his lips. Someone had screwed up. He could see the bite marks on the woman's neck, so yeah, she'd been a vamp chew toy, but—

But she hadn't been a vamp.

The movies and TV shows had vampire killings all wrong. When vamps were staked, they didn't age or shrivel or explode into dust.

Nothing so fancy.

But the change *was* there. You just had to know what you were looking for to see it.

At death, well, their second death, anyway, a vamp's elongated fangs retracted. The darkness in their eyes—the darkness that came when they hunted—faded away.

Their bodies stiffened, hardening immediately so that when an ME looked later, the TOD was never right. No way could you determine the time of death for a vamp, just couldn't happen.

Their skin whitened, not slowly turning ashy and yellow like a human's. No, the skin drained of color until the flesh was the starkest of whites, and the drain was nearly instantaneous.

Those signs were always dead giveaways that you were dealing with a vamp. Those indicators, and the wooden stake that was generally lodged in the chest. Hard to miss the stake.

"Oh, man, is that who I think it is?" The uniform next to Antonio pressed in a bit too close.

Antonio slapped his hand against his chest. "Don't even think about screwing up my crime scene." Like things weren't screwed up enough. That tip they'd received . . . *"Two women fighting, screaming, someone needs help at Belmont and Queens. The crazy bitch was screaming about vampires."*

Screaming about vampires—and now the victim had been staked.

"Captain, don't you recognize her?"

He turned to stare at the uniform. Red spots blotched the kid's face. "Should I?" Another body. Another case that would give him heartburn. Couldn't the supernaturals ever back off?

A quick swipe of the cop's tongue. "She's Lisa Durant. You know, Senator Durant's niece. I saw—I saw her on TV a few weeks back. She was . . ." His gaze fell to the body. "Hot."

Not anymore.

Antonio's back teeth locked. *Senator's niece.* Oh, hell. Keeping this quiet would be a bitch.

He glanced back at the stake. His eyes narrowed. "Jon . . . is that what I think it is?" Not enough light to tell for sure from this angle, but that looked like—

The crime scene tech who'd crouched beside the body shot him a grin. "Bloody fingerprints. Hell, yes."

Antonio's hand ran over his face. "Run 'em, and give the report to me." His eyes held Jon's. "Only me, you got that?"

Jon gave a grim nod.

"Good." Because he had a feeling the supernatural shit was about to hit the fan in his city.

"Dee."

Somebody shook her. Hard.

"You've got to wake up. That hit you took to the head left you concussed. You can't sleep."

But she really wanted to, just a little longer anyway.

"Dee!" Another shake. One hard enough to rattle her teeth.

She managed to crack open one eye. "Should you really . . . shake a woman with a . . . concussion?"

A brief grin turned up his lips. "It was either shake you or maybe let you slide into a coma."

Something wet and cold pressed against the back of her neck and Dee sucked in a fast breath. "What the hell?"

The grin flashed again. Was the guy enjoying her pain or what? "The ice will make the giant knot go away sooner."

Both of her eyes opened. Dee realized she was on a couch, propped up against some cushions, and Simon, he was over her, *around* her. One hand held her shoulder, urging her close, while the other anchored the ice pack at the base of her skull. Mere inches separated their faces. His smoky eyes were so deep and intense. She noticed his lashes then. Really long, dark lashes. Weird, because his face was hard and—

"You back with me this time?" he murmured.

She blinked, realizing that though her skull still throbbed, the grogginess of before was gone. "Yeah, I . . . think so." If she could stop being an idiot and gazing into his eyes like some lovesick teen with a crush. Jeez. Dee fumbled for the ice pack. Her fingers tangled with his. "I've—I've got this."

His jaw locked.

Okay, so maybe she wasn't being the most gracious victim. Good southern manners had never been her strong suit.

Simon's hand fell away and she pressed the frigid pack against her head. "Don't worry . . . about me," she managed. "I'm a fast healer." For a human, anyway. She dragged her gaze away from him and scanned the room. Bare walls. No photos, no paintings. A TV, DVD player, game consoles. And in the corner . . . what was that? A porn magazine? "Ah, your place?"

A grim nod.

The ice shifted beneath her fingers. "Look, Simon, I appreciate you trying to come to my aid—"

"I saved your ass, Dee, *again.*"

True, though she was a bit sketchy on the details. "I don't . . . I can't remember what happened after I left the alley." The vamps had jumped her. She'd fired her gun. Run out of bullets. Started staking.

Too many of them.

They'd knocked her down. Her head had thudded into the ground and—

"I woke up in her blood." She didn't even know the woman's name. Another vic. So many nameless faces.

Simon began to ease back. Dee's left hand grabbed for him. "I didn't kill her."

His head cocked. "Thought you just said you didn't remember."

Dee swallowed and hoped she was telling the truth. "I wouldn't kill a human."

"You had the stake against her heart last night."

"To *scare* her, not to kill her!" Oh, bad idea. Shouting made the throbbing much worse. "Simon, trust me, I-I wouldn't kill a human, not after what happened to—" She broke off, clamping her lips together. So, what? A bump on the head had made her super chatty?

"You want me to trust you?" he asked.

Dee realized her fingers were digging into his wrist. With an effort, she unclamped and nodded.

"You tell me why you're so gung-ho against the vamps, and make me believe you'd never stake an unarmed woman. *Then* we'll see about talking trust."

The ice had begun to melt. A trickle of water slid down the back of her neck. "My story's not so different from yours."

He didn't speak.

Fine. He wanted her soul naked—that was the way it would have to be. Because right now, she needed him. *Until I can find out what the hell is happening.* "When I was fifteen, I came home to find a bloodbath at my house."

Mom? Mom? Where are you?

Dee ignored that soft voice whispering in her head. The voice of the girl she'd been a lifetime ago.

She cleared her throat and said, "My date dropped me off at the door. My first date." He'd wrapped his sweaty palms around her shoulders and given her a kiss. Wet, sloppy, but her first kiss. Then he'd hightailed it out of there when he heard a thump from inside.

Vince had thought her dad was coming. The ex-marine, tough as nails guy who'd been cleaning his gun before they left.

"Dammit, I loved him so much," she murmured. That stupid gun. She'd begged him to put the thing up before Vince arrived. People didn't really do things like that, but he'd—

"The boy you were—"

A hard shake of her head. "No. Forget it." She swallowed.

"The lights were on when I went inside, but I couldn't find anyone." But she'd smelled a thick, hard odor.

Blood and death.

"I found my dad first. He was in the hallway. His throat had been ripped open." So much blood. She hadn't screamed when she'd seen him. She should have, she'd even tried, but her breath had been gone.

She'd dropped to her knees next to him. His precious gun had still been in his hands. Her dad never loaded the thing so it hadn't done him a bit of good.

Simon's fingers skated down her cheek and Dee realized she'd dropped her gaze. His hand curled under her chin and he forced her to look at him again.

Better him than the past. "I found my sister next." She paused, felt the pain. "She was seven."

They'd killed her in her bedroom, right there next to Sara's pretty pink bed and her tall, white doll house.

"Some vamps get off on children's blood. They think it makes them stronger," he said. "Dee, look at me."

She was, but she could still see Sara. "She used to drive me crazy. I was so much older and—" And Simon probably didn't care. He didn't want to know what a bitch she'd been to her kid sister. Didn't want to know that she'd run straight to Sara's room after finding her father, her heart burning her chest. When she'd found Sara, she'd fallen.

The scream had come then. Breaking from her mouth and shattering her.

"I screamed for her, for help, and then I heard the footsteps coming."

So stupid.

"They would have heard you the minute you entered the house," Simon said and his face hardened. "The bastards were just playing with you."

She knew that now. They'd let her find the bodies, let the terror and grief break her, and they'd crept out to watch her. Sick, twisted freaks.

Then they'd attacked.

"Their mouths were stained with blood. When I saw their teeth, I-I didn't believe what I was seeing at first."

Because who would believe vampires were real? That they'd just slaughtered your family?

"*We've been waiting for you, little Sandra Dee, waiting so long.*"

Dee jumped and the ice pack tumbled from her fingers. "What? What the hell did you just say?"

His fingers fell away. "I said they were waiting for you, probably trying to make sure you were alone before they attacked. It's the way the bastards work."

Yeah, it was.

"How did you get away?"

Because of a miracle. Or, no, maybe because the devil had gotten bored and decided to stir up hell on earth. "My mother came down the stairs."

Still alive. Dee had gasped those words. One vamp had held her right arm, another her left. She'd thought they were going to rip her apart. And the other vamp bastard—the one with the blond hair, coal black eyes, and the lying, kind face—he'd watched her with a smile.

Her mother had stumbled down the steps. Thick, gaping wounds covered her neck. "The vamps hadn't been easy with her." A rusty, broken laugh. "When are they ever easy?" A kind kill wasn't generally an option for vampires. They liked prey to suffer.

Blood had soaked her mother's shirt. Her face . . . "She was so pale. Trembling. And her eyes, they were—" Changing. Fading from a brilliant gold to dark shadows. She hadn't known what that darkness meant. Not then.

"They laughed when they saw her. Told her that she couldn't have a drink." *Mom doesn't drink.* The stupid thought had been the fifteen-year-old's. Her mother never touched alcohol. Never.

His jaw locked but his gaze never wavered. "Finish it," he gritted.

She didn't want to. Dee squeezed her eyes shut.

Darkness.

Just like her mother's eyes.

Were all vampires really bad?

Some hunters claimed a vampire lost his soul when he was transformed. That goodness died and only evil remained. A shifter had told her that once—he'd said the decay and the rot that he smelled from vamps came from the decay inside, where a soul should be.

Maybe the old fox had been full of bullshit, but she'd asked Jude and he'd said he caught the same stench any time a vamp was near.

Except once, he'd told her about a vamp in LA who—

"How did you get away?" he repeated.

Dee opened her eyes. "She—she had a weapon. That thump I'd heard before, she'd broken a table. I guess they didn't think she had any fight left, but she did." A bit of pride there. "When she reached the landing, she lunged and stabbed the lead bastard in the back."

A moment of weakness. That was all she'd needed. Just a moment.

"*Go, Sandra Dee. Go,*" she whispered her mother's last words. A sad smile curved her lips. "And I did. I ran and I left her there." To die.

Rage and fear had twisted her stomach as she rushed down the hall and out of the house. "I left her," she repeated, voice still soft. The other vamps had turned on her mother when she'd stabbed the leader, and their attack had given Dee that one moment to break away.

Kill them. The thought now was the same as it had been then. *Kill them.* She hadn't wanted to get help. She'd wanted to find someone to kill the bastards in her house.

"I ran outside. Went to a neighbor's." They hadn't been close. Not close enough to hear her first scream. If only.

Mark McKenley and his wife Julie had wanted to go to her house, right away. They'd called the cops, and Mark had taken off with his old hunting shotgun. Dee remembered rushing after him, screaming that the gun wouldn't be enough.

"Something happened in my house." She licked her lips. "Fire . . . the smoke, I saw it the minute I went back outside."

Mom!

"Fire burns fast, you know. So fast." Greedy flames, licking up the side of her house, peeling the paint away in thick bubbles, eating at her home.

"I know," his gruff whisper.

Julie had held her back. Mark, sixty, with stooped shoulders and shaking hands, had burst into the burning house, screaming her mother's name.

He'd stayed inside, until the firefighters arrived and dragged his body out.

Dead. Like the others.

My fault. She hadn't even been able to look at Julie after that.

"The cops and firefighters didn't believe me when I told them what happened." Not that she could blame them. Hell, they'd probably thought she was crazy or high. "The story ran in the paper a few days later." She'd read it with tears streaming down her face. "They ruled it a murder-suicide. After the fire stopped, the only remains they found inside were—well, they said they could identify Mom, Dad, and Sara." *Not her. Not now.* "No sign of the vamps, of course."

"Fuck." Understanding in the guttural word. He knew where this was going.

"They said my mom killed Dad and Sara, then she shoved a knife into her own throat."

Bullshit. Not her mom. Not the woman who'd sacrificed her own life so Dee could get away. "No one would believe me." The steady throb in her head was driving her crazy, but she'd deal.

She always did.

"What did you do? Where did you go?"

To the streets. "I took off on my own." With the stupid idea of finding the vamps who'd attacked her family and killing them. But, at fifteen, she hadn't known how to live on the streets. She'd been close to starving a week later, dirty, cold.

Her jaw locked. "I managed to get by." A shrug. Like she could shrug away those dark years. "Then I met Jason Pak." No, he'd *found* her. Stalked her and found her in that roach-infested apartment she'd bleed to pay for.

"Pak." He echoed the name. Most folks in Baton Rouge knew of Pak, even if they hadn't personally met the guy. Bad reputations carried too easily.

"The first thing he told me . . . He said I wasn't crazy." But she'd thought he was.

"And the second?"

Her fingers fisted. "He said he'd teach me to kill the bastards."

Pak had always been a man of his word.

"I haven't found *those* vamps yet, but I will." One day. Then maybe she'd stop hearing Sara's screams late at night. Maybe. Or maybe she'd just hear them until she died.

His gaze roved over her face. Her neck. "They didn't bite you that night?"

"No." Adamant. A good thing, too, because most folks didn't understand just how dangerous even a little nip from a vamp could be.

Once a vampire took a victim's blood, he had a psychic link with his prey. If he was strong enough, he could steal thoughts, memories, and send seductive whispers in the hours of darkness.

Some of them—those ancient Born Masters—it was possible they could even control their prey. Get humans to follow their every twisted command. Like sick, freaking puppets.

Dee never wanted to be a puppet. Never.

Taking a deep breath, she shoved off the couch. Their thighs brushed and she fought to ignore the wave of heat from that quick touch.

Her knees shook a little when she stood. For just a second, black spots danced before her eyes and the nausea rolled in her stomach.

"Dee?" He was there, rising, too, and putting a bracing hand on her shoulder.

Careful. Don't get used to him being there.

Alone. That was how she lived her life. How she'd keep on living it.

She stiffened her spine and lifted her chin. "I'm all right." Not a total lie. Dee was pretty sure there was no immediate threat of death.

Slowly, she turned to face Simon. She looked up at him. "After what happened to my family, do you really think I'd ever take a human's life? I couldn't do that. I'd be the same as—"

Them.

The vampires. Stealing life, spilling blood.

"I don't remember what happened in that room, but I know I wouldn't have staked her." The vampires. Had they made her watch and she couldn't even remember it? Had the woman begged her for help?

Simon weighed her with icy eyes. Silence filled the room, heavy and thick, then he gave a grim nod. "If you'd wanted to kill her, she would have been dead on the ground last night."

Not a ringing endorsement, but she'd take what she could get. "Thanks for that much, at least."

Then it was her turn to pause because this part, yeah, it would be awkward. Well, hell, not like he hadn't already had her naked. "I need a favor." She'd bared her soul to him, a small favor really wasn't so much to ask in return. "I played your game, told you the hell from my past, now I want one thing from you."

"Fair enough."

She thought so.

"What do you need?" He gave a shrug. "You know you can crash here until we find out what's—uh, Dee?"

Her shirt hit the coffee table. The pounding in her head kicked up a notch. No help for it. She'd had to yank the shirt off. Blood had stained and hardened the fabric, and she never wanted to see the shirt again.

Dee toed out of her shoes. Jerked open her jeans and—

"Just what kind of favor do you need, babe?" His voice had thickened, darkened, and when she glanced up, Dee saw that those smoky eyes of his didn't look so cold anymore. No, not cold at all.

She shoved down the jeans. "I don't remember what happened—that means they could have done anything to me." *No, no, no.* "I . . . need you to check me." She licked her lips. It would have to be a full body check. No way could she take chances.

"Check you?"

Her gaze held his. "For bite marks."

Chapter 5

Oh, but he'd sure like to take a bite. Simon swallowed and let his gaze slide over Dee's pale flesh. The woman knew how to strip, fast. A simple black bra and matching panties covered her. Well, covered what he most wanted to see, and she stood there, shoulders back, small breasts out, and told him . . .

"I'm going to need a full body check."

Yes. He cleared his throat. "I'll do my best."

"This is serious, Simon. It's not like a damn mosquito. If I've even got one bite, I'll—"

"What?" Real curious now. "If they bit you, there's not a damn thing you can do about it now."

"I know." Soft. Her hands lifted, hovered between them. "I just—" Her eyes widened as she stared at her fingers. "Her blood's still on me. On my hands."

Her fingernails were tinted red. Steaks of blood had dried on the back of her hand.

"Sink." Snapped out.

He pointed to the bathroom and watched her dash away as he enjoyed the tight ripple of her ass. He followed slowly, the better to enjoy the view. *Nice.*

Dee wrenched on the water and, with his temperamental faucet, it flew everywhere. But she didn't so much as flinch beneath the lash of what he knew to be icy cold water. Simon stalked closer and watched as she grabbed his soap and began to all but scrub the flesh off her fingers.

After about five minutes, he told her, "I think you've got it."

She stiffened. Dropped the soap. The rush of the water seemed too loud to him. Always did, though.

"Check me." She growled the words. "I've got to know."

He eased up behind her, and he saw her elbow move as she turned off the water. But Dee didn't turn to face him.

The lights blazed in the small bathroom, giving him a perfect view of her body. Small, fragile . . . sexy. Even though she was small, the woman really had a fine ass. Maybe it was those panties. They hugged her curves so very, very well.

"Simon."

His fingertips skimmed her shoulders. "Hold still."

He caught the sharp inhalation of her breath. His gaze lifted from that sweet ass and scanned the rest of her body. Okay, his cock was so hard that it was about to bust through his jeans, but he'd hold onto control and manage to focus for a while. He had to, for her.

This—his fingers trailed over her small shoulder blades— *was important.* To her and to him.

Because if she'd been bitten, then she'd been compromised. She'd be a risk to herself, to her friends.

To him.

Not that a bite would change his plans. No way would he abandon her now. Not when he'd really just found her.

"The bra's got to come off." Guttural. Too bad. Not like he could manage much more than that. Simon figured he was lucky to be able to speak right then. His fingers slipped under the straps, then trailed down to the hook. If the vamps had fed on her, they would have tried to hide the mark.

They wouldn't want her aware.

The better to keep track, to torment.

He unhooked the snap. Pushed the bra off her shoulders and let it fall.

Simon had one damn good idea why the vamps had let Dee keep breathing and why they'd tried to set her up.

Word on the street was that certain vamps had plans for Sandra Dee. Plans of pain and madness.

Death would have been too easy.

His mouth hovered over her, right above her shoulder. The skin looked so tender. He could—

"What do you see?"

Simon jerked back. "Let me check your front."

A huff, but she spun around.

His eyes widened when he saw her tight nipples. Still wet from the spray of water. Pointed, arching right up to him.

Fuck. The woman had a concussion for shit's sake. He couldn't devour her now, no matter how hungry he might feel.

He wasn't that much of a bastard.

Was he?

Her hands clamped on him. "Check." Breathy there. Hungry—*just like me.*

Because she felt it, too. The lancing heat of lust. Always there. When she was close, he burned.

He slapped his hands against the sink, caging her. He let his eyes touch her flesh, the way his hands and mouth wanted to do so badly. "Lift your arms."

Of course, the move just made those breasts arch more.

Dammit. *Con-cus-sion.*

His gaze raked across her flat stomach. Down to the black bikini panties.

"Trust me, Simon, I'd know if I'd been bitten there."

His lips curved. Couldn't help that. "Fair enough." He sure didn't need that sensual temptation then, anyway.

He wrapped his hands around her waist and he lifted her. He put her down on the counter—probably with a bit too much force—and reached for her legs.

"*Simon.*"

He pinned her with his stare. "You wanted this."

A grim nod. Her pupils were too big. Her eyes so dark. Almost like a vampire's. Almost.

He caught her right leg. Curved his fingers around the flesh and stroked upward. No breaks in the skin. No tears. No blood.

Her skin was so silken and soft. As he touched her, his heart slammed into his ribs. Simon pressed a kiss against her thigh. *Can't help it.*

A soft rasp came from Dee.

His fingers stilled around her knee. "If I find something, what are you gonna do?"

Her lips parted.

The question had to be asked. Had to be. His fingers rose.

Her eyes narrowed. "I'll get as far away from those bastards as I can."

Good. The more distance, the less control they'd have. A lesson he knew well.

"Did you find something?" She whispered and there was a quaver of fear in that husky voice.

"Not yet." He caught her left leg. Stroked her calf, worked up her leg and curved his fingers over her thigh. "I don't think they touched you."

They wouldn't have dared. Not if they were following orders, and he suspected that there were definite orders out for Dee.

They'd jerked her around. Had their fun.

Break her, but don't taste. Not yet.

An old order he'd once heard a vampire give. Sick bastard.

He left his hand on her thigh. Such smooth skin. Such strong muscle beneath the silk.

His teeth ground together. Only one more place to check, and she'd already told him that sweet spot was off limits. "You're clear," he gritted and shoved back.

Dee blinked at him. Then her gaze dropped, fell to his crotch, to the bulging hard-on he knew there was no hope of hiding.

Not like he wanted to hide the thing anyway. He wanted Dee. He'd have her. But not when she was still spinning from an attack.

He stepped back, giving her some room, and yanked off his shirt. Simon stared at those breasts. *Want them in my mouth.* Her scent surrounded him. That deep, rich scent that was Dee.

His cock throbbed.

Could have found her corpse. The stake could have been lodged in her heart.

Then what the hell would I have done?

What. The. Hell?

Simon tossed Dee his shirt. "Cover up." The thing would swallow her.

Her fingers fisted in the material, catching it easily. "Simon, I—"

"Get. Dressed." He sucked in a harsh gulp of air. "Or get fucked because, babe, it is a very near thing." A gentleman, no, he'd never been that. The woman might not realize it, but he was *trying* for her.

Trying to protect her. From the freaks out there who were after her, and even from himself.

Slowly, taking her sweet time about it, Dee stuck her arms into the sleeves of the shirt. She hadn't put her bra back on— what, did she want to torture him? He could see the tips of her nipples and he hadn't gotten to taste them and—

Simon spun away from her. "Just so you know," he growled. "I was an idiot the other night." *Should have taken her. Would have made things easier.*

"Huh." A pause. "So what's your excuse now?"

His head swung back toward her. "The concussion that has you trembling, your eyes dilated, and your speech still slurred." Okay, not really slurred. He'd just thrown that one out for fun and to make his point. The woman was barely on her feet, if he took her, no—*no*.

"So, when I'm healed, it's game on?"

What? His eyes slit. "Count on it." Was this some bluff? Some tease? She'd learn soon enough he wasn't the teasing kind.

"Good." Her smile punched him in the gut and had him almost weaving. "Because I'm tired of waiting on your hard-to-get ass."

The laughter came from him, a little rusty and a little too hard.

That smile of hers widened, showing her pretty white teeth. Then she laughed with him, even as she put up a hand to touch the base of her head.

Oh, shit. He couldn't look away from the fullness of her lips. *I'm in trouble.*

Headed straight to hell, following a woman who would never be an angel.

Antonio entered the Night Watch building just before dawn. Hunters milled around, voices buzzed. The place was always the busiest at night.

The darkness was the best cover for catching prey.

He hurried past the line of back offices, a file gripped tightly in his left hand.

Rounding a corner, he headed down that last, lonely stretch of space—

"Sir? Sir, may I help—"

New assistant. Antonio halted. Great. Leave it to Pak to be breaking someone new in now.

Turning slowly, he eyed Pak's new PA. The woman looked to be pushing seventy. Her hair was a white mane, and her dark eyes were narrowed behind her wire-framed glasses. Her shoulders had stooped with time, just a bit. The woman looked like a small wind could slam her against the wall.

She also looked like she was someone's grandmother.

But, knowing Pak and the folks he liked to employ, odds were good that the woman was a witch. A demon. Or . . . who the hell knew what else.

Flashing his badge in a quick move, Antonio said, "I need to speak with Pak. It's urgent." Or else he wouldn't have dragged his butt across town. He would have been at home, in bed, dreaming of—

"Why you want to see him?" Her head cocked. Her thin lips pursed.

His brows rose. "Can't say, ma'am. This is a private matter." For now. But when the news got hold of this story . . .

"Hmmmph."

Pak's door opened down the hallway. A soft creak that had Antonio's shoulders stiffening.

"Antonio, come on in."

He inclined his head, casting one last glance at the woman. "Ma'am."

She moved her head in the faintest of regal acknowledgments.

He marched into Pak's office. The door closed behind him with that same creak.

Pak didn't sit. The guy just stared at Antonio with his dark, can't-read-me eyes. After about thirty seconds, Pak asked, "Where is my hunter?" And Antonio knew they were on the same page.

He handed Pak the file. "Don't know, but we damn well need to find out." He exhaled and fought to keep his voice flat, unemotional. Hard, that. Because he cared about Dee. More than he'd ever cared for another woman. "We've got trouble, Pak."

The guy that *was* Night Watch grunted as his eyes scanned the typed notes. "Her fingerprints were on the murder weapon."

"Doesn't mean anything," Antonio said, even though he knew he shouldn't. He should at least pretend to be impartial, but—this was Dee. "Someone could have lifted one of her weapons. The lady's got too damn many stakes. I've been telling her that for years." But Dee always had the weapons. She hid them around her apartment for God's sake. Not that he really blamed her, with her past.

Pak's fingers whitened around the file. "Someone saw Dee attack the victim on the previous night?"

Yeah, and that shit was the part that was biting them all in the ass. "I've got two witnesses who told uniforms they saw

Dee fighting with a woman matching the victim's description the night before. They were behind Onyx. The bartender there ID'd Dee."

"She was working a case." A fierce growl. "You know she doesn't hurt humans."

Dee's number one rule. Yeah, he knew it. That was why he was there. "She left the crime scene. We've got hair samples that I'm sure will match her." Had to match, everything else was so nice and neat. Like it had been gift wrapped for him. "Her leaving . . . man, that doesn't look good."

Pak glanced up at him. Those eyes were as dark as a demon's. Well, when a demon let the glamour drop anyway. "We're not sure Dee left willingly."

What?

With steady fingers, Pak placed the file on top of his perfectly arranged desk. "There's been no contact from Dee since she was last seen by Zane on the mission. Her car is still at the bar. She hasn't gone back to her house. She's made no attempt to contact the agency."

His stomach knotted. "Is she alive?"

One shoulder lifted. "At this point, I can't say for certain." A pause. "I *can* say that Dee would never kill a human."

Not intentionally, anyway. "What if things got away from her? What if there was an attack and she was fighting the vampires and the woman—the woman attacked her, too?" Made sense. He'd sure been over all the different scenarios a dozen times. *Trying to find a reason, an excuse.* "She would have acted to defend herself. She would have—"

"She wouldn't have left on her own. If that's the way it went down, she would have stayed, waited for the cops."

True. That was the way Dee worked. Or so he'd thought. "You're looking for her," Antonio said, statement, not question.

A nod.

"We've got to be careful with this, *very* careful." The wrong word, the wrong ear to hear it, and the town would explode. "The vic, she was the niece of Craig Durant—the senator.

He's already been calling the PD, talking to the DA." He shook his head. "This case won't disappear easily." If at all.

No expression crossed Pak's face. "Thank you for coming to me with this information. I'll remember how helpful you were to me."

"Yeah, right." He ran a hand over his face. His eyes were so grainy they hurt. "When my ass gets tossed off the force for sharing confidential info, I just hope you have a job for me." He turned away, marching for the door.

"Don't worry." Pak's soft voice. "I will."

Pak waited for the cop to leave. A good guy, if too grounded in human ways.

He glanced at the manila file, then picked up his cell phone. Dee's number was one of the few automatically programmed in the phone because she was one of the few who mattered to him.

The text message was short. Simple.

Don't come in. Cops are hunting you.

Dee wouldn't go to jail. He'd never let that happen.

Stick to the case. Kill the Born Bastard.

Before the Born succeeded in killing her.

"Why didn't they kill me?" Dee asked as the first rays of dawn began to appear on the horizon.

Dawn. Her favorite time. She loved it when the light kicked night's ass across the sky.

Simon sat next to her. They were on his back porch. Small, compact. Two old rocking chairs that reminded her too much of her past.

At her question, he turned to her and his eyes seemed shuttered. "Why do you think you're still breathing?"

"Don't know." She wouldn't have asked the question if

she knew. What was this, some kind of Freud crap? "They're setting me up, and—"

Her pocket vibrated. No, her phone. She'd jerked on her jeans earlier, knotted Simon's shirt at her waist, and tried to feel normal. She'd even found her phone, checked the battery, and thought about calling Pak.

She'd also realized that if the vamps were truly setting her up, he might be ass-deep in cops. So she'd waited.

Protocol for an agent in trouble was to wait, stay low for twenty-four hours, then seek contact.

Unless a superior from Night Watch contacted first.

She pulled out her phone. Punched the buttons until she saw her text, then her breath whistled out. "Damn."

Simon rose. "Trouble?"

Of course. Like good tidings followed her. Dee licked her lips and glanced up at him. "Can I . . ." Yeah, his gaze had definitely heated with the swipe of her tongue. Her heartbeat kicked up a notch. "Can I stay with you? Just for a day or two?"

His gaze was still on her mouth. "I already said you could. Stay as long as you want." The words were a dark rumble.

Oh, they would so be getting into bed soon. Her head was better now. The swelling had eased. No more black spots danced before her eyes.

Simon had pushed for a visit to the hospital, but she hadn't wanted to risk that.

Vamps loved hanging out in hospitals. Talk about free and easy access to a blood supply.

If she'd had double vision, if she'd passed out, if she'd vomited on Simon's sexy self, then, yeah, she would have found a doctor.

But it looked like she'd pull through.

And that she'd get to jump Simon soon.

"You keep saving me," she told him. Weird. Usually, she did the saving. The protecting. She wasn't quite sure how to act with him. But twice, *twice,* he'd saved her butt from the flames.

"You'll do the same for me." Absolute certainty.

Her eyes narrowed. That phrasing . . . it was off. Not, *you'd do the same,* but *you'll do.* She forced a laugh. "Don't worry. I always pay my debts. In fact, I—"

He caught her arms. "We need to go inside."

His hold seemed too tight. "Uh, okay."

Simon's lips thinned. "I'm . . . sorry. I'm tired. Hell of a night, you know?"

Oh, yes, she did.

He eased his grip.

And Dee realized he looked tired. There was an edge of darkness under his eyes. The faint lines near his mouth had hardened.

Only fair, considering I probably look like warm hell.

She followed Simon inside. He bolted the back door, rolled his shoulders. Then he asked, voice distracted, "You want some food?"

She'd already had a shower, and sure, food sounded real good right then "Yes, why not?"

His head shot up and his gaze zeroed in on the front door. *"Fuck."*

An icy stillness settled over her. "Uh, Simon?"

"Company."

Understanding hit hard. "And here we are without a welcome mat out." *Weapon.* Simon had to—

The windows exploded. Glass shattered, raining into the room as bullets ripped through the panes.

Shards hit her, cutting deep, and the rapid fire thunder of the guns echoed in her ears.

Sonofabitch.

Dee hit the floor just as the wooden front door burst apart. Bits of wood flew across the room, some biting into her flesh, some scraping the skin right off.

She crawled behind the couch. Pitiful cover, but it was better than nothing. Simon inched toward her. A long trickle of blood ran down the side of his face.

Dee sucked in a quick breath. Whoever was firing—the bastards were sure doing a fine job of shooting up the place.

Where was her gun? Back in that blood-soaked room? Perfect time to be unarmed.

Simon grabbed her shoulder. "We've got to run for it," he whispered.

That didn't seem like the best option, but then, sitting there and waiting for the assholes with guns to come and shoot her right in the face didn't seem like such a fine plan, either.

He pointed to the right, to a closed door. "Garage," he mouthed.

Five feet away. Maybe six. But where were the shooters? Still outside? Or working their way in?

The faint groan of wood reached her ears. The porch was wooden. Old, faded wood. *Fuck.* Their attackers were getting too close.

"Go!" Simon heaved her up, moving at the same time to cover her back. Dee lunged for the door. *How had they found them so quickly? How had—*

Bam. Bam.

One bullet cut right across her shoulder. *Sonofabitch.*

Using her left hand, she jerked open the door.

Simon hit a button on the wall even as he fell into her. They tumbled down three steps, hit the concrete, hard, and staggered up in a tangle of limbs and curses.

The Mustang waited. Black coat gleaming. Dee jumped into the passenger seat even as more bullets flew. Simon took the wheel.

The garage door was opening—must have been a door control that he hit before—

"Here." He dug under the seat. "Get those bastards off our backs."

A gun. A sweet, black Beretta that fit perfectly in her hands.

Two assholes in black appeared, heading down the steps into the garage. Ski masks covered their faces and their guns were up.

Simon jerked the gear shift into reverse. Dee hoped the garage door was open enough.

Bullets plowed into the windshield. One. Two.

Dee shot right back. The bullet hit the guy high in the shoulder. Not a flesh wound, a deep thud of bullet into muscle and bone. And so down went one jerk in black. The other dove for cover.

"Fuck! Behind us!"

She spun around. Two more men, revealed now by the opening in the garage. Guns up. *Since when did vamps hunt in the daytime? And wear ski masks?*

"Hold on," he growled and the car flew backward even faster.

Because he was aiming right for the men.

They jumped away at the last second, flying to the overgrown side of the road before the Mustang rammed them.

Simon shifted quickly. The Mustang snarled forward, horses pounding away.

Dee stared back at the men. Not giving chase. Not yet. Too busy picking their beaten butts up off the ground.

And the way Simon was driving . . . hell, no, they wouldn't be following them anytime soon.

The Mustang was easily pushing one hundred on the long, empty stretch of road.

Dee took a deep breath. The first she'd had since she'd risen from her cover in his den. Her shoulder burned like a bitch. Carefully, she unlocked her white knuckled grip and clicked on the gun's safety before she put in on the floorboard.

Wincing, she touched the wound. Okay. A lot of blood, but the bullet hadn't gone in the shoulder, just grazed her. No big damage. She'd keep living.

Dee eyed Simon. "Are you hit?"

He growled at her. Seriously, *growled*.

Dee reached for him. "Simon?"

His head jerked toward her. "Back off." His teeth snapped together.

What? Her hand hovered in the air between them.

He shook his head even as his knuckles whitened around the wheel. "Don't touch me now."

Her fingers fisted, then fell. "I-I didn't think someone would come after me." Not so quickly. But, hell, she should have known. Someone could have easily followed her and Simon from that death pit.

And that someone had wrecked his house. Nearly killed him.

Yeah, because all that will put a smile on a guy's face. No wonder he was growling at her. She'd just brought her usual death and danger into the guy's life.

"You didn't ask for this," she said, even as she glanced back to make sure they still weren't being followed. This time, she was alert enough to spot a tail. Being unconscious had really slowed down her game before. "I-I'll contact Zane at the first safe stop. Get him to come for me and—"

"The hell you will." Guttural, but without the dark fury of before.

"Dammit, don't you see what being with me is doing to you?" He had to see it. "Those bastards were after *me*, Simon, they wanted—"

"Fuck what they wanted." He spared her a burning glance. "I'm not letting you out of my sight."

What?

He shifted in his seat, flinching a bit. "And those weren't vampires, babe. Since when do vamps hunt in the daylight? And use guns on prey?"

Hardly ever. Vamps didn't explode in the sunlight. That was just some BS myth Hollywood had invented. Good old Bram had been right when he'd said that vampires could walk in the daylight. They were just weaker in the hours of light—human weak. Dee had always figured Bram must've had the inside track on the vamps.

As for using guns . . . why shoot your prey? For vampires, that was just a waste of good blood. Dee swallowed. "Why would vamps send humans after me?"

"After *us*."

Her eyes narrowed. Sweat beaded Simon's upper brow.

"They know I'm helping you," he muttered. "Now they're trying to shut us both down. Not. Gonna. Happen."

The car jerked a bit. "Simon?"

He shook his head. "All . . . right." His fingers tightened around the steering wheel, but his eyes began to drift shut.

"No, you're not." Her heart slammed into her ribs. "You're hit, aren't you?" *Don't touch me now.* Gruff and angry. Had to be man slang for *I'm hurting*. "Stop the car, let me see what—"

"No! Won't . . . let them . . . take you . . ."

Uh, being all macho and protective was kind of sexy, especially since she was usually the ass-kicking one, but . . .

The car swerved off the road and headed straight for the line of twisted pines.

"*Simon!*" Dee lunged for the wheel.

Chapter 6

Simon stared at the grim-faced reflection in the broken gas station mirror.

He'd fucked up. Gotten distracted by a sexy smile and curvy body.

He hadn't been on guard, hadn't known the attackers were going to hit until it was too late.

Running—his only option. He *hated* to run.

When the gun had fired, he'd taken the hit. Taken it hard, right in the back. A human would have died.

Good thing he wasn't a human.

Dee had saved *his* ass when she taken the wheel. A head-on crash with trees. Never good.

But if he didn't do something, fast, Dee would be stalking her pretty little ass into the dingy restroom and demanding answers.

She knew he was hurt, but she hadn't figured out how badly. Not yet.

If he had his way, not ever.

Simon jerked off his shirt, gritting his teeth as the pain knifed into his back. He spun around, craning his neck to see the wound in the mirror.

Dee waited just outside the door. She'd tucked the gun into the back waistband of her jeans and the woman was standing guard.

But he doubted he had more than a few minutes time until she burst in to see what the hell had happened to him.

The wound was open. Deep as hell. The bullet had lodged inside. No way could he get it out now. Eventually, he'd find someone to dig it out. He just had to stop the blood loss now.

Because if he didn't stop bleeding, his ass would be in serious trouble.

Human attackers. That bastard Grim was playing smart. He hadn't sent his vamps because they would have been weak in the growing sun. But humans, probably puppets desperate for that immortal kiss, had done his dirty work.

And really screwed Simon over.

The door squeaked open. The scent hit him instantly. Cigarettes. Coffee.

"Hey, hey, buddy!" The door swung closed behind the guy. Balding, but young. Fit. "What the hell happened to you?"

Simon cocked his head. *Shouldn't* . . .

But there was no choice.

"Do you—do you need some help?" Ah, a good Samaritan. Wouldn't those guys ever learn?

The Samaritan crept closer. "There's a woman outside. I can get her to call for help—"

"No . . ."

The Samaritan moved a few more precious inches closer. Perfect.

Simon's hand whipped up and caught the guy right around the neck, closing off his airway. "I can't let you call for her at all."

The fear came then. In the widening of the man's eyes, in the fast drumming of his heart.

"Don't worry," Simon said, "I'm not going to kill you."

"Simon?" Dee's worried voice as she rapped on the door. "Everything okay?" The rusty door began to inch open.

"Fine!" He yelled back. "Be right there."

The door froze.

He stared into his prey's eyes. "I won't kill you," he repeated again because the guy had really only wanted to help.

And that was exactly what he'd do.

Three minutes later, Simon left the Samaritan sleeping in a bathroom stall. The *cleaner* stall. The one that didn't have feces floating in the toilet.

Dee still waited outside for him.

"We need to hit the road," he told her, trying to brush past her.

"No, you're hurt. Let me help you—"

He shook his head. "Flesh wound, just like yours." The scent of her blood hung in the air between them. Not as much of a temptation though, not now.

She braced her legs and cocked her chin. "Let me see it."

This part, he'd expected. Dee Daniels was one stubborn woman. He lifted his shirt. Twisted a bit, and showed her the long gash on his lower left side.

Not really a mark made by a bullet. One he'd carved himself, using his claws.

He and Dee were sure going to have to talk soon. No way would he be able to keep hiding his true self from her.

Just wanted her to trust me first.

Trust. Such a hard thing to earn and so easy to lose. One word. One wrong move and she'd turn away from him.

"They've got some bandages inside," she said. "Let me get some, clean you up better."

A grim nod. If that was what she wanted. "Only if we do the same to you." They'd have to hurry. Simon didn't want to risk any more unexpected company. Not until his strength had fully returned.

Dee turned away from him, but he reached out and snagged her arm.

A frown pulled her brows low when she glanced back at him. "Simon?"

"Trust me, Dee."

She blinked. "I don't—"

"I know, you *don't*." That was the problem. "I just want you to try. I'm not one of the bad guys." Well, depending on your definition of bad. "You and I—we want the same thing."

For the vampires who were hunting her to pay.

"I know you're after the Born," he told her, deciding to cut through the shit.

Dee's gaze darted around the deserted lot. "Not here. We can't talk about this now—"

His back teeth clenched. "Then let's hurry and get to safety, because we damn well have to talk."

And maybe, just maybe, confess.

Can't. Lose. Her.

Safety was her grandfather's cabin. A place he'd built by hand long, long ago.

Her parents had sold the place when she'd been a kid, but she'd gotten lucky and been able to buy it back two years ago. *The only tie to my family.*

Winding dirt roads took them back to the two-bedroom shelter. The old wood gleamed in the bright sunlight.

"Not much," she murmured. "But I installed a generator up here a few months ago. So, we'll have power, a roof over us, and time to figure out our next move."

He eyed the cabin. "Can the vamps trace this place back to you?"

Dee slammed her door and ignored the throb in her shoulder. "No, Night Watch made sure this place was buried for me." Because she'd wanted a retreat, no, a haven.

Pak had made certain she was protected.

She found the key she'd hidden so carefully on her last visit. The scent of pine teased her nose. Birds chirped from their nests high in the trees. "Come on," she said. "We're both about to crash." And after the night they'd had, the crash would be *hard.*

A flick of her hand and the key slid into the lock. The door opened soundlessly and the place was just as she'd left it. Rocking chair, faded rug, the quilt she'd—

"Uh, are those stakes?"

A smile lifted her lips as she stared at the glass gun cabinet. "Stakes . . ." She crossed the room and spun the lock, turning the code automatically. "Knives, guns. Everything we need to be ready for those bastards."

Her hand lifted and opened the door. Then her fingers smoothed over the wood and tested the sharp points of the stakes. If she'd been better armed before, they wouldn't have been on the run now. No way would she be caught unaware again. Out here, every sound was magnified. Human ears or not, she'd hear the assholes coming long before they stepped onto her small porch.

"You hate them, don't you?"

At his soft question, Dee glanced back and found Simon watching her with hooded eyes.

No need to ask about the "them" in question. "Don't *you?*" She fired back. "I know what happened, Simon. I know they killed your family. Slaughtered them, just like they did mine."

His jaw tightened and he slammed the cabin door closed with his heel. "I want those bastards. I want them to *pay.*" He wrenched the lock into place and stalked toward her. "I took some of them out already. Hunted them down . . ." He reached behind her, grabbed one of the deadly stakes, "and made them beg for death."

Her breath caught. *Vengeance.* How long had she wanted it?

"How long have you been hunting the ones who killed your family, Dee?"

"Since that night." A stark whisper. But she'd been little more than a kid. She hadn't known where to hunt. Hadn't known how to track. By the time she'd learned, they'd been long gone from the city. "I won't stop," she told him and her gaze darted to his hand. The stake was so sharp. So deadly. "Not until I find the bastards." Because she'd never forget their faces. Never.

He pulled back a bit and lifted the stake between them. "How many vampires have you killed? How many did you stake because you were trying to punish the ones who hurt you?"

Her eyes narrowed. What was this? She wasn't in the mood for some kind of therapy session. Not her thing. "The vamps I staked were killers. They got off on fear, on torture—"

"So vampires are all evil? They all have to be put out of their misery and given a one-way ticket to hell?"

"Aren't they?" He'd hunted, too. *Just like me.* She caught his hand and wrapped her fingers around the stake. "I've never met one who wasn't addicted to the power." That was the problem with vamps. As humans, maybe they'd been okay, normal even, but when they woke as vampires, the power rush got to them. Human life lost its meaning.

Humans became nothing more than prey. No, *food.* And so many vamps enjoyed playing with their food.

He grunted. "I have."

"What?"

His lips thinned and pulled away from her, dropping the stake onto the floor. "The vamps who went after my family. Hell, yeah, they were freaks. Sick, twisted bastards who deserve hell, but I-I've met vamps who aren't pure evil."

She stared at him, waited.

Simon exhaled. "You need to open your mind, babe. You got a raw deal. We both did, but hating every vampire isn't gonna bring your folks back." A pause. "Killing 'em all won't either. Trust me, I know."

Dammit, she knew that, too. But when she'd first started hunting, the rage of revenge had been all she'd had.

She hadn't wanted to live. When the remains of her parents, and, God, Sara, were hauled out the next day, she hadn't wanted to take another breath. She'd fallen to her knees, wished for death.

Even thought about—

Dee shook her head, hard. Her mother had died for her, no

way would she have taken the easy way out. "Sometimes vengeance is the only thing that keeps you going." Especially once you found out the world wasn't the happy, picture perfect postcard all the TV ads promised you.

His hands fisted at his sides. "There's more to life than death, Dee."

Her lips trembled at that. Not a smile. Not yet. "Tell that to the vamps."

"I'm telling it to you."

She swallowed. "Why are you here? Why did you track me to that vampire hell? What do you—"

"Would you rather I'd just left you in the pool of blood? Left you with the body and with the cops on the way?" His shoulders stiffened. "Well, fuck, next time I'll know to just leave you the hell alone."

He spun away. She reached for him. Her fingers brushed over his shoulder.

Simon stilled.

"I'm not good at this emotional stuff," she told him, and felt rough, awkward. "I know how to fight. I know how to kill. I don't know how to—" *Love.* No, no, they weren't talking about love.

Don't go there.

But he wanted more from her than she was used to giving. That need was there in his eyes, in his voice, in the rough demand of his questions. Simon wasn't going to settle for small offerings from her. He wasn't that kind of guy. She'd have to open up to him if she wanted to keep him.

And she wanted to keep him with her. Maybe the best way to do that was to start by being *civil.* She could do that. She could drop her guard and try being normal.

So she let the armor fall and jerked up her big girl panties. "Thank you for pulling my butt out of that place."

He glanced at her. "Hard, wasn't it?"

Uh, yeah.

"You're not used to needing anyone else."

No, even at Night Watch, she usually worked on her own. She liked it that way. If you had a partner, you'd start to care too much.

Then it would hurt like a bitch when the partner left . . . or died. Hunters at Night Watch didn't always have the longest life expectancy.

Slowly, he turned fully toward to her. His hand lifted, skimmed her cheek. "I told you I knew about the Born coming to the city." His fingers were light, but strong. His thumb brushed over her lips. "Every vamp in the city is lit up because of him. Some are scared shitless. Some are thrilled."

Because some loved to see death and chaos.

"He'll bring hell, Dee. Born Masters have too much power. He'll bring the vamps he's turned, all those . . ." A gritted jaw, then, "*puppets* that he controls, and he'll burn down the city if he can."

Borns didn't come out and play much in the States. Not much at all. Because when they played, life ended.

"I'm going to stop him," she breathed the words against his fingertip. She would stop him. Dee was certain of that. Maybe not too sure of the *how* part of the equation, but she'd find a way to stop him. There wasn't any other choice.

"No."

She blinked.

"*We'll* stop him." A vow. Then he kissed her.

Just what she'd been wanting.

Dee rose onto her toes, locked her arms around him, and held on tight.

So she sucked with emotions and nice words, but getting physical was definitely her strong suit.

His tongue thrust into her mouth and she moaned, loving that strong glide. His lips were firm, hard, just what she wanted, and her nipples tightened as need burned through her.

The aches, the pains, the fears—all faded away.

Lust. Hunger. Need—all that remained.

His hands slid down her back, curled over her ass, and jerked her up high against him.

No mistaking the swollen ridge of his cock.

Good, I'm not alone in this.

His mouth tore from hers. "Not stopping this time."

"You'd better not."

His lips pressed against her throat. Oh, Christ. Her sex creamed. Yeah, her panties were about to get really wet. Good thing she wouldn't be wearing them much longer. "Bed," she gasped. Not real big, but it would do. "Next . . . room."

He'd had her naked, but she hadn't seen him. Not yet.

Soon.

Flesh on flesh. Pleasure fighting the darkness. *That* was what she wanted.

Because the darkness always followed her, even in the daylight.

They fumbled their way to the bed. Kissing. Stroking. Hands sliding over flesh and making the lust spike.

Not stopping. Not!

He hit the button for the lights. No windows in this room. You had to have the lights to see.

She definitely wanted to see everything.

Dee shoved him onto the mattress and laughed when his eyes widened.

Then she stripped. Nothing fancy, because she wasn't the strip tease type. Her borrowed shirt hit the floor. No bra. Not like she really needed one.

She kicked off her shoes. Pushed down her jeans—

"Damn, Dee." He licked his lips. "I could eat you."

No, this was *her* turn. Her panties fell to the floor.

His nostrils widened, just a bit.

"You've got too many clothes on," she told him.

He jerked off his shirt.

"Nice start." Her gaze darted to his jeans. "But I'd like to see more."

He held out his hand. She so didn't need a second invitation. Dee climbed onto the bed. Onto him. Straddled him. Her fingers trailed down his chest. Tight, strong muscles. A few scars, faint white lines of raised flesh.

Dee hesitated at the sight, all too aware of the marks on her own body. She wasn't perfect, not by a long shot. Especially not after that last tangle with the wolf.

But to her, Simon was perfect. The marks just meant he was a fighter. A survivor.

Like me.

As she stared at that expanse of muscled flesh, Dee realized she'd never seen a man look so good or feel so right. She bent and licked one taut brown nipple.

His breath hissed out.

He liked that. Good. She used her teeth on him. A little nip. Nothing too hard, she didn't want to—

Bite.

The whisper, almost a command, slipped through her mind and Dee jerked back.

Simon stared at her, eyes so intense. She shook her head.

His fingers rose, cradled her breasts. "You're so beautiful."

Lust could make men so blind.

Dee managed to unsnap his jeans. Being careful, though, because she didn't want to jar the bandage she'd placed on his—

"Don't go easy with me, babe." He pushed up. "Trust me, I can take anything you've got."

They'd see about that. His zipper came down with a hiss. No underwear. Her kind of man.

His cock was long and thick, bulging up toward her. The tip was dark, round, and smooth to the touch. She eased back, sliding her bare legs down his jean-clad thighs.

"Dee—"

Her turn.

Her mouth closed over his cock. Her tongue licked the broad head, tasted the saltiness of his flesh.

"Fuck me."

She would. Eventually.

Dee took his length into her mouth. Looked up at him and saw his narrowed eyes, his clenched jaw, and the naked need on his face.

Just the way she wanted him.

Her tongue and lips teased. Took. Her cheeks hollowed as she worked his length.

She liked his taste. Liked the feel of his flesh and the jerks of his breath and—

His hand curled under her chin. "Can't . . . not much longer . . ."

One more lick, to prove that she'd do what she wanted. Then, one more because what she wanted was him.

"Dee!"

A caress with her lips, then she freed his flesh. But she still tasted him on her tongue. "Why should you get all the fun?"

In a flash, he flew forward, and Dee found herself flat on her back, near the edge of the bed. His mouth was on her breast. Sucking, licking, tasting, and taking.

Okay, so this was . . . damn . . . fun.

His fingers pushed between her thighs. Stroked her sex, thumbed her clit.

"So wet," he muttered, sending that lust-filled stare her way. "You're gonna feel fantastic."

So would he. Her teeth clenched and her heels dug into the bed. A few more strokes and she'd be coming. Just a few more.

A strong finger drove into her.

Dee bit her bottom lip.

"No!" He glared down at her. "Not this time. I want to hear every sound you make. Every sound."

Her mouth dried. *No holding back.* She always held back. Pushed her partner, but kept her own control as she—

"I want everything." Two fingers. "And I'm gonna have everything."

Her head fell back. So she'd come this way first, fine with her. The second time, he could be inside, he could—

"No, babe."

Her gaze snapped to him.

"Not without me."

He shoved a hand into the back pocket of his jeans. Pulled out a small foil packet.

She loved a man who was prepared.

Of course, she'd also picked up some condoms at that run-down gas station. Just in case.

Because she liked to be prepared, too.

He ripped the foil with his teeth. Rolled the protection down his thick length.

Then he pushed her thighs apart. Wider. He stared at her flesh. "Beautiful."

Simon drove into her, thrusting his cock balls deep into her sex.

She let her moan out, full and loud, because he felt *great*. And because she wouldn't hold back, not with him. Her nails dug into his arms.

He withdrew. Thrust deep. Again. Again.

"Harder." The coil within her tightened. Release—so close. *So close*.

Sweat slickened their bodies. Her hips rose to meet the plunge of his body. Faster. Stronger.

He stretched her, drove deep and had her shuddering for more.

Pleasure, that sweet release, was temptingly near.

Her legs curled around him. He pressed a hard kiss against her lips. His tongue thrust into her mouth.

Her sex quivered around him—that full, hard cock, driving so deep.

His head lifted. His teeth were clenched. Eyes glittering.

His neck was close to her. The strong curve of his shoulder. Close enough to—

Bite.

Her teeth snapped together. *What the hell?* Not during sex, she'd never wanted to—

His cock eased back, almost to the entrance of her straining sex.

She flattened her hands against his chest. *Push away. Fight the—*

His hot flesh slammed into her.

She came, screaming, "Simon!" Her muscles clenched as the white-hot wave crested. Her sex rippled around him, contracting as the pleasure blasted her.

"Better," he growled and his fingers dug into her hips. He lifted her up, arching her toward him and thrusting fast and deep. "So much better."

He bent toward her, pressing his lips against her neck. Tasting and licking her flesh. The muscles in his arms bunched. So much power there, so much strength.

He came on a long shudder, pumping out his release.

Her sex throbbed around him, the aftershocks of pleasure reverberating through her core.

Dee sucked in a breath. Then another one. She licked desert-dry lips.

His tongue skated over her neck.

She shivered. *Nice.*

His hold tightened around her as the sound of her drumming heartbeat filled her ears.

Oh, yeah, she'd known it would be that good. When a guy oozed sex like Simon, a good time was pretty much guaranteed.

Her hands skimmed down his back, and Dee realized that his muscles were locked tight. "Simon?" He'd come, she knew he had.

His lips pressed against her neck once more. A bit harder this time, then his head rose. His eyes were such a turbulent gray. Stormy.

"I don't ever want to hurt you," he told her, voice gruff.

Her brow pulled low. "Then don't." Simple enough.

A finger rose and traced her cheek. "You cried when you came."

Dee blinked. "I—" Okay, now she didn't know what to say.

"One tear drop. Just one."

"I don't usually—" Hell, she *never* cried. Not in years, anyway.

His lips pressed against hers. A soft, gentle touch after the wildness of the lust. His cock was still lodged in her, and swelling.

His mouth lifted, just an inch. "You can trust me," he breathed the words.

She'd already trusted him with her body. What more did he want?

But she could read the answer in his eyes. *Everything.*

And suddenly, even the heat of his body couldn't warm her. Because everything—she'd never had that to give a man.

They slept. Finally. Dee drifted away in Simon's arms. The sleep was deep, heavy, and filled with the soft whispers that haunted so many of her dreams.

Go, baby, go! Get out. Hurry! Her mother. Always warning her.

Dee—Dee, why didn't you help me? Sara. Always blaming her.

So many voices. So many.

Why, bitch, why'd you come after me? The vampires. Their last words haunted her.

Fucking whore. More of my kind will come. More. You can't stop us. Twisted murmurs that followed her into the darkness.

She couldn't escape the voices. No matter how hard she tried, she couldn't—

"Dee. *Dee.* Wake up." Strong hands shook her.

Her eyelids flew open. Simon stared down at her, his hair tousled, his face grim. "Someone's here."

A surge of adrenaline had her out of the bed and dressed in

moments. They ran to the outer room. Dee grabbed two stakes and a gun.

Simon didn't reach for a weapon. Funny, she'd actually never seen him armed.

She killed the lights and inched toward the window. A car door slammed outside. Gravel crunched beneath someone's feet. Carefully, she pushed the curtain back, just a tiny crack of space.

Darkness without, to match the blackness within.

Night had fallen.

The vampires would be at full strength again.

But since when did vamps come right up to your front door when they wanted to attack?

Her eyes adjusted almost instantly to the dark and she motioned with her hand, pointing for Simon to take up a position on the left hand side of the door. The right side would be hers.

As she watched, the door knob began to turn. *What? The bastard had picked the lock?* Skilled SOB.

Not that lock-picking talents would save his ass.

Dee waited in the darkness. Silent. Steady.

The door swung open. The scum walked inside.

Dee attacked.

She moved fast and came in hard. She caught the guy with a hard punch in the gut, then slung him back and rammed him into the wall.

Simon slammed the door closed. Good. Who knew how many of the bastards were out there? Better to separate them and make them weaker.

"Start talking," Dee ordered, pulling out her stake. "How many of your asshole friends are out there waiting for their turn to jump me?"

The guy moved, shifting from a hunched shadow to the tall, strong form of a man. Dee stared at him, frowning as—

"Dammit, Dee! Why the hell do you always have to punch first?"

She *knew* that voice. "Simon, hit the lights."

A bright flood of light lit up the room, and Dee stared at an all too familiar face. "*Tony?* What are you doing here?"

He pressed a hand to his stomach. Groaned, then said, "I'm here to arrest you for murder."

Chapter 7

"The hell you are." Simon lunged forward. No one would be taking Dee away from him. *No one.*

And sure as shit not the bastard who'd been her lover.

Captain Antonio Young lifted his chin and glared at him. "Who are you?" His hand still rubbed his wounded stomach.

"The guy who's been watching her ass." Simon let his lips curve into a feral smile. "And there's no damn way you'll be taking Dee out of here." But if the cop wanted to try . . .

Come and get some.

"Simon." Dee caught his hand. The cop's eyes dropped at the move, narrowed. *Oh, didn't like that, huh? Too bad.*

She bit her lip. "Are you . . . are you okay, Tony?"

He instantly dropped the hand he'd been pressing against his stomach. "Fine." Bit off. "I thought you were up here alone."

Ah, so that's why Lancelot had come bounding to the cabin. "How did you know I was even out here?"

Dark eyes flickered over her face. Too much emotion there. "I know you pretty well, Dee. I knew where you'd go if you wanted sanctuary." He held up a key. "And I stayed here with you before, remember?"

The hell he had. Simon's vision bled to red. So what—Dee had a habit of bringing lovers here?

Not any longer she didn't and if that pretty boy kept looking at her with his puppy dog eyes, he'd plant a fist in the guy's face.

Dee glanced at Simon, then looked away quickly. "I remember. That was a long time ago."

Good to know, and Simon didn't want to hear any more about *that*. "Dee didn't kill the woman."

The cop blinked, then looked over at Dee's left hand. Her fingers were clenched around a wooden stake. "Evidence says otherwise."

"It was a setup," Simon gritted. "The vamps want to take her down."

"Why?"

Dee jerked away from him and marched toward the weapons cabinet. *Some women collected figurines, Dee—*

Instruments of death.

"Why the hell would they go to all that trouble?" The cop, Tony, shook his head. "Vamps don't work like that. They kill, drain a vic dry, and—"

"And some of 'em are sick freaks who get off on playing with their prey." *Not all, though. Not all were like that. Dee would learn that truth. Eventually.* "They want to break Dee. Not just kill her. By setting her up, they rip her out of her nice, safe world." Not that Dee was much for safety. "They tear her away from her friends, isolate her—" He broke off, shaking his head. No, he couldn't say any more.

"I was fighting a pack of vamps behind Onyx." Dee's voice was flat. She crossed her arms over her chest. "My head hit the pavement, and the next thing I knew, I was in some stinking, dark room. Blood was all around me and your victim—"

"Lisa Durant."

"Was dead." Her shoulders tensed. "I don't remember anything that happened in between that alley and that room. I just remember—"

"I was there," Simon spoke, holding the cop's gaze and daring him for a challenge. "I saw the vamps kill the woman. They left Dee in her blood. I saw it all."

"Bullshit." Tony stepped forward. "I don't buy that—"

"It's my story." A brief pause. "The one I'll tell everyone I see if you so much as even *think* about hauling Dee away from here." Not going to happen. His temples throbbed in a sickening, painful rhythm.

No one could threaten Dee. She was too important.

"Oh, so you're just gonna fucking *out* the vampires?" Disgust had Tony's lips tightening.

"They outed themselves." Maybe it was time for the whole world to stop pretending. Feeding rooms were cropping up in most cities—and dumb humans were stumbling inside, some quickly getting addicted to vamp bites. Some never making it back out. Lucky for the vamps, they'd perfected the body ditch over the years.

"There's a Born Master coming to town," Dee said and she tilted her head. Simon's eyes narrowed. Yeah, that was his mark on her neck and he knew the cop saw it. No blood drawn, no bite since Dee didn't like that. But a sweet suck had done the trick. "I'm the best vampire hunter at Night Watch. You take me out of this game, and there's no telling what hell will come to the city."

Tony's eyes widened. Ah, so the dick hadn't ever come across a Born? Then he didn't know what hell looked like. "You can't kill Borns the way you can most vampires." No, they were so much harder to slay. He'd once heard of a Born who'd survived a stake to the heart *and* a partial beheading.

Their bodies were tougher. They healed ten times faster than the Taken. When you were changed into a vampire, you brought some of your human weaknesses with you.

But when you were *Born* a vampire . . .

There was no weakness for you. Not once the powers kicked in and the bloodlust began.

"*Who are you?*" Tony demanded again.

"Ease up, Tony. Simon's not the bad guy here." She unfolded her arms. "He knows what I'm up against. He can help me."

"And I can't?"

"No."

Tony flinched.

"You're a cop. You protect innocents." She shook her head. "But your job isn't to kill vampires."

"Some days it is," he fired back.

Simon's brows shot up. So the cop had some bite, did he?

"I know things look bad right now," Dee said.

"You *ran*, Dee. Innocent people don't run."

Okay, his fault. Simon rolled his shoulders. "I didn't give Dee much choice. When I hauled her out of that pit, she was barely conscious. Sirens were wailing—I just couldn't risk her."

"You couldn't, huh?"

"No." Nothing more to say on that. "The woman on the floor was dead. Dee wasn't. My priority was getting her to safety."

"Yeah, cause getting in her pants had nothing to do with it, right?"

Fuck him. Simon attacked. In a second's time, he had the cop pinned to the wall as his fist twisted the front of Tony's shirt. "Don't . . . talk about Dee like that."

A tap on the back of his shoulder. "Ease up. Tony just turns into an asshole when he's worried."

"He needs to watch that tendency. It'll get him into trouble soon." He held the cop's stare. "Real soon." He unknotted his fingers.

"Christ, Dee, where'd you find him?" Tony muttered, straightening his shirt.

"In an alley, one littered with bullets." She pushed in between the two of them. "Same place I found you a few years back."

A grunt, then his lips started to curl, just a bit.

"Tony, we were attacked right before dawn. Some guys in ski masks found us at Simon's house. They shot up the place." Her hand lifted to her shoulder. To the wound Simon had all but forgotten when he'd had her in that bed. "We were lucky to get out alive."

"*Hell.*"

"Yeah, that's where we are." She swallowed and Simon heard the soft click. "But I'll be damned if I stay here. I'm not going to keep hiding out, waiting for the vamps to strike. We needed to rest. We needed to recover—done that."

Simon knew where this was going. Knew, and didn't like it.

"Now it's time to hunt these bastards," she said. "Because I really don't like it when jerkoffs try to kill me, especially when I'm already down."

"Can't say I like it much, either," Simon added.

Tony's gaze snapped to him, then back to Dee. "You really think you'll be able to find the vamps?"

A little shrug. "It's what I do." Her chin was up. The woman was cute when she was promising death. "I was weak before, I'm not now."

Yeah, um, humans didn't recover that fast from concussions and gunshots. Maybe she was feeling all good and vampire-pumped-for-killing, but the woman still wasn't 100 percent.

Neither was he.

Not yet.

"Brass is leaning on me like a tree about to fall." Tony blew out a hard breath. "It's those witnesses who say they saw you fighting with the vic at Onyx. They're nailing your coffin shut."

Her gaze darted to Simon. "That part's right, Tony. Lisa . . . met me behind the bar. She was working for the vamps."

"A lure?" the cop asked.

"More a messenger," Simon said. "You know, the cheery kind that comes and says *You're going to die. Beg for death.* Blah. Blah."

Tony blinked.

Dee gave a little shrug. "She pissed me off. I lost my temper."

"That's the problem." Lines of worry tightened the cop's face. "Too many folks know about that temper of yours. It's not a leap to think you met up with the woman again, and got angry one more time, so angry you didn't stop yourself when the stake came out. After all, it's easy to kill, isn't it? So easy."

The guy sounded like he was speaking from experience. As if he could ever compare. "Give us time and we'll prove Dee's innocent." The words snapped out. *Not* what he'd been planning. Simon rubbed his temples. The throbbing was getting worse. The sleep hadn't been enough for him. To recover fully, he'd need so much more.

"The DA knows the score about this town," Dee told them. "Pak told me, after Erin Jerome's case . . . the DA *knows*."

Erin Jerome. Simon knew the name. Erin was the assistant district attorney. She was also involved with one of the Night Watch hunters, Jude, the shifter.

"Figured the bastard knew more than he let on." Tony ran a hand through his hair. "Too many cases that seemed to disappear before court date."

"This one has to disappear, too." Dee's body vibrated with tension. "I'll bring you a witness. I'll bring proof that I'm innocent, and I want Clark to make this thing vanish."

"And the vamps?"

"I'll make them vanish."

Big promise. Real tough to keep.

Tony stared at her. Too deep and way too long.

"Tony, give me this time. You know me."

Too well it seemed.

A grim nod. "Forty-eight hours."

"Tony—"

"It's all I can do. I'm not the only one on this case and I won't be able to hold the others back longer than that." A muscle flexed along his jaw. "Forty-eight hours—and you bring me a vamp who'll convince Clark you're clear or else I'll have to lock you up."

She whistled. "Not giving me much time to work, are you?"

"I'm giving you all that I can." He stepped toward her,

cupped her cheek with his palm, and very nearly lost a hand. "The last thing I want is to have to take you in, but I might not have a choice."

Simon gave him a long, level look. "There's always a choice." Always. Might not be the *right* choice, and that was the problem.

Tony dropped his hand. "Guess you're gonna be her back-up?"

"Guess so."

"Then you'd better take care of her or I'll be coming to kick your ass."

Doubtful.

The cop headed for the door. "Better hurry out of here," he tossed back, "the way I figure it, two squad cars will be pulling up in about thirty minutes."

Dick.

"You sent the uniforms after me?" A whistle. "Damn, man, you really did come to toss me in jail."

The dick in question glanced back at Dee. "No." A hint of sadness there. Regret. "I came to give you a chance, one I knew the others wouldn't. And that's why the uniforms won't be arriving until you're gone." A flash of white teeth. "So move that sweet ass, Dee. Get out there and find those vamps."

"So where the hell are we headed?" Simon asked, and tightened his fingers around the leather steering wheel. They'd been staying to the back roads, trying to fly under the radar as they headed back to the city, and the silence—thick, heavy— was getting on his last nerve.

Was Dee having regrets? Maybe seeing the old boyfriend had made her hesitate. That jerk had the worst timing.

"There aren't any feeding rooms in Baton Rouge."

Feeding rooms. His back teeth clenched. The places set up to look like bars but, deep inside, they were just all-you-can-eat buffets for vampires. Folks went inside and some never came back out. Others got addicted. They became controlled by the vamps, and they would do *anything* to go back into the rooms.

"Why aren't there any?" he asked. "I thought those places were in damn near every city now." Some said they were safe houses for vampires. And those *some* just really knew how to bullshit.

Not a safe house. More like a slaughterhouse.

Even though humans were the preferred prey in the feeding rooms, the vamps never had to worry about the humans turning on them and shouting to the authorities about the new night club that served up blood. After all, one bite, and a vampire could link with a human's mind.

A link meant control. You didn't turn on those who controlled you.

For the humans, it was all too easy to get hooked on the thrill of the bite.

If the vamp wanted the victim to feel pain, the bite could hurt more than a knife wound or gunshot.

The bite could also feel better than sex.

It was all up to the vampire. Pleasure or pain.

Simon slanted a quick glance at Dee's still figure.

Almost better than sex.

"I've made a point of shutting down any feeding room that tries to spring up."

Oh, yeah, he bet she had. "So where do we start then?"

He felt her eyes. Didn't have to look, just knew those chocolate eyes were on him. "I thought you had vamp contacts in this town."

Careful now. "Ah, the vamps I know scattered when word came down about the Born Master."

"Why? If they weren't linked to him, there'd be no need to flee."

The link. The screwed family tree that connected vampires. A Born Master took a victim, and formed a psychic connection with his prey. But if the Master turned that prey into the

Taken, and the new vampire took another victim, the Born Master's connection would trickle into the new prey, and keep trickling down through every blood exchange. Like freaking tentacles, reaching out for minds and spirits.

A Born Master wasn't just stronger physically than other vampires. He was like a psychic black hole, sucking in all the prey he could find.

And controlling them.

A Born Master didn't just pick up the thoughts of those in his link. He could whisper his thoughts to them. Compel them. Rule them. His army of helpless minions. Good, bad, everything in between. All his for the taking and for the killing.

The Taken were never truly free. Not until the Born Master who'd started their blood lineage was dead.

Never an easy feat.

"Huh. Well, if your contacts are out, then I guess we'll just have to do it the old-fashioned way."

Simon knew he was not going to like this. "And that would be?" He braked at a Stop sign, one that had been spray painted a garish yellow. They'd reached the edge of the city. The part where the good folks never visited. Too many criminals. Too much darkness.

Too much evil.

Simon glanced at Dee. Yep, her eyes were on him. "We find the perfect prey," she said simply. "Then wait for the vamps to take the bait. When they come up for a bite, we nail their asses."

"Interesting plan." His fingertips pounded a fast, hard beat on the steering wheel. "You really think it's going to work?"

One shoulder lifted. "Figure I've got a fifty-fifty shot with it. If it doesn't, then I have a witch who owes me a favor. Maybe I can get a summoning spell."

A *summoning spell?* Now she was talking spooky shit. You had to be damn careful when you used dark magic. You never knew what in the hell would hitch a ride on that darkness and come traveling straight to you.

As he watched her, thinking about his own darkness, a shiver worked over Dee's body. "Uh, Dee? You okay?"

"Fine. Just cold. Can we turn the heater up?"

Because summers in Baton Rouge were *cold*. Right. But he still flicked on the heater. Didn't matter to him. "Maybe we should wait." He sure wasn't feeling up to kicking major vampire ass right then. Perhaps after a meal or two.

"No time." She criss-crossed her arms and rubbed her flesh. She had on a light blouse, one of her shirts she'd found at the cabin. One that gave him a nice glimpse of her breasts. "We've already lost a few hours. We hunt, now and—*there*."

He followed her suddenly sharp gaze. A man had stepped out of the shadows. The faint red glow of his cigarette lit the night. "Who the hell is that?"

"An informer." She tilted her head and his stare snapped back to her and to that beautiful bared throat.

Focus.

But the drumming was back in his temples. Harder, more painful than before.

"Ian knows this city. He'll be able to tell me the latest whispers on the vamps."

Control. Simon sucked in a deep breath.

"I knew he'd be here." She unhooked her belt.

"And how'd you know that?" He gritted, turning off the engine.

Dee pointed toward the hollowed-out husk of a building on the left. "Because his brother died in that fire a year ago. He comes here every Friday. He comes to remember."

Simon narrowed his eyes and looked once more at that glowing cigarette. "Uh, yeah, how'd that fire start?"

"You don't want to know." She pushed open the door, then hesitated. "Ian doesn't take too well to others. Just stay here, okay? I'll only be a few minutes."

Staying in the fucking car. Was that what he'd been reduced to?

But the woman was gone. Running across the street. Disappearing in and out of the shadows.

Staying in the fucking car. No. Not his style.

He was there to watch her back. Not to be left behind.

He opened his door soundlessly, then, moving slower than her, but keeping to the same shadows, he began to follow her.

The smoke from the cigarette drifted to her nostrils. Dee stepped into the faint streetlight, deliberately placing herself in Ian's path. With Ian, you had to identify yourself fast—or he'd attack.

And sometimes, he attacked no matter what.

"Ian." She made her voice quiet but calm. "Ian, I need your help."

He was half-hidden by the darkness. The cigarette dangled from his fingertips. He wasn't smoking. Hadn't smoked in a year.

"Dee?" The tip of the cigarette bobbed and ash drifted into the night. "That you?"

Okay, he wasn't coming at her with fists yet. A good sign. She'd told Simon to stay back because one look at him, and she knew Ian would have broken.

The guy just hadn't been the same since the fire. Not that she blamed him. No, not at all. "Yeah, Ian, it's me."

He shifted his stance a bit, bringing the right side of his face more into the light. A strong, hard face. "Heard you killed a human, Dee." He shook his head. "Bad move that."

"I didn't do it, Ian."

"Humans are supposed to stick together. All those paranormal assholes out there want us gone. We have to fight 'em."

More ash drifted away.

"I want to fight them tonight, Ian." She had to keep Ian focused. So hard. The man already had one foot in the grave. Maybe *that* was how he did it because she sure as hell wasn't sure how he found out all his information about the *Other.*

Ian was psychic. She'd always known that. But since the fire, it was like he was some kind of open channel to the darkness in the city.

He took a step forward, and the light drifted across him, across the ruined, twisted, and reddened flesh on the left side of his face.

Dee kept her eyes on his. "Help me, Ian."

"The vampires are coming for you, Sandra Dee." His voice had hollowed and taken on that empty tone that came with his visions. "Inching ever closer. Closer than you know . . ."

Simon caught the scent in the air. *Blood.* Fresh blood. He jerked to a halt, his nostrils flaring. Dee stood about ten feet away from him, whispering to the bastard in the shadows.

But the blood scent was coming from the left. Drifting from the mouth of that alley. Garbage and decay—and sweet human blood.

He hesitated, his gaze on that yawning opening.

"Help . . ." The faintest of whispers.

Simon closed his eyes. An attack. Right there, so close.

Close enough for the blood to tempt him.

Dee had been right. This was the perfect place to hunt. But not for them.

These hunting grounds belonged to the vampires.

"Help . . . m—" A choked gurgle. A death cry.

Shit.

Simon ran for the alley's entrance.

Dee's head snapped up at the thunder of footsteps. *Simon.* She spun around and saw him run into an alley. Where the hell was he going?

Ian grabbed her hand, the hard flesh of his burnt fingers and palm scraping against her. "Coming from the inside, Sandra Dee. The thing you fear will take you tonight."

And just like that, the odd chill she'd felt in the car was back. "You telling me I'm going to die, Ian?"

His muddy gaze drifted back to the burnt house. "Saw the fire, you know. Dreamed it."

Ian always had his dreams. Dreams that had sent him to the edge of sanity and beyond. "I know about your dreams." Everyone knew, human and supernatural.

"Told Brian it wasn't safe. Told him to leave."

Brian. Ian's twin. Addicted to crack and eaten away by cancer.

"But then I felt the fire start, and I had to go to him. I knew—I *knew* he hadn't left."

He'd walked into the flames for his brother. Faced death.

And still Brian had been taken by the flames.

But Ian hadn't died. Not fully.

"I saw Death that night." He turned away, so that only the perfect side of his face remained. "I see him now. He's with you. Standing so close."

This wasn't the tip she'd wanted.

His lips rose in a humorless curl. "Don't worry, Sandra Dee. You won't be alone. I'll be right there with you. Every minute."

She rocked back. Shook her head. "I'm not dying tonight."

But that lop-sided smile didn't fade. "We both are," he whispered. "I dreamed about us last night. Sweet, beautiful dreams full of blood and screams."

A scream pierced the thick silence of the night, and Dee ran for the alley, Simon's name on her lips.

I'm not dying tonight.

Simon grabbed the vamp and threw him against the wall. The scent of blood flooded his nostrils and the hunger he'd tried so hard to fight bubbled to the surface.

Weak. Just need to feed once more.

No! Dee was too close.

He spared the screaming woman a glance. Blood trickled down her throat. "Get the hell out of here," he snarled. If the woman had sense, she would already be running.

He opened his mouth and bared his own fangs. "Get. Out."

But at the sight, the redhead just screamed louder.

And another vampire jumped him.

Dee ran fast, her heart slamming into her ribs. She caught sight of Simon, fighting with another man, both of them spinning and thrashing on the ground as—

Simon's attacker opened his mouth and sank his fangs into Simon's shoulder.

"*No!*" The scream burst from her.

Simon threw the vampire off him, sending the guy hurtling a good ten feet into the air. *What—how in hell had he done that?*

Some woman was screaming in a continuous howl, the sound piercing Dee's ears as the chick huddled near a Dumpster.

The vamp rose. "You think you can attack *me?* Chase, I'll fucking cut your heart out, you don't be—"

Simon ran straight for him. Tackled the bastard. "You won't do a damn thing to me!"

And then he sank his teeth into the vampire's throat.

Sank his *fangs* into the vampire's throat.

Dee froze, every muscle in her body hardening. No, please, Christ, no, this couldn't be happening.

The screaming snapped off, the silence rough and jolting. Dee wrenched out her stake. Realized her palms were soaked with sweat when she nearly lost her weapon. "*Simon?*"

He dropped the vampire and whirled toward her. Blood dripped from his mouth.

She'd wondered if he were fully human. Thought perhaps he might be a hybrid. Or a demon. Maybe a shifter.

In the end, she'd been leaning toward him being a charmer, like Pak.

But she'd never thought he was a vampire.

Not a vamp. Not him.

He licked his lips. *Licking the blood away.*

"You're a fucking vampire." What had Ian said? Shit, stupid, he'd said—*He's with you, Dee. Standing so close.*

Simon had been with her from the beginning, sneaking under her skin. Getting too close.

The perfect setup.

She'd trusted him. *Vampire.* No, no—

"Easy." Simon held up his hands. "I'm on your side, Dee."

No, he wasn't. He knew the vamp he'd just attacked. "You've been setting me up."

"No. I swear, I've been trying to help you."

Cigarettes and old smoke burned her nose. Ian had come to join the party. "It's time," he called out and Dee didn't glance his way. Fucking crazy Ian. He'd been insane since he and Brian shot up on that bad batch years ago and—

"It's time, bitch," another voice growled and Dee's gaze shot to her left. The woman—the one in the skin-tight dress and the spike heels, the woman with blood soaking her neck and a weird, trembling smile on her lips—that crazy chick lunged at her.

And sank a knife into Dee's chest.

"No!"

Dee's knees gave way and she hit the ground, hard. The bloodstained bitch stared down at her, that stupid grin still on her face. "They said you wouldn't fear me. What? Didn't you think a human could kill, too?"

Dee's fingers fumbled with the hilt of the knife. Fire pulsed from her heart.

Her heart . . . slowing, slowing . . .

"Dee!" Simon shoved the bitch out of the way. He grabbed Dee's shoulders, his fingers biting into her flesh. "Oh, shit, babe, hold on!"

She blinked and tried to focus on his face. *What big teeth you have.* "Vam . . . pire . . ." A croak. She tried to jerk free from him. Weapon. She needed her weapon.

Dark spots danced before her eyes.

"I won't hurt you! I won't! I swear, I'd never—"

Vampires lied.

Everyone lied. Even the victims. No, the victims didn't just lie. They stabbed you in the fucking heart.

Laughter. The bitch's laughter.

Dee's fingers curled around the hilt.

"*Dying! We're dying tonight...*" Ian's stupid singsong voice. "*Death's here. Standing right here...*"

"Dee..."

"Thanks for telling us where to find her." The bitch was talking again and Dee blinked, sure she was speaking to Simon. *He set me up? Why?*

She'd... trusted him.

And been so damn blind.

Ian laughed. Loud. Deep. Crazy. "Doesn't matter what I said, nothing could have changed. Nothing ever changes. Death is coming... for *you*, too..."

Ian had told the woman where to find her? *I dreamed about us last night.*

Ice numbed her body, gentled the fire in her chest.

"You'll be all right." Simon. His fingers were still on her flesh, but she could barely feel them now. No, she couldn't feel much, but she could still see—him. Fangs out and gleaming. Eyes—pitch black. A vampire's eyes.

She wrenched the knife out of her chest. The fire roared to life again and her heart—

Dying.

"*Dee, babe, no—*"

She fumbled. The knife slipped from her fingers. "Bastard," she whispered. "Why... didn't I... see y-you?" She'd been too weak with him, from the beginning. Needed him, wanted him—

Cared.

So dumb. She should have known better.

"You won't die. I won't let you!" His bared fangs came toward her throat.

"No," a breath, because that was all she had.

"We die tonight!" Ian yelled. "*Tonight! Brian, are you waiting for me?*"

"We're getting the hell out of here," Simon growled and then he grabbed her, jerking her up against his chest.

Vampire. Dee tried to shove against him. Failed. Her hands just weren't working right now.

"You're not going any damn place, bastard."

Dee's head fell back against Simon's shoulder as he turned to face the mouth of the alley. The exit that was blocked by easily half a dozen vampires.

Trap.

The human had been the willing bait. *Lure.* Should have known.

Stupid fucking rookie mistake. But she'd been so busy watching Simon, that she hadn't seen the threat screaming in the shadows.

Simon.

She tried to speak, but choked on her own blood.

One of the vampires grabbed Ian. "Thanks for the tip, asshole." The vamp yanked Ian's neck to the side and sank his teeth deep.

We die tonight.

Ian's gaze pinned her. "*Ready?*" His lips moved in a near soundless whisper.

No.

"Give us the bitch!" A vamp spat at Simon. "Hurry, before she—"

"You won't touch her. *You. Won't. Touch. Her!*"

Huh. Sounded like he cared. Lying bastard.

The drumming of her heart didn't echo in her ears anymore.

No more.

Her neck began to sag. *No, I'm still here! I can still think, still—*

So very dark.

But she could hear the snarls. The vamps were readying to attack.

And there wasn't a damn thing she could do.

This is the way it ends.

Hello, Death.

Ian, you bastard, I'd better not see your sorry ass in the afterlife.

Chapter 8

Simon kicked open the main door at Night Watch. His arms curled tightly around Dee's limp body and blood dripped on the floor around him.

Her blood and his.

He'd had to bite and claw his way through that gang of vampires. He'd taken as many of them down as he could, then he'd run like hell.

Staying and fighting hadn't been an option. Not with Dee bleeding out all around him.

The shifter must have caught the blood in the air because Jude Donovan came charging down the long corridor, barreling past the guards who had their weapons up, but who stared with wide, shocked eyes at Dee's prone body.

Donovan shoved one of the guards out of his way. "*What the fuck—*"

Simon's hold tightened around Dee. She was so damn still.

Donovan's hands reached for her. Simon clenched his jaw and let the tiger shifter take her away. *No choice.* The vamps would be coming for him. He had to leave her someplace safe.

It didn't get much safer than a hunters' den.

Her lashes cast dark shadows on her cheeks. Such pale cheeks.

"*Pak!*" Donovan bellowed.

One of the guards ran behind the shifter, grabbed a phone, and immediately called for an ambulance.

"Won't do any good," Simon said, voice grim. "Doctors can't help her now."

Donovan looked up, his teeth lengthening, his nostrils flaring. "What did you do?"

Ah, now there was the problem. He reached out and trailed his fingers down Dee's cheeks. "Not a damn thing." Her flesh was warm. No longer chilled as she'd been in that alley.

Life, not death.

Why was it so hard for people to understand?

Footsteps thudded down the hallway. More hunters, coming to the aid of their fallen friend.

His thumb brushed over her lips. Those soft lips were stained red with her blood.

Simon dropped his hand. "Tell Dee . . . tell her I didn't do a damn thing."

Pak rounded the corner. Maybe he'd heard the shifter's bellow or maybe one of the guards had buzzed him. Pak staggered to a stop at the sight of a limp Dee in Donovan's arms.

Don't leave her. Stay. The command came from inside, from the soul he'd all but forgotten in the last few years.

Stay. A temptation that almost broke him. She'd wake up. Confused. Angry.

She'd need him. She'd need—

No. The vamps could track him. They couldn't track her.

This time, it wouldn't be about what he needed. Simon met Pak's dark eyes. "You'll know how to take care of her."

Pak flinched as understanding hit. "No . . . Dee?"

His head inclined in the briefest of nods. Then, one last look. Couldn't help it. He had to see her once more.

Dee.

Donovan had dropped to his knees and spread Dee out on the floor before him. His hands were at her chest, jerking open her shirt and pressing against the wound.

It wasn't bleeding, not any longer.

Simon swallowed. The game hadn't gone according to plan. Not at all.

Fuck.

"Good-bye, Dee." Simon turned away and went back to the darkness.

The darkness always waited for him.

And now, for her.

Dee opened her eyes and sucked in a sharp, hard breath. A fierce pounding filled her ears. Hard, too loud. A dozen scents assaulted her nose. Perfume, too strong. Cigars. Mint. A wild, animal scent and—

Voices buzzed in her ears. Dozens of them. The buzzing grew, louder and louder, turning into a mad roar—

"Dee! Dammit, Dee, look at me!"

She blinked at the thundering voice and her gaze flew to meet Pak's glittering stare. Pak? How had he found her? She'd been in that alley, bleeding all over the place—

Blood.

Simon.

Vampire.

"Easy, Dee." Hands were on her shoulders. Holding her in place. Holding her down? She glanced to the right. Saw Jude, his face white, his jaw clenched. There was something in his eyes as he looked at her, something—

Pity?

"I-I-" She sounded like a freaking frog. A really *loud* frog. "I was . . . dying." Her hand fumbled, reached for her chest.

Her shirt had been cut away and she touched skin. Smooth, unmarred flesh right over her heart.

No, no, that wasn't possible.

"Breathe, hunter. You'll still need to breathe," Pak told her softly.

Well, of course she needed to breathe. Everyone did. She took another hard breath and swallowed and realized that she was thirsty.

Very, very thirsty.

Her teeth began to ache.

"Are you in control?" Pak asked.

Dee could only stare blankly at him. *Why am I alive? Did the knife miss my heart?* Maybe the wound hadn't been as deep as she'd thought, but there had been so much blood.

Blood.

The drumming in her ears pounded faster, louder. Her hand rose higher, brushing over the edge of her bra, and her fingers circled her throat. So dry. It hurt to swallow.

"Drink this." Pak shoved a black mug into her left hand.

Pak had never led her wrong. Dee lifted the mug, and the liquid, sweet and rich and oh, God, *good*, slid over her tongue and down her parched throat.

More.

Greedy, desperate, she drained the mug in three swallows. "*More!*" The taste lingered on her tongue. Pak had been holding out on her. He'd never given her anything like this before and—

"Maybe we should give her the whole bag." Jude's voice. Deep and booming, except maybe he'd been whispering.

Her gaze slanted to him, and she found him holding up one of those bags, kinda like the IV drips you'd see in a hospital, only—this one was filled with red fluid. No, with blood.

Give her the whole bag.

Dee licked her lips and the mug dropped from her hand, shattering onto the floor.

She vomited then because she knew what they'd just given her. What she'd eagerly taken.

"Fuck! Get towels in here!" Shouted to someone, somewhere, then, "Everything is okay, Dee." Pak, still trying to be reassuring.

No, everything was *not* okay. Her head fell back even as her tongue skated over her teeth, caught the too-sharp edge of her canines—

No, Christ, no! "Pak?"

Jude moved toward her, holding that damn vampire take-out, and Dee shuddered. Her hands came up. Her short nails were turning into claws. "What did he do to me?"

Simon.

The vampire who'd held her in her last moments. The lover she'd stupidly trusted. "*What did he do?*" But she knew. Oh, dammit, she knew.

Jude lowered his hand. "He said he didn't do anything."

"Look at me!" She screamed as the voices droned in her head and the smells blasted her nose. "I'm not human any-more! That bastard changed me." *I've become what I hate most.*

"Dee." Pak, calm, trying to talk her down. No talking down from this.

The blood—so close. She wanted more.

No, no, she was going to be sick again—

Blood.

Her gaze rose to Jude's throat. To the pulse that throbbed beneath the skin. Fresh blood would be better. So much better.

His brow furrowed. "Why you looking at me like I'm your meal, hunter? Stay in control, you got me? Stay in—"

She shoved her hand against her mouth. The hunger was so intense she nearly doubled over. A vampire. Just like those bastards who'd slaughtered her family. No. Never this. *Never.* "Stay away from me," she growled, and didn't look at him. Couldn't, because he tempted her too much.

"You have to drink more," Pak said, voice smooth as silk. Calm, steady Pak. Acting as if nothing were wrong. As if her world hadn't just gone to hell thanks to a sexy, lying vampire who'd set her up from the beginning. "The first hunger can be too strong for some. I can't allow you to attack anyone, Dee. You have to drink."

She threw out her hand. Another mug was pushed against her fingers. She lifted the cup, guzzled the blood. *Keep. It. Down.*

I'm drinking blood. Nausea rolled inside her, the human remnants fighting what she'd become.

Empty. She pushed the mug back at Pak. It was refilled almost instantly.

She swallowed the dark liquid. *Keep. It. Down.*

Again.

Again.

Dee drank and closed her eyes. Her cheeks were wet, but she didn't care. She'd never cried in front of the other hunters. Never cried, period. But this was different. This was hell.

Her teeth ached. Her stomach knotted. She still drank. Drank until the vicious need pounding through her body eased, until she could breathe without wanting to sink her teeth into Jude's throat.

Until the monster inside had quieted.

"No more." Pak took the cup from her. Dee swiped the back of her hand over her cheeks. Stupid tears—what good would crying do her? She glanced at her hands, frowning. Wait, was that blood? She'd cried tears of blood?

Dee's chin came up. "Where's Zane?" She wasn't stupid. She hunted vampires for a living. She'd known that a day like this could come, probably *would* come, sooner or later. She'd hedged her bets to make sure that she wouldn't turn into one of those killers who preyed on innocents. So many vampires just lost control and killed . . . *killed.*

Because the bloodlust could flare so strongly.

Zane was her safety net.

"He's with the cleanup team on Bymore."

She'd been on Bymore, right before the attack. "Ian?"

"Bastard's dead, and so is some cop, a female who'd been working vice."

The bitch who'd stabbed her. And she'd been one of Tony's girls?

"The place is a fucking mess, blood everywhere, dead vamps torn apart—"

"What?" With the hunger slaked, she could think better. "Did Night Watch get there to—"

"Not our kills." Pak crossed his arms over his chest and

stared down at her. "We found the bodies like that and thought maybe you'd managed to take some of the bastards out."

She shook her head. "No, no, the cop stabbed me. I was down for the count." Should have been, anyway.

You won't touch her. Dee could still hear the rage in Simon's voice. "He brought me here?" Dumped her. He'd changed her, then dumped her.

She swallowed, aware that the knowledge hurt. The jerk still had the power to hurt her.

Dumped me like garbage. Why?

Because he knew she'd be coming after his ass.

"Chase wanted you taken care of. He knew you'd be safe here."

But the hunters weren't safe. She was too unstable. Too—

"You know the first forty-eight hours are the hardest." Pak, still with those crossed-arms and quiet voice. "We're going to have to keep you under lockdown until we can make sure you're not—"

Insane. Driven crazy by bloodlust and power. A freaking killer who would slaughter everyone and everything in her path.

"I know you gave Zane kill orders," Pak said and Jude sucked in a sharp breath.

"What the hell?" Jude's claws sprang out.

"But you're not dying yet," Pak told her.

"I'm *already* dead!"

He jerked his head toward Jude. "Lock her up. And, do whatever you have to do, but keep that demon away from her." A pause. "For now."

Because if she went bad, if she couldn't keep her control, Zane would come for her.

He'd given her his word, after all, and one thing about that demon, he always kept his word.

Unlike Simon . . . *I'll find you.* Sooner or later, she'd find her lover and make him pay.

* * *

"You don't smell like a vamp," Jude said four nights later when he led her out the back door of Night Watch. His nostrils flared a bit and he leaned in close. "Damn, woman, you just smell, hell, like you."

Dee glanced his way, then turned to stare at the long, dark street. Since the moment she'd awoken, Pak had kept her under close scrutiny. He'd watched her. Fed her. Helped her to focus the chaos in her mind that came from the enhanced senses and the fears.

Just like before, Pak had taught her.

Not how to hunt this time.

How to live as a vampire.

"Pak told me that a vamp's scent changes," Dee said, not sure she understood why she wasn't reeking like a corpse. "Those bastards that hunt and rip apart humans, they stink of death and decay."

"Because they have no soul left," Pak's soft voice, coming from behind them. Dee didn't glance back. She'd known he was there. It was too easy to catch even his soft footfalls now.

"My grandfather once said that when the Taken lose their humanity, they become no more than the walking dead."

His grandfather had been a Choctaw shaman, so Dee figured the guy had known a thing or two about the walking dead.

"You still have your soul, Dee. Your mortal life is gone, but you're still the same inside."

Yeah, right. She just had a few flashy additions on the outside. New teeth. New nails. New eyes.

Taken. Why had Simon changed her? "Why not just leave me to die?" she asked the night, her hands clenched into fists.

No answer. Dee hadn't really expected one.

"You'll hunt now." Pak sounded certain.

She would, because there was still a job to do.

"For some reason, the Born Master left the city."

A great stroke of luck for them. Because she sure hadn't been up to hunting the last few days.

"We can't risk him coming back," Jude said, voice grim.

She uncurled her hands and glanced down at her new claws. "He won't be back."

"You can't take him down alone!" Jude snapped. "You'll—"

"Die?" She finished and gave him a tight smile. "Been there, done that." Her eyes darted around the street. No sign of Zane. He hadn't come to Night Watch, not once during her little "stay." She would have known. Would have caught his scent just as she'd caught all the others.

But he'd come for her, sooner or later.

Just like Tony would be coming. Her time had expired for him, and the little matter of her being undead wasn't going to stop him from taking her down.

She stepped into the night.

"Never the innocents, hunter. Remember that. *Never them,*" Pak ordered.

Dee gave a nod. The prey she'd be hunting first, well, he wasn't innocent.

She doubted if he ever had been.

Sure, she'd track the Born Master. Find him, do her damned best to kill him. But first—

First, she had some personal payback coming.

Her nostrils widened as she scented the night. "Come out, come out, Simon Chase." *I'll find you, wherever you are.*

The hunt was on.

Following the scent of blood was ridiculously easy. Fighting the urge to let her fangs out, to take a bite, not so easy.

But the need for blood had been slaked under Pak's watchful eye. Control, yeah, she had that now. He'd gotten her through that first mad rush of blood hunger. The rush that drove some vampires crazy and pushed others beyond that thin good/evil line.

She'd survived. She wouldn't need to feed for weeks now, and when she did feed, the thirst wouldn't be as overwhelming.

The first time—it was always a bitch in vampire land.

So she had her control. For what it was worth. Once she got her hands on her lying lover, Dee wasn't real sure how long it would be before that old wall of control started to crack.

The first stop on her little hunt was his place. Not that she expected Simon to still be hanging around town. No, once he'd dumped her ass, he'd probably hit the road as fast as he could.

Why change me? Why? That question had haunted her every moment. Was this some kind of sick punishment? Another way of torturing her? Damn vampire. He'd probably thought turning her into what she hated most was hilarious.

His house stood at the end of the road, lined off by garish yellow police tape. She could see the color of the tape so clearly in the darkness. Could see everything so clearly. The bullet holes in the siding. The broken shards of glass. The front door that swayed drunkenly on its hinges.

Dee hunched down and slid under the police tape. No sign of any uniforms. No sign of anyone. Maybe she'd find something inside to lead her to the vampire bastard.

Getting inside was easy—the front door was pretty much gone. The TV lay smashed on the floor. Stuffing from the couch cushions covered the room.

And to think, she'd actually been happy here, for a brief, stupid moment of time, she'd been happy.

The floor creaked. A groan, more vibration than sound, and she caught the faintest hitch. *Breathing.* Coming from the bedroom.

Claws out, she sprang forward.

And slammed into her lover's chest.

Dead lover's chest.

Dee took him down, hard and fast. Simon's head rapped against the hardwood. Her hips straddled him and she pinned his arms to the floor. Oh, yeah, vampire strength, baby. Payback was going to be hell.

"Dee." Why was he saying her name like that? All husky and hungry. Like he hadn't royally screwed her.

"Asshole." Her fangs were growing, sharpening, and she wanted to sink them into his throat.

Bite.

The whisper she'd first heard here, with him. She should have known back then what was happening. Vampires were highly psychic. He'd been the one broadcasting that need, not her. *Him.*

"You should have let me die," she growled and her fingers tightened around him.

His eyes flashed to black as fury hardened his face. Finally she was seeing the real man. Not the fake veneer. "I did."

"What?"

He lunged up, breaking her hold and rolling them in a tumble of limbs. In the next second, Dee was on the floor, he had her caged, and his teeth glinted down at her. "Haven't taken straight from a source yet, have you, babe? That was a mistake. You won't be strong enough to—"

Dee tried to head-butt him, but Simon pulled back, shaking his head. "Still thinking like a human. You can't do that, Dee."

"I told you *no!*" She knew her fangs were out. Didn't care. Her words were starting to lisp, just a bit. Still not used to those damn teeth. "I knew what you wanted, at the end." That part was seared in her mind. "I told you no!"

The memory of his voice rumbled in her mind. *"You won't die. I won't let you!"* Then his bared fangs had come toward her throat. Must have been her imagination, or maybe just the insanity brought on by dying, but she'd sure thought the man sounded scared then. Afraid, for her.

His jaw clenched. "I didn't—"

"You played me all along. Lied to me! Tricked me! You were the one who set all this shit up, weren't you?" Her hands jerked against his, but, he was stronger and he wasn't letting up.

"Thinking like a human," he muttered again. "Dee, calm down."

She was so sick of people telling her to *calm down, relax, or go easy.* She was a vampire for fuck's sake! She didn't have a cold or a broken hand—she was a *vampire!* Dee rammed her knee up and caught him right in the groin. His hold loosened, a moment was all she needed, and she hurled him back.

He flew five feet and thudded into the wall.

Sometimes thinking like a human wasn't bad.

She bent low and jerked her stake from her ankle holster.

He bounded back to his feet and shook his head. "You didn't come here to kill me."

Straightening, she tested the weight of the stake. "I want to know where the Born Master is." If she had to get physical with him to find out the location, so be it.

A rough laugh burst from his lips.

Her fingers tightened around the stake. "Don't push me." Her control had begun to waver the minute she'd seen him.

But the man stepped forward and a hard smile curled his lips. "I made you scream for me. I took you and you came and you screamed for me."

She'd screamed his name. A growl built in her throat. "The Born Master."

The smile wiped away. "I got you out of that alley. Those vampires wanted to rip you apart. *I* got you out. *I* kept you safe."

She lunged at him and closed the distance instantly. She shoved the stake right above his heart, not breaking the skin, not yet. But it would be all too easy to go in for the kill. "You should have let me die." *And let me stay dead.*

His hands came up, moving in a fast blur, not to push her away, but to wrap around her wrist, and to hold that stake close. "I did."

He'd said the same thing before, but this time, a shiver worked over her. "Someone else made me?"

His hold didn't waver. "Don't get it, do you? I thought Pak would have told you before he sent you out to hunt."

The stake pressed into his flesh. "Told me what?"

His gaze tracked over her face. "It's you. *You.* You were *Born* in that alley. You died—" He sucked in a sharp breath. "Right in my arms, but *then you came back.*"

And Simon almost died then because the roaring in her ears blasted her mind apart and the stake was suddenly so light in her hands—

He shoved her back. She should have fallen to the floor. She barely stumbled. "That's bullshit."

"No, it's the truth." That black gaze bored into her. "In certain circles, the truth about you has been known for a long, *long* time."

"Certain vampire circles?" Her stomach rolled.

A slow nod.

"You're lying," she spat the words. Had to be. There was no way she was *Born.*

"What do you hear?" he asked and he didn't advance toward her. A rivulet of blood ran down his chest. The scent was so ripe and rich, better than the strawberries she'd always loved and Dee wanted to slither closer, to taste. "*What do you hear?*"

"Your heartbeat." The myths were wrong. The hearts of vamps still beat. They still breathed. Still fucked. Still did everything that humans did. Because vampires only died for a moment of time, then they came back—they just came back different.

Wrong.

"What else?" he pressed.

"Cars." Far away. Zooming on the road. "Insects." Couldn't focus on them or their buzz would drive her crazy. She'd learned that lesson in the first hour of her new life. Death. Whatever.

"And what do you feel?"

Hunger. Lust.

Looking at him, Dee knew she should hate him, but the need simmered below the surface. He'd lied to her, betrayed her, but the vamp inside looked out from her eyes and lusted.

Blood.

Sex.

Prey.

"You don't feel the call, do you?"

Her eyes narrowed.

"You don't feel the pressure." He sounded certain. "You don't hear it, right? The nagging voice in your head, telling you to come, to *listen*, to *heed?*"

No, there was nothing in her mind like that. Just the lust and the need.

And the strong urge to rip the guy apart.

"The Taken are linked to the Born, you know that."

Vampire 101. Every hunter learned that lesson early.

"You don't have a link. If you did," his hand clenched, "you'd be about to go as fucking crazy as I am because the Born we're after is calling his vamps to him, calling 'em in a frenzy because the bastard is scared as hell."

The Born we're after? She could see the tension in Simon's body. The faint sweat on his brow. She'd thought that was fear, fear of her. "You're telling me that you're linked to the Born who was in Baton Rouge?"

The barest of nods.

Her breath exploded, and for a moment, she saw red. Literally saw him in a wall of blood. *Betrayed.* Dee attacked. Not with the stake this time, but with claws and teeth.

She slammed into him and they staggered to the floor. She wrenched his hands down and her mouth went for his throat.

Her fangs scraped across his flesh.

It took a moment for her to realize that he wasn't fighting her. His body was held too still, taut, like a wire, and he was just . . . waiting.

"Do it," a rasp and he bared his throat. "This is why I hunted you, why I fought for you."

Nothing was making sense to her.

"I killed for you, and I would have died. *Died.*"

The blood flowed so close, right beneath her teeth. Her tongue slipped out, tasted that flesh.

Should have stayed with Pak longer. Not ready for this.

But she'd never be ready for this.

"*Bite me.*"

The bite gave a vampire power. Why would he want to be weak?

That blood ... so close.... She shuddered against him, fighting the beast she'd never known until now.

"I wanted you from the moment I saw you. I want you *now.* I fought like hell burning for you, don't you see that? Woman, don't you—"

He jerked forward and her fangs pierced the skin. Accident! No, she hadn't meant—

His blood slipped over her tongue. Warm and sweet.

A groan tore from his lips.

Her fangs sank deeper. The blood flowed faster. *More, more.* Her breasts pressed against his chest and she freed his hands, the better to drag her fingers through his hair and hold his head so she could take.

His hands curled around her hips and yanked her tight against him, the aroused length of his cock shoved between her legs. Thick, hard. She arched her hips, loving that pressure even as she drank from him.

Sex and blood.

"More, Dee, take more!"

Helpless, she did.

His fingers fumbled with the button of her jeans. He jerked the fly open, managed to push his fingers between them and shove down her jeans.

Heat pooled in her sex, and a hungry, vicious need ripped away her reason as she fed from him. Fed, for the first time on a living being.

Addiction.

Power.

Lust.

This was what Pak had warned her about. This was why she'd given Zane kill orders. Dee couldn't pull back. She wanted her teeth in Simon's throat and she wanted his cock driving into her.

What he'd done to her, who he was—didn't matter. She needed, so badly.

Take.

More.

Mine.

Her body began to heat, from the inside out, and a rush of power and euphoria swept through her. She could have anything. Do anything. The world was hers. There was no stopping her. She could take and take and—

Her hands joined his and they jerked her jeans and panties down even as she kicked off her shoes. But Dee didn't free his throat. No, there was no way she'd stop drinking that wonderfully sweet blood.

His zipper hissed down. Her legs widened. The touch of his bare cock had her jolting, but not stopping. No, not stopping.

She was undead. No protection required. No diseases. No pregnancies.

Just need.

The need that had her sex slick when she should have been horrified. The need that had her nipples tight and her back arching, the need that—

Simon thrust into her and she slammed her hips down on him at the same moment.

"Dee!"

Shouldn't be doing this. Shouldn't be. She didn't trust him. Didn't even like him.

But the vampire didn't care.

Blood and sex. A vampire's wet dream.

Their bodies strained together. His cock was long and thick and every frantic move of his hips had him sliding deeper inside. She was wet, more than ready, and he filled every inch of her core.

Her mouth tightened on him, fangs in deep.

He drove harder, shoving up with his hips, and Dee took every straining inch of his shaft and wanted more.

His fingers thrummed her clit.

Her knees tightened around him. She pushed down harder, wanting to take, *take*.

She exploded around him as her sex contracted on a wave of pure pleasure that had her trembling, quivering, coming with the best orgasm she'd—

Simon bucked beneath her and climaxed, jetting out the hot splash of his release deep inside of her.

This time, he was the one who screamed. No, more like a roar.

Her name.

Her mouth gentled on his neck. The driving rush of blood-lust began to ease and the haze of red cleared from her mind.

What have I done?

Oh, Christ, what had she just done? She hadn't come to screw him. Not part of her plan. She'd come to find out what he knew about the Born and to make him pay for changing her.

Two bodies on the floor. Man. Woman. Older. Graying hair and sightless eyes. Blood around them, oozing from their torn necks.

Her hands clamped on Simon's shoulders. Her claws dug deep.

Simon, running to them, falling to the floor, slipping in their blood.

Dee tried to lift her head. This was wrong. She shouldn't be seeing—

"Told you there was no choice, Chase. You're ours now." A tall, pale vampire. Beautiful and perfect. Laughing as he stared at the dead bodies, blood dripping from his mouth.

"I'll fucking kill you!" Simon's bellow of fury.

Simon.

His memories. His mind. His blood.

What was she doing?

Linking. The way of the vampire.

Dee jerked her mouth away from his throat. She scrambled away, shaking, the taste of him still in her mouth, on her tongue, and her sex quivering for *more*. Dee shoved back her hair and she stared at him.

What have I done?

No, no—*what have I become?*

Blood and sex.

More.

He smiled at her, a sad, painful sight, and said, "Welcome to my world."

Chapter 9

"Sandra Dee Daniels rose."

The words fell into the silence of the room. The Born Master didn't glance up, he kept his teeth buried in the neck of his prey and her blood flowed over his tongue.

One minute stretched to five. Then ten.

The prey stopped moving. No more whimpers. No more tears.

He kept feeding. Kept drinking. Until nothing was left.

Only a shell.

His head rose and he licked his lips. "I'll need another." The hunger was never satiated for him. Never.

His glance drifted back to the woman. Pale limbs. Limp neck. Hair a long, straight black.

Death had been kind to her. No fear showed on her face. Her eyes had closed, and she almost looked like she might just be sleeping.

Kind. He wasn't usually kind, but this human had helped him.

In return for luring, she'd wanted immortality.

Too bad.

Turning, he glanced at the Taken in the doorway. "When?" He'd known this day would come. But just because the little hunter had finally turned didn't mean she was a threat. Sure he'd hoped to have her head so she wouldn't *become*, but failure didn't mean the end for him.

There was no end for him.

"About four nights ago." A pause. "We had her, but Chase stopped the team. He took her away."

Fucking Chase.

The asshole had been a thorn in his side for too many years. "The bastard needs to burn."

A grim nod.

"So does she." He shoved the body out of his way as he stalked to the window. "Take the bitch out with him." Because the demon seer he'd used so long ago, another bitch who'd tried to screw him, had told him a great deal about Sandra Dee.

A new Born breathes on this earth.

A new Born? He hadn't believed her, not at first. The youngest Born was over two thousand years old.

But the demon had been certain. She'd seemed to know so much about Sandra Dee.

Her strength lies close to her heart.

So when he'd attacked, his first move had been to cut her heart out. He'd killed her family. Let her walk in their blood.

And later, when he couldn't kill her, he'd set plans in motion to separate her from the friends she'd come to know so well.

The killing of the human in Baton Rouge had been the first step. He'd planned to force Dee into solitude. To make the others turn on her. Alone, Dee would be weak. The demon had said so.

He'd *made* the seer tell him about Dee's weaknesses. Torture was so easy for him. He'd learned at the foot of a master so many centuries before. He knew exactly how to make prey break.

The demon had broken for him. Two days, and she'd broken. But the whore had made one last prediction, right before he used his fangs to slice her throat wide open. *"She'll kill you when she rises. Drain you. Make you see the fires of hell."*

Fear.

As the demon had bled out, fear had trickled through him because the woman had been so certain.

Death wasn't an option for him. He knew what waited after this world. No, death *wasn't* an option.

He rolled his neck and shoved away the past. "Burn her," he said again. Fire was always the easiest way to kill his kind. "Make sure Chase dies with her." *Simon Chase.* A stupid mistake made by one of his blood.

Some just weren't meant for the darkness.

A soft muffle reached him. Glancing back, he saw the new girl who'd been brought to him. Young, maybe eighteen. With bright red cheeks. A smile curved his lips. He could hear the fast drum of her heart.

Some weren't meant for the darkness.

And some were.

"You know where they are?" he asked, eyes on the girl. She stared back at him. No fear in her light gaze. Excitement. She knew what was coming.

"We followed her the instant she left Night Watch."

"Good." He licked his lips, already tasting his pleasure. "Then have her dead by dawn."

Simon raised a hand to his throat, and touched the blood that dripped down his neck. His pants were open, his cock out, and rising by the moment.

Dee stared back at him, her eyes slowly changing from black to that deep chocolate he loved.

Her mouth hung open. The tips of her fangs peeked at him.

A vampire. A Born. The witch he'd sought had been right about her.

He should probably lower his head. Do some dumbass bow or head incline like all the vamps did whenever a Born was close. A sign of subservience. Of submission.

Because Borns could rip apart the Taken if they wanted.

But he'd just let her take his throat and his body. And he'd taken *her.*

Simon wasn't exactly feeling real submissive right then.

So he held her stare and knew that she felt the new link between them. A link she'd forged. Not him.

Already, the call that had haunted his mind for weeks had begun to soften. *It will work.* He'd been right to think she was the key. Dee would be able to change the game, to give him back his life.

Well, what was left of it, anyway.

She stumbled to her feet. Grabbed her jeans. Jerked them up. No panties. He'd remember that. Her curls disappeared beneath the denim. Pity.

Setting his shoulders, he began to rise.

But fell right back on his ass.

"Simon?"

Weak, in front of her. Because of her. "Give me a minute."

Her footsteps creaked across the wood. "I took too much." Not a question.

But he managed a nod anyway.

She edged closer to him. "I-I— didn't mean to hurt you."

She hadn't. The woman had given him one hell of a rush with her mouth and then the tight clasp of her creamy sex had driven him close to begging.

"What can I do?"

He looked up at her. Standing over him, blond hair mussed, always mussed, eyes so steady and . . . afraid? Dee? Since when did that woman fear anything? She'd stared straight at death with her eyes wide open and never flinched.

While he'd been so scared he'd almost bitten her. *Because what if the witch had been wrong?* Losing Dee hadn't been an option for him. The woman wasn't a pawn anymore. Hadn't been, maybe from that first night.

She was . . . everything.

Not that she'd believe him. Not when she found out the secrets he'd kept.

His eyes began to drift closed.

"Simon!"

The crack in her voice had his lashes lifting. So beautiful. Had he seen the beauty the first moment? Or the strength?

"What do you need?" She asked again.

The last part of the puzzle. Careful. Had to be so careful here. "Blood."

Her delicate jaw worked.

He let his shoulders slump. Not really hard with the weakness spreading through him, weighing down his limbs.

"You drink, then you explain, got me? Everything, *everything.*" She held out her arm, turned it, and exposed her wrist with the thin line of blue veins visible just beneath the surface.

He'd be her first.

His hands shook when he reached for her wrist. The shaking was from the blood loss, of course, just that. His fingers curled around her flesh and brought her offering close. Eyes on her, he opened his mouth and sank his teeth deep.

Fuck. His tongue slid along her wrist and the blood flowed into his mouth. Sweet, so damn sweet. A wild rush poured through him at her taste. His cock jerked, his muscles strained, and power, wild, rich power, heated his body.

Nothing like a Born's blood. That was the whisper. The rumor. Blood straight from a Born was power. Pure power.

Her breath caught and her eyes began to darken once again. The scent of blood hung in the air between them, but Simon's nostrils widened and he caught the heavier aroma of her slick cream.

"*Enough.*" Her whisper.

One more swipe of his tongue, then a press of his lips, and Simon pulled back.

Her chest rose and fell quickly. "What the hell am I doing?"

Getting ready to change the world.

Simon rose, too easily this time. He righted his clothes, hard that, with his dick bobbing toward her. But he'd promised Dee answers, and from here on out, he'd be keeping his word to her.

"I didn't change you in that alley." Her chin tipped back as she stared up at him. His neck throbbed from her bite and his body burned for her. Always, for her. "And I damn well didn't let any of those other bastards touch you."

The understanding was in her eyes, but Dee shook her head.

Time for some brutal truth. "Do you know how long it's been since a new Born came into the world?"

Her lips trembled. "Borns are ancient. There haven't been any for thousands of years. They were some kind of genetic mutation. A messed-up mutation that gave rise to the vamps."

To us. "What all do you know about Borns?"

The fingers of her right hand rubbed the wrist he'd bitten. Slow, steady strokes that she didn't even seem to be aware of making. "I hunt vampires. I know everything there is to know—both about the Born and the Taken."

"Not everything," he said, voice soft.

Eyes narrowing, she snapped, "They're young. I mean the Born change young. They're strong. Stronger physically and psychically than the Taken. They can—they can control other vampires. Summon those in the line they create."

Points for her. Time for hell. "Those vampires came to your home all those years ago for a reason, Dee. It wasn't some random attack."

"No, they wanted blood. They didn't care who they hurt—"

"They came for you."

She paled. "What are you saying?"

"I'm saying that about sixteen years ago, a level-nine demon made a prediction." She'd been the strongest precognitive alive. Of course, after her prediction, the demon's body had been found, minus her head.

One less precog demon around.

"The demon said a new Born was in the world, and that one day, she'd change, just like the others had changed so long ago." Not so subtle emphasis on the *she.*

Dee's lips parted. "No."

No sympathy. No remorse. "The vampires came to your home because *you* were the predicted Born. They had to kill you while you were young, before you could change."

"*No.*"

The air seemed to thicken around him. "They were under orders not to drain you. They were supposed to cut your head off." No chance of her changing that way. "They weren't sure when you'd transform, and the bastard leading them didn't want to take any chances."

She backed up a step. "Stop this! This is bullshit, I don't—"

"They killed your family because they wanted you to be alone. Helpless."

A tear leaked from the corner of her eye. Blood red. Borns always cried tears of blood. "If what you're saying is true, why didn't they come back and kill me? Why let me keep living all these years?"

"At first, because you disappeared." And because Grim had killed his all-seeing demon. No one had been around to tell him where to find a missing girl. "Then Pak took you in." Most vamps knew better than to cross him. "Others did come for you, but by then, it was too late. You'd learned to kill, and you were ready for the change."

"Ready? Ready how? Simon, I don't—"

Now he did lift his hand. His fingers brushed over her face. The clean, smooth lines of her face. She should have seen this for herself. "You stopped aging."

She swallowed.

In her thirties, but she looked like she was in her early twenties. The woman hadn't even realized it. She'd been too busy fighting. He cleared his throat. "You probably began to heal faster from your injuries, too, didn't you? And killing, I bet it became easier."

"So much easier." A bit of sadness.

"You didn't transform fully because you were still alive." Tricky part here. "You couldn't become a vampire until your human self died." A little rule not everyone knew.

Her lashes fell. "Like I did in that alley."

No denial now. She just sounded tired. Sick.

"Yes."

She swiped away the tear and left a smudge of red on her

cheek. "Why should I believe this crap? Why should I believe you? You've been lying to me from the beginning."

"Yes." Again, a simple response.

She growled at him. He shouldn't have, really shouldn't have, but Simon found that small growl sexy.

"This could be some kind of sickass mind game you're playing with me."

"Could be, but it isn't."

Her hands went to her narrow hips. "Then how do you know all this? *How do you know?*"

His gaze drifted over her face. He suspected she knew this, but he'd tell her anyway. If she wanted the words, he'd give them to her, and he'd brace for her attack. "Because I'm blood linked to the Born Master who killed your family. And from the moment I became a vampire, I've known there was a bounty on your head."

The hunter—she didn't know it, but all along, she'd been the prey. Prey who'd taken down every vamp who'd come for her.

And who'd made the Born bastard afraid.

Dee drew back her fist, and Simon knew the punch would be hard. He probably deserved it, though, all things considered.

Before the blow could land, a long, loud whistle split the night.

Dee spun toward the front of the house. "This is not my night—" She froze. "*Tell me that's not gasoline.*"

But it was. The scent was thick and heavy in the air, because some bastards were out there, getting ready to torch the house, to torch *them.* "They followed you."

"What?" Her claws were out. Not as long or deadly as a shifter's, but still able to do a whole lot of damage. "No way, I'm always careful."

He shoved past her and headed into the small den. The gasoline scent was stronger here. Not much time. "You weren't careful enough."

"Simon—"

Something flew through the already broken front window. A Molotov cocktail. *Shit.* "Dee! Get the hell out!"

More burning bottles. They slammed into the floor. Into the walls. Into the broken remains of his prized TV.

Then the flames sprang up like greedy bitches, racing across the floor and devouring everything in their path.

Trying to burn us out. No, just trying to burn them. He grabbed Dee and shoved her back into the bedroom. The flames chased them. The smoke thickened the air and he tasted ash on his tongue. He could see flames through the blinds on his window. Tall, dancing, red flames. They'd surrounded the house. Smart assholes. They'd circled the house with a ring of fire before sending the flames inside.

The better to trap them.

Vampires and fire didn't mix. He'd seen too many of his brethren fall to the flames.

It wouldn't happen to them. Not to Dee. He grabbed the tangled covers from the bed.

Dee jumped up and kicked the glass from his window. No fresh air came in, just more billowing smoke.

She hurtled through the broken glass and Simon lunged right on her heels.

Couldn't see the sky. No stars. No moon. Only that hungry circle of flames, burning closer.

"We're surrounded." Dee's tight voice. And they were. The vamps had planned well, and he'd been so distracted by Dee that he'd let them get killing close.

Won't make that mistake again.

They'd fed the flames, poured so much gas on the area that the air tasted rancid on his tongue.

"*Burn, bitch, burn.*" The words echoed in the night, crackling above the flames.

Not on his watch. He threw the covers over Dee, heard her grunt as he grabbed her and tossed her over his shoulder.

Then he jumped through the flames.

The fire bit his arms and licked across the side of his face.

Touching hell. The white-hot pain seared him, singeing skin and lancing flash in the seconds it took to leap through the fire.

They hit the ground. His arms were burning. The cover surrounding Dee blazed with fire. He rolled her, pounding at the fire, and the dirt flew around them.

The pain—*aw, fuck.* He sucked in a breath, choked on smoke, and took the hot agony. Used it.

Dee shoved out of the cover. "Simon, what the hell were you—"

"Fucking bitch," a snarl, too close.

Simon's head jerked up and he saw the vamps closing in. Four of them. The survivors from the alley.

Shouldn't have let them live. But his priority had been getting Dee the hell away from that place before any of the vamps had been able to make her death permanent.

Mateo came in first. The big, thick Italian was at least a century old, and he had one serious addiction to pain—giving it and hearing the screams of his prey.

He came at Dee, the claws of his left hand swinging toward her neck even as he brought up his right hand, a hand that Simon knew would be clutching a stake in that bulging fist.

"No! Dee, watch out!"

She twisted, her legs still partially trapped in the smoking covers as she fought to rise.

Simon jumped in front of her, and Mateo's claws sank into his chest.

Shit. His teeth snapped together. Oh, but the bastard had been begging for a killing for far too long.

He slammed his head into the vamp's. Handy little trick he'd learned from Dee.

But Mateo just laughed and that stake came up even as the claws twisted in Simon's chest.

Okay, a little help would be good right then. "Dee!"

Mateo's eyes widened. His lips opened, a high keening cry gurgling up in his throat.

Then he slumped forward.

Simon looked over the stiff man's body. Saw Dee. Saw her jerk the wooden stake from Mateo's back. "Don't worry, I got the heart."

Uh, yeah, he bet she had.

He wrenched the vamp's hand and the claws ripped from his chest.

Pain blasted through him.

Take it. Use it.

Simon didn't look down at his body. Couldn't. Not then. If he saw the damage . . .

"What are they waiting on?" Dee whispered.

His head shot up. The other three vampires stood less than five feet away. Their claws were out, their fangs glinting in the firelight.

He knew them all, just as he'd known Mateo.

Katya, the Russian vampiress, an ex-mob boss's lover. She'd gutted the fool who'd loved her.

Vince, the newbie who'd turned less than a year before. So much bloodlust there, burning in his eyes.

And Leo, tall and dark, standing and waiting with that damn twisted grin on his face.

Waiting, all of them, just waiting.

"Who the hell are you assholes?" Dee demanded and damn if the woman didn't put herself in front of him.

Aw, well, wasn't that sweet. But, considering the way he was starting to waver on his feet, maybe it was necessary, too.

"We're the welcome wagon, sweetheart." From Leo. He crossed his arms, raked his gaze over her, and seemed to ignore the flames.

"Uh, yeah? Well, here's a tip. Flowers work well. They say, 'Hi, here's a present.' Fire, ummm, not so much." The stake was in her hand. Dripping blood.

Leo's black stare drifted to Simon. "You sure this is the side you want to choose, buddy?"

Before he could speak, Dee growled. "*Buddy?* Hell, Simon, tell me you don't know these freaks."

A laugh from Leo. Should have been a warning. It was. "I'm the one who changed Simon, and Katya—"

Katya smiled. *Don't go there. Don't!*

"She's the one who gave him his first vampire fuck."

Oh, great. Like he needed this shit. "Let's just kill 'em, okay?" The talk was part of Leo's technique. The way to distract. To weaken.

Dee glanced at the redhead. "How about that." She fired Simon a hot stare. "Bad taste. You go for killers? Cause Katya, I've heard about you." The Russian liked her bloodbaths, so that was no surprise.

"I didn't screw her, Dee." The bloodlust had been riding him hard when Leo had brought him in to the pack. But he'd fought the dark temptation and Katya.

Katya wasn't the kind of vampire he wanted. Dee was. "I'm not like them." Could she see that?

Her eyes held his a second longer. "I know."

"*Bitch.*" Katya pulled two knives from the sheaths on her hips. "I'm going to cut your head off." Fifty years and the woman's accent still rolled Russian.

A sigh from Dee. "Bring it."

Katya lunged forward, knives up, fangs bared, she went in quick for a brutal attack and—

Dee drove her stake into the vampiress's heart.

Katya fell to the ground.

"Next."

He blinked. No, she hadn't just said—

Vince screamed and barreled toward her. Oh, right, rumors said Vince and Katya had been an item since his change.

Dee scooped up Katya's knives. Sliced fast and deep.

Another body hit the ground. This one, um, minus a head.

"You ready?" Dee asked a no-longer grinning Leo. "Or do you want to make things interesting and try to run?"

Yes. He'd been right about her. She'd be more than strong enough to kick Grim's ass. The Born Master would go down.

This nightmare could end. Finally.

Sirens wailed in the distance. The cops were coming. So someone had finally noticed the giant ball of fire that was eating its way into the night?

"More will come for you." Leo spat on the ground.

One shoulder lifted. "Let them."

"You and the traitor—you'll both die, screaming."

"Uh, wait, let me guess." A pause as she held up her hand. "Begging for death? For mercy?" A hard shake of her head. "Not my style. Didn't do it the first time, won't be doing it the second."

Bright red lights filtered through the smoke. The loud blare of a fire truck's horn had Leo jerking. "It's not over."

"For you, it is."

Simon's knees hit the dirt. "Dee . . ." Too much pain. Too much. Mateo's claws had dug too deeply into his chest. He glanced down now, finally, and—*bastard almost took my heart.*

This wasn't good. "D-Dee . . ." He tried to call her again.

But Dee, with her slightly scorched hair, shot forward and slammed her fist into Leo's face.

Then Simon slammed face first into the ground.

Chapter 10

He woke on a gurney. A mask covered half of his face and some crazy woman had her hand pressed hard to his heart. Simon's hands jerked, snapping through the binds that held his wrists in place.

"Wow, easy!" That hand pressed harder. The woman stared at him, hazel eyes steady. "You go jumping up, you'll ruin all my fine work."

He heaved up anyway, and winced at the pull of—stitches? Yeah, she'd sewn up his chest.

"I didn't do anything for the burns." No, he didn't want to look at those, but the woman, an EMT, trailed her fingers down his arm.

Pain pulsed through him and Simon sucked in a hard breath.

"Easy." She glanced over her shoulder at the swarming cops and the firefighters with their blasting hoses. Then her eyes came back to him. "I stitched you up to stop the blood loss. I figured the burns would heal either before or on your next rising."

Rising. A vampire term. So the lady with the curly brown hair knew what he was.

"I gave you blood," she said, leaning in close and pointing to a bag that dangled near his head. "It took four bags to wake you up."

"You mind giving him some room, Samuels?" Dee's annoyed voice.

Simon almost smiled. Almost.

The EMT did.

"Jeez, I swear, if I didn't know you were screwing that charmer, I'd think you were hitting on my vamp."

Her vamp? Since when?

Serious progress.

Samuels eased back and Simon got a good look at his Born.

Soot marked the right side of her face. The ends of her hair had been scorched, so the cut was even more screwed than normal. Her lips were red. Her eyes big and dark. And when those eyes landed on him, horror filled them.

"Oh, hell, Simon, I didn't know it was this bad." She jumped into the back of the ambulance and hurried to his side. "What the hell were you thinking? Vamps can't jump through fire. You know the skin of a vamp burns too fast."

A weakness. One of only a few his kind possessed.

Her breath came out in a long hiss. Her fingers hovered over the red, raw flesh.

He caught her hand. "Don't look at it."

Her gaze rose. "Your face . . ."

Then he remembered the flash of agony along his cheek.

But her eyes only flickered for a moment, then held his. "Tough guy, aren't you?"

Like this was the worst that had ever happened to him.

Not even close.

"You've got to stop trying to protect me." Her fingers lifted and brushed back his hair. Simon knew his hair had to be singed like hers. That, too, would vanish with the next rising. "You know I'm stronger than I look," she said.

A hell of a lot stronger. "You killed them all?" A guy could hope, because those assholes were trouble.

Her hand fell away. "No, your sire's still breathing. Kinda, anyway."

He flinched. This was the last thing he wanted. "What? Why? And where the hell is he? Humans are here!"

"Easy." *Why was everyone telling him that?*

She glanced back over her shoulder. "Tony has him. He's

taking him to a private holding cell." Her eyes returned to his. "Can't really have him blending with the general population in jail, now, can we?"

Not unless they wanted a slaughter.

Someone slammed the ambulance doors. The siren shrieked on, wailing over his head. "I can't go to a hospital! You know what will happen once they get a good look at me."

She crouched and locked her fingers with his as the ambulance took off. "We're not going to the hospital." Her eyes didn't waver. Didn't look at the skin on his face that he knew had to look like it had been touched by hell.

"Then where?"

A faint curve lifted her lips. Samuels watched them, but said nothing as she fiddled with the bags of blood, one of which still drained into Simon's veins. "We're goin' to that private holding cell. Tony still needs his proof that I'm innocent, and before the sun rises, Leo will give him that proof."

"You think Leo will turn on Grim?" He managed a hard shake of his head. Pain knifed through his body, white-hot agony snaked up his arms, but he was getting stronger. Every second, he was getting stronger. "Never gonna happen."

"Aw, but you don't know just how persuasive I can be." A bigger smile, one that showed the tips of her fangs.

He swallowed.

"Grim," she repeated the name, as if tasting it. "That the name of the freak after us?"

"Yeah." One of his names, anyway. When you lived as long as Grim had, the names changed over the centuries. "He's not an easy mark. You've never come across another like him." He had to warn her. The fight wouldn't go down like others had in her past.

"Huh." A pause, too long, then, "If you haven't been bull-shitting me, and I'm really a Born—"

"*Oh, Christ,*" the whispered exclamation came from a suddenly wide-eyed Samuels.

"—then I can make that bastard Leo talk. One way or another."

Yes, she could.

He fell back against the gurney. "It's not bullshit."

"No," soft, thoughtful. "I don't think it is." Her fingers traced up the edge of his arm, carefully skirting the bright red blisters. "Where do you fit into all of this? Their side? Mine?"

His gaze darted to Samuels. He didn't know her. Didn't trust her.

He caught Dee's fingers. Brought them to his lips. "I'm with you, babe." That simple—he fit with her.

She hesitated. He knew she didn't trust him yet. But she would. Soon. Even if he had to step through fire for her once more.

Simon closed his eyes, pushed back the pain, and wondered who Grim would send after them next.

"You burned for me," she said, her voice barely reaching his sensitive ears.

He didn't open his eyes. "I told you, I'm with you." *Hers.* If she only knew.

Dee didn't speak again. Neither did he.

The ambulance stopped at an old factory on the outskirts of Baton Rouge. A train whistle echoed in the distance and the scent of rain carried on the wind.

When Simon climbed out of the ambulance, Dee tried really, really hard not to wince. The wounds were healing, almost right before her eyes, but, oh, damn, they were vicious.

And the man was standing. No, walking, as if he hadn't just been comatose, with second-degree burns covering a good portion of his body.

Vampires.

He saved me. Again.

"Dee!" Tony's voice. Demanding and a little nervous. Since he was human, he should be nervous. Very nervous.

She walked toward him, with Simon at her side.

I'm with you, babe.

If only things were that simple. If only she didn't think the man still had secrets that could come back to bite.

Tony shoved open the doors to the factory. Rats squeaked and Dee was pretty sure about six roaches ran over her feet.

Oh, hell.

"Got him chained in there." He jerked his thumb toward a room on the left. "He's waking up, and even the blood loss isn't going to slow him down for long."

Her chin lifted. She'd managed to get some good swipes in before the cops pulled up, and she'd managed to knock out Leo just in time. She'd been the only one left conscious when the uniforms swarmed with their guns, so she'd been able to make some bullshit explanations, fast.

Lucky for her, Tony had been on the scene, barking orders and getting the cops he trusted—two charmers—to take the bleeding Leo into custody.

She'd leaned in close to Tony at that scene. Too many ears had been there, so she'd had to be careful, and she'd told him, simply, "My proof."

He'd done the rest. Cleared the area. Taken Leo to the new "interrogation" room that had been cleared for supernaturals. Made sure that Samuels was there to treat Simon.

Simon.

Tony eyed him. "I can't believe you took up with a vampire. I mean, seriously, Dee, a bloodsucker? Come on, I thought you had standards. You know that you and I could—"

Her stare shut him up. "Let's get this over with, okay? I want my name cleared and I want to find out if more jerkoffs are gonna be coming to attack." *He didn't know.* Tony thought she'd just had one really kick-ass fighting night because she'd had those before.

You were getting stronger.

What would Tony do, when he saw what she'd become?

Growling, she shoved by him and went after her prey.

Leo stood in the middle of the room, his arms lifted and held in thick chains so that he dangled a good foot off the ground. The chains were hooked up to some kind of pulley, and one of the charmers stood near the master machine, sweat coating his brow.

"*Bitch.*"

Her brows lifted as she faced Leo. "Aw, you're trying to sweet-talk me."

He snarled and tried to lunge for her.

Stupid move. Even he wouldn't be strong enough to break those chains.

He spun a bit, looking like a fish on two big hooks.

Leo's teeth snapped together. "You should have killed me. I'm gonna get free—gonna come after you! *You should have killed me!*"

"Don't worry, you'll die." From Simon. Hard. Cold. *Ice.*

"*You.* You fucking bastard! You think you found your damn golden ticket, don't you? Think you can get away just because you're screwing the new queen bitch?"

"Queen bitch?" Tony asked softly. "That's . . . ah . . . different for you, isn't it?"

"The bloodlust will get her," Leo screamed. "Only a matter of time, then she'll fuck like crazy and she'll drink from any fool she wants. Drink, drain, and fuck—and you'll be just as screwed as before!"

Dee flew at him. Not deliberate. Not really. She'd just seen the stiffening of Tony's body and—

And, shit.

She launched at the vampire and slashed her claws down his chest. He howled and the blood flowed.

And the scent tempted.

Dee began to shake.

"What the hell? Dee? Dee, you're not—"

She turned toward Tony and knew that her fangs were out. Fangs, claws. Bloodlust.

"*Fuck!*" Tony scrambled for his gun.

Simon punched him, a driving, brutal punch right in the jaw. Tony staggered back, hit the wall, then the ground.

Snick.

The two charmers had their weapons out and aimed.

"Won't do you any good," Simon told them, coming forward and—what? The guy was blocking her. Shielding her.

Again. Kind of sweet. Kind of— "You know bullets won't stop us."

No, but Dee wasn't exactly excited about testing that idea. She'd been shot as a human, could still remember the fiery blast, and didn't want to go through that again, thank you very much. "Don't even think about firing at me," she told the charmers, aware of Leo laughing softly behind her. Laughing—*freak*.

"Hold your fire." Tony rose slowly, rubbing his jaw. His gaze traveled over her. *"Dee?"* His dark eyes snapped to Simon and fury hardened his face. "You did this to her." He had his gun out and aimed in an instant.

Simon, bastard, spread his arms wide as if to say, *yeah, I can take it, so—*

"Not to her!" Tony roared.

Damn.

Dee grabbed Simon's arm and shoved him.

The bullet tore into her shoulder.

Her eyes squeezed shut. *Still hurt like a bi—*

"Dee!"

Her eyes cracked open. Tony ran toward her. "I didn't mean—"

Simon caught him, lifted him by the throat. "You. Never. Shoot. Her."

Um, he just did.

"I was aiming for you, asshole!"

More wild, loud laughter from Leo.

Screw this. "Lower the bastard," she ordered. The charmer near the switch hesitated. *"Lower him."*

A choked gasp. Tony's face began to purple and the whir of the pulley filled the room.

"Simon." Dee kept her voice soft. Too much tension. Too much rage. Simon walked a fine edge, and one push . . . "Simon, I want you to let him go."

He dropped the cop.

Tony heaved, trying to suck in air.

Dee licked her lips and fought to ignore the throbbing in

her shoulder. The bullet had gone straight through, she'd heard it clang against one of the metal pipes behind her. At least she didn't have to worry about digging the thing out.

Just the blood loss. She had to stop that.

And she had to forget the pain. If Simon could stand there, with the hell he had to be feeling, then, somehow, so could she.

"Dee?" Tony's voice, hoarse. Sad.

She couldn't deal with him then.

"They'll all turn from you now," Leo taunted. She faced him. His feet touched the ground. "Every one you care about—they'll turn away. They'll see what you are, and they'll come to kill you."

Zane.

"You'll be the one hunted now. You'll be the one who's scared and desperate and—"

She stepped forward. Smiled a bit. Then sank her teeth into his throat.

There was an instant of revulsion. Of horror. Of what-the-hell-am-I-doing.

Because she didn't want his blood. Not like she'd wanted Simon's. Didn't want his taste in her mouth.

She'd longed for Simon. No revulsion. No fear. She'd been desperate to take from him.

This—this was just business.

And the woman inside, the woman who'd feared and hated vampires for so long, she shuddered and a scream rose in her throat.

Can't do this. Can't live like this. No. No.

Images came to her then. Flashing one right after the other.

Leo, covered in blood and grime, standing on an old battlefield. A sword lay cradled in his hands. The dead surrounded him and a wild smile stretched his face.

Dee forced herself to take more. Keep. It. Down.

Leo, drinking a woman dry as she screamed and screamed—a woman in a long, flowing white dress, with her hair so long and loose around them. A tall man with bright blond hair, braided on the sides, watched, a smile on his lips. "The first blood taste is always the sweetest."

Leo lifted his head.

"Want more?" the blond man asked.

A quick nod, but a tear leaked down Leo's cheek.

"Don't worry, your wife doesn't even feel the pain now."

Laughter.

Madness.

Rage.

Pain.

She ripped her mouth away from his flesh. Her lips were wet. Blood trickled down Leo's neck. His eyes had gone glassy and the guy had stopped laughing. Finally.

"The voice is quiet . . ." Leo spoke, a whisper.

Okay, so he seemed to be calming down, always a nice bonus and—

He lunged forward and sank his teeth into her shoulder. Dee howled and shoved him back. He shot away from her, but the chains groaned and jerked him up short.

Leo licked his lips. "Got you."

Her teeth snapped together. "You—"

A shake of his dark head. "I-I can remember her . . . now."

Dee rubbed her throbbing shoulder, then she punched him, because that shit *hurt.*

"Dee." Simon's voice. Steady and too controlled. Where was her big, bad protector when she'd actually needed his butt? She fired a glare at him, then nearly winced. *Still damaged.*

"Dee, he needed your blood, just like I did."

She blinked.

"What the hell is going on here?" Tony shouted.

"I'm a vampire, you just tried to kill me, and I'm having one real pisser of a night." Good sum-up. Dee narrowed her eyes on Leo. "And if you come at me again, I'll take your head."

A tear leaked from his left eye. "I can see my Sonja again."

Uh, great.

"Your bite and blood diluted Grim's control," Simon said. "Ask him now, he'll tell you everything you want to know."

Really? That easy? Well, not really easy considering she'd had to bleed for her answers. "Are you one of Grim's Taken?"

"He changed me." Whispered. "Bound by his blood."

Vampires. Couldn't they ever just say things simply? "Okay, you're one of his goons. Were you in on the setup? Did you kill that woman and leave me in her blood?"

His eyes squeezed shut, then flew open. Midnight black. "She was easy to kill. She thought I'd give her forever."

"Guess you did, didn't you?" Forever in a pine box somewhere.

"It was quick." A shrug. "She didn't suffer."

"Yeah, I'm sure there were plenty more who suffered over the years because of you."

His lips trembled. "Not what I wanted. Never wanted."

What? "Listen, buddy, *you* were the one killing. The one biting and draining—"

"Wasn't strong enough." His gaze darted to Simon. "You know what it's like. When he gets inside . . ."

He. *Grim.* The big badass that Simon had warned her about.

"He takes control," Leo said, giving a slow shake of his head. "His needs became mine. You have no idea how strong he can be."

Footsteps shuffled closer behind her. "Tell me this freak Grim isn't in my town." Tony's voice cracked a bit. Fear would do that to a guy.

Leo didn't answer.

Dee grabbed his bloody shirt front. "Where is he?"

His eyes narrowed on her. "Fled. Knows what you will do."

Okay, so now his voice was getting a bit sing-songy. Was she doing that? Or was it his blood loss? Maybe both.

"Uh, what's she gonna do?" Tony asked.

Simon and Leo answered in unison. "Kill him."

Simon caught her hand. "Or at least, I hope to hell that she will."

"If not," Leo breathed, staring straight at her with his hunting black eyes, "then he'll tear you apart, Born. Rip your world away and tear you apart."

Ah, nice visual.

A shrill beep cut through the air. Tony swore and jerked out his phone. Leo sagged back against his chains. "Death," he whispered.

This was the tough SOB who'd nearly taken her out earlier? He looked . . . beaten.

No, broken.

"It's your blood," Simon said, his voice carrying only to her ears. "It's diluting Grim's hold on him, making him remember who he was and everything he's done."

Tony let out a hard expulsion of air. "What? When? Christ. How many dead?"

Dee ran a hand over her face. "If Grim has this much power, why weren't you like"—she shot her thumb toward the trembling vampire—"him?"

Simon's face had begun to heal. The blisters were starting to vanish, the skin lightening to pink instead of the fiery red. "Grim didn't change me directly. Leo did. So the bond was weaker."

"Liar, liar . . ." A weak chant from Leo. "I know what you did, Simon. *I know, little brother.*"

"Dee!"

She jerked at Tony's snapped call. She eased away from Leo. He looked like he was down for the count, but she didn't trust him.

Tony lifted a hand, reaching for her. Then he hesitated.

Dee's chin lifted. *I'm still the same.*

Maybe. She hoped.

Tony's hand shot out and he snagged her wrist.

A growl built in Simon's throat.

Tony didn't glance his way. "There's been an attack."

Yeah, well, sadly, in this city, someone was attacked every day.

"Less than half an hour ago, vampires took out two hunters at Night Watch and they killed one of the assistants, a woman named Grace."

Her face iced. "*What?*" Not Night Watch. No one would dare to go into headquarters and attack the hunters there.

Not unless they wanted hell on their trail.

"I've got to go—"

His fingers clamped tighter around her flesh. "I can't have you at the scene. Not . . . with the way you are."

Fangs and claws. Bloodlust. Her jaw locked. "Who—who are the hunters?" Not Jude. Not Zane. No, not them, *please*.

"Spade and Gomez."

Bile rose. The taste of blood—way too strong in her mouth. *Monster. I've become just like them.*

"Spade was DOA, his throat had been ripped open."

"Fuck." A snarl from Simon and suddenly he was there, wrapping his uninjured arm around her, holding her close.

"Gomez is en route to the hospital, but he's bad. *Real bad.*" Tony inhaled. His fingers brushed over her wrist, over the pulse that raced too fast. "Looks like the vamps jumped them all right after they left Night Watch."

There would have been too many hunters inside. The vamps wouldn't have been stupid enough to risk a fight like that. So they'd hid in the shadows. Struck in a weak moment.

"This isn't your fault," Simon told her, voice roughening. But even before Tony's lips parted, she knew he'd prove Simon's words a lie.

"They left Gomez alive so that he could deliver a message."

She kept her chin up. Kept her shoulders back.

Leo, crazy screwed-up bastard, started to laugh again. So much for her blood helping him. "What message?" she asked.

Tony's lips thinned.

"Tell me!"

"That you're next, baby. The blood will keep pouring in the streets, and they're coming after you."

She took the blow. Took it, even as her stare darted to

Simon's tense face. "They knew the first hit wasn't successful." Knew she'd still been living while the vamps hit the ground. "How?"

His fangs were out. "Because word travels fast in this town and his men—" He spared a hard glance at Tony. "Know more about this city than he thinks."

A leak. No, a spy. One who reported to Grim's vampires. One who wanted that sweet promise of immortality?

Why did everyone want to live forever?

"I'm going to the scene," Tony said, "and I'll see if I can figure out just what we're up against."

Easy. A Born Master and his gang of bloodsuckers. Guys who liked to drink, drain, and torture for fun.

"Harper, Post," he fired at the two charmers. "Watch this freak."

"Run, little vampire," Leo murmured. "Run fast. Grim's coming for you, and he won't stop until he has your head."

She glanced back at the prick.

But found sadness in his eyes. Gray eyes now, not black. "Even being Born won't save you," he told her. "Run, while you can."

Chapter 11

They needed sanctuary, and they needed it fast.

Simon and Dee ran down the deserted streets in the heart of the city. Pink strands of light crept across the sky. Dawn, bitch that she was, would be there soon.

He needed to crash. Needed the healing sleep that would come.

So did Dee. And with her fresh wound, she'd need blood. *Mine.*

The cop bastard had gone off to investigate the attack, ordering them to stay away.

Not much choice. For now.

"Here," Dee said, and Simon stopped in front of an all-too familiar bar. No, no way were they going to seek shelter from—

The glass doors swung open. "Dee?" A woman with long, pale blond hair stood just inside. Her eyes glittered, and her hands, bare and small, fluttered in the air. "I was wondering when you'd come to me."

The woman—the witch—lifted her eyes and met his stare. "And when I'd be seeing you again, Chase."

Hell. He had such shitty luck.

"Don't even want to know right now," Dee muttered and shoved past Catalina. "Cat, I'm calling in my favor. I need a roof, a bed, and protection for the day."

Catalina smiled at Simon and motioned for him to enter

the bar. "I see you found your key, and you thought I was just bullshitting you."

She'll be all that you need.

But there's a price for her. One you may not want to pay.

He'd agreed to pay everything. To trade everything, for the chance to have full control of his soul once more.

And for revenge. Sweet, sweet revenge.

Catalina closed the door behind them. She flipped the lock, then whispered a fast spell. "One day," she said, turning back to face them. "I don't want to get in the middle of your war."

A broken laugh slipped past Dee's lips. "A war? Is that what I'm in?"

"Honey, you've been in a war for years." Sad. "You just didn't know it."

"And you did?" Snapped fast. "Thanks a hell of a lot for telling me, Cat."

The witch's lips tightened. "Some things you weren't ready to know." She swallowed, then pointed to the back of her empty bar, to the door with the gold EMPLOYEES ONLY sign. "Take the second room at the top of the stairs. Chase can have—"

"He'll stay with me." Flat.

Simon's brows shot up.

"Ah, like that, hmm? Fair enough." Catalina tossed him a smile, one brittle around the edges. "Told you what would happen, didn't I?"

"But you didn't tell *me*." Not flat now, furious. Dee's hands slapped down on the bar. "I trusted you, Catalina. Watched your back for years. I never came in your bar. I respected your surface rules, never tried to push your spell—"

The spell that made all the humans walk right past Delaney's. The spell that only let supernaturals gain entrance to the bar.

"—but you and me—I thought we were friends."

"We are." Soft.

Simon knew better than to get between two fighting women.

"Friends don't keep secrets."

"You didn't want to know this." Catalina's long hair floated behind her as she walked around the bar, poured a whiskey, and drank it in two gulps. "When I scryed and found out— *you didn't want to know*."

"My choice." Dee threw this over her shoulder as she marched toward the marked door. "You took it away."

Catalina's fingers clenched around the glass. Dee shoved open the door. Simon followed, slower.

Glass shattered. "I didn't take it away." He caught the whisper of the witch's voice. "I gave *him* to you, and I gave you a fighting chance."

Dee didn't glance back. Maybe she heard the witch. Maybe she didn't.

Right then, he guessed it didn't matter.

She awoke to hands on her flesh. Slow, stroking fingers that pushed up her shirt, skated over her stomach. Gentle. So gentle.

Her lashes lifted. Darkness surrounded her, but she could see so well.

See him.

Healed now. Not even a scar to mar his face or the bare flesh of his arms. He leaned over her, eyes intent, fangs gleaming.

Dee reached up and touched his chest. "I dreamed about you." Yeah, vampires dreamed. Or, in her case, had nightmares.

The flames, burning Simon's flesh. Killing him.

He'd walked through the fire for her. Whatever agenda the guy was working, he'd sacrificed for her, again.

His gaze held hers. His fingers were a warm weight on her flesh. No aches troubled her body. No pains. Healed, just as he was.

But . . . hungry.

The bloodlust, rising again.

She'll drink from any fool she wants. Drink, drain, and fuck—and you'll be just as screwed as before.

No, Leo had been wrong about her. She *would* have control and she would have Simon. "Stop risking death for me," she whispered and the words stuck in her throat.

A sad smile twisted his lips. "Don't you understand? I'd risk any damn thing for you."

He kissed her. Still gentle. Still soft.

And the hunger grew.

Her hands clamped around his shoulders and she pulled him closer.

His tongue thrust into her mouth. She moaned, eager, and arched toward him.

Taste.

His hands eased up, sliding under the shirt that still covered her breasts. His fingers skimmed over her bra, over the nipples that were pebbled and hard, thrusting up against the cotton.

She could smell her own need in the air. Feel him all around her.

Simon's head lifted. "I want your throat."

Drink.

Asking, not taking. The lust was there, brimming in the eyes gone black.

For vamps, blood was about power, control, life.

In Simon's eyes, she just saw need. The same stark need that she knew would be reflected in her own gaze. Dee tipped back her head.

Should have been repulsed. Horrified. Even with what she was—

His teeth scraped over her neck.

Her sex clenched.

Should have been afraid.

His teeth pierced her flesh. Her nails dug into his skin. "*Simon!*" A bolt of pleasure shot straight to her core. Her belly quivered, her knees shook, and she wanted.

Dee's hands pushed between them. Fumbled with the snap of his jeans.

Dee wanted his flesh beneath her fingers. She needed more. So much more.

Her hands shoved inside and she found his cock. Fully erect, thick, so hot to the touch.

"Inside," she managed to gasp, "Inside, Simon, I need—"

His tongue swiped over her neck and he lifted his head. "Take from me."

Her lips parted and her tongue pressed against a fang. Sweet blood.

Simon.

She rose, and her hands pressed him back against the mattress. He went willingly, letting her have the control she needed then.

Power.

No, not about power.

The hunger. The lust.

Craving.

She didn't take his neck, though he offered his throat to her. Dee yanked off her shirt. Tossed her bra aside, then straddled him, her legs resting over his powerful thighs.

Her fingers trailed down his chest and she leaned forward. A dull thudding filled her ears. Her heartbeat? His? Her mouth pressed against his flesh. Not in a bite. A kiss.

Pleasure.

She closed her lips around his nipple. Swirled her tongue over the hard nub. His cock pushed up between her thighs, rubbing at the crotch of her jeans, and the pressure had her rocking back and forth.

More.

"Take, Dee. *Take from me.*" Guttural. A demand.

But he wasn't in control anymore.

Her tongue swiped over him and she let him feel the press of her teeth. Not a bite. Not yet.

Maybe he'd beg for that.

His hands clamped over her hips and he ground her against his cock. Oh, damn, but that was good. Just not—

Enough. Not even close.

"Don't play." An order given as her fingers crept down the

hard plane of stomach. "You don't want to push me, you don't want—"

She looked up at that and knew her eyes would be black. "I want everything."

"Then you'll get it," a harsh whisper. "Hope you're ready."

So did she.

But she had the power, she'd be in control.

Her teeth sank into his chest. His growl filled her ears even as the hot warmth of his blood slipped over her tongue.

Life.

Power. So much power.

Her hips lifted and her fingers curled around his cock. She pumped him, once, twice, felt his length swell even more in her grasp. Felt—

Dee stood in an alley. One hand on her hip. A vampire hissed at her, and that preppy fool holding the vamp blinked his eyes.

"Just how long do you think it's gonna take me to shove this into your heart? A minute? Less?"

She pulled back from him. Her memory, seen from his eyes. No, his memory. "Simon, why do I—"

"Not now," he gritted. "Ditch the jeans or I'll rip them off."

She didn't have any backup clothes then and—

"Fucking rip them off."

Dee rolled off him. She shimmied out of her jeans and panties even as she licked her lips and tasted him.

His hands, warm, strong, closed around her thighs. He pushed her legs apart and his breath blew against her damp curls.

"Your smell." His nostrils flared. "I could devour you."

Um, now, since he was a vamp that could— *Oh, damn.*

His mouth took her sex. Lips, tongue. Tasting, claiming. Her hands fisted in the sheets. Dee heard a hard rip. Didn't care.

That mouth.

His tongue swiped over her clit and Dee nearly came off

the bed. She squirmed, trying to get away, no, get closer, but his hold stayed tight and strong.

And he took. His tongue drove into her sex.

She climaxed against his mouth. A long, hard wave that trembled through her body.

But he didn't stop. That tongue tasted and licked and stroked and Dee realized she was calling his name.

Nearly freaking begging. Her.

She swallowed and her nails dug into his back. "Simon!" Demand there.

Command.

One more swipe of that tongue. Her calves stiffened. Oh, sweet hell.

Then he rose above her. Positioned his cock and drove into her.

Yes.

Her legs clamped around him and when he began to thrust and retreat, she shoved right back at him. Harder. *Harder.*

The bed banged against the wall. Simon's gaze burned hers. So much fire there. So much need.

He lifted her hips higher, plunged deeper even as his fingers bit into her flesh.

Marking her.

She'd marked him.

Another climax bore down on her. Her sex trembled, tightened, and she tossed back her head.

Simon came, pouring into her.

She watched him. Watched the pleasure, the near-pain of it sweeping over his face.

Then she came, pulsing, throbbing, breaking, beneath him.

Pleasure. So much pleasure.

Enough to nearly die from.

Good thing they were both already dead.

Zane Wynter didn't glance to the left when he exited the Night Watch building. He didn't need to look to know that blood still stained the sidewalk.

The blood of hunters.

The scent teased his nose and a growl built in his throat.

Vampires. Hitting *here*.

Come and get me.

The stakes he'd taken from Dee's stash were slung in a pack that dangled from one shoulder. He hadn't needed to sharpen them. Dee always kept her babies in such fine form.

He'd find the assholes, all right.

An eye for an eye. He'd always thought that way.

"Zane!"

He swore at the call. Not one from another Night Watch hunter, but from the cop he sometimes called friend.

A mistake that. Taking humans for friends just led to trouble.

Tony hurried to his side. The guy's badge flashed. It hung from Tony's hip. All official-looking. The cop had to be on the clock.

Or hunting, just like he was. Pity they didn't always play by the same rules.

"I need to find Dee," Tony said the minute he reached him.

Zane didn't stiffen. Just stared back at him. "Good luck with that." *Dee.* Pak hadn't called him in when she'd been hurt. Hadn't told him about what happened, not until the bastard had given Dee a running start.

Pak had always had a soft spot for her. He wouldn't do what needed to be done. The guy just didn't understand . . .

"I—if something ever happens, you'll come for me, won't you, Zane?" He could see her so clearly. One hand tight around a stake as she stared down at the still body of a teen, a young girl with blond hair and blood all around her. A girl who'd gone on a killing spree and attacked her two younger sisters. *"I'd never want to be like them."*

Dee's nightmare. One some bastard had made come true.

Pak said she'd adjusted. That she'd maintained control. And that she had a pack of vampires after her ass.

But could any vampire maintain real control? What happened when the bloodlust grew too strong? What happened when Dee turned on an innocent?

"You'll come for me, won't you, Zane?"

Good thing they'd never fucked. If they had, knowing what was to come would have made the job so much harder.

Impossible.

Tony grabbed him and shoved Zane back against the side of the building. The bricks bit through his shirt. "I need to find her!"

Tony had slept with her. There was pain there. In his eyes. On his face. "Haven't seen her." Truth. Though he had a good idea where to start looking.

Dee would be licking her wounds. She'd need shelter. Someone she could trust.

Mistake.

Tony's face mottled. The guy had always been so in control. So restrained. One of the reasons why he and Dee hadn't lasted.

She'd needed a guy who didn't understand control.

"That bastard Leo bit his own wrists open and the fucking guards didn't check on him. He was in a padded cell, they thought he was safe. The vamp bled out, *bled out!*"

Zane blinked at that. Yeah, vamps could die from blood loss, but he'd never heard of a vamp taking his own life that way.

You had to want death pretty badly to take that route.

"Last night, he said some SOB named Grim was after Dee. She needs help. I've got to find her, help her—"

At that, Zane knocked the cop back. Tony staggered, nearly fell to the cement. "And how are you gonna help her?" He demanded. "Offer to be her snack?"

A muscle flexed along Tony's jaw. "She's not like that. She wasn't crazy, she was just . . . Dee." Sadness again.

Fucking shame.

Tony's chin jerked up. "I don't want her to wind up like Gomez or Grace. I don't want—"

He stiffened. Okay, yeah, this was one of those moments in life that sucked. "Grace was working with the vamps. She lured the hunters out, got them to lower their guards." Then served them right up to the vampires.

A woman he'd known for years. He'd laughed with her. Talked with her about her dumbass dog. Stolen her coffee more days than he could count.

And she'd set them up.

"What? No, man, she was a vic, same as the others, Grace wouldn't—"

"We hacked into her hard drive today. Did interviews with family, friends, and we got her doctor to talk." Patient confidentiality, his ass. That old rule stopped the moment the patient got zipped up in a body bag. "She was dying. Cancer. She had about six months left to live."

"Christ."

"You know humans," Zane said softly, watching the cop carefully. "Once the clock starts running out, they get desperate. They'll try anything."

"Hell!" His throat worked. "Grace saw Dee." He ran his hands over his face. "She was here. She saw Dee change, survive—*live*."

Vampire. "Guess it was too much temptation for her. The bastards sent her an e-mail. Told her to bring a trade outside to them. The vamps promised her a new life."

But just gave her death.

"They're going after Dee. You know they won't stop until she's dead."

No, they wouldn't. "It's time for you to step back, Tony. You're not strong enough to handle the hell that's coming." Not with a Born Master playing in the game.

"I'm not leaving her alone."

His brows shot up. "Who says she's alone? Word I have is that Dee's got a new lover, a vamp who risked the fire for her." Interesting. In his experience, vamps really didn't like to burn.

"I don't trust that bastard."

Neither did he. "You think he's setting her up to die?"

Grim. That was the Born's name. Old as frigging dirt. And the older the vamps were, the stronger they were and the harder to kill.

Dee was a newbie. So easy for her to die.

"No," Tony gritted out. "I think he's setting her up to kill for him."

Footsteps shuffled and a woman with short, red hair appeared, rounding the corner. She drew up when she saw them, her eyes widening.

The scent of smoke teased Zane's nose.

She hurried past them, and he caught a whiff of . . . blood? Hell of a combination.

"*Zane.* Shit man, forget about your dick right now, okay?"

He yanked his gaze off the woman's ass and zeroed his stare back on Tony. "Go home. Leave Dee to me."

But the cop's head started shaking, hard. "I'm not abandoning her, I'm not just—"

"You want to be her prey?"

"*What?* No, she's not like that!"

"Every vamp is 'like that' when they get hungry enough." He jerked his thumb over his shoulder. "You want to find her? Go inside and talk to Pak. You know that guy always has info about this city."

Tony's dark stare measured him. "And where the hell are you going?"

He brushed by him. Didn't meet his stare. "Hunting."

"Who are you hunting?"

Zane ignored the question and kicked up the stand on his new motorcycle.

"*Who are you hunting?*"

A flick of his fingers, a press of his foot, and the engine roared to life.

"Not her, you got me? Not. Her!"

The motorcycle shot away from the corner, racing right in front of an old, gray truck.

*   *   *

"Tell me about your change." They probably didn't have time for this. She should be getting dressed. Finding weapons. Figuring out what the hell they should do next.

But she needed to know more about Simon. Wanted to know and she didn't want the blood link to tell her. She wanted him to talk. "Your parents, the vampires attacked them." Killed them. Just like they'd killed her family. "Is that when you changed? Did they trans—"

He rolled away from her.

A chill rose on her flesh. "Simon?"

He sat on the edge of the bed, giving her a view of his strong, powerful back. "Don't make me into something I'm not, babe."

She pulled the covers up to her chest and waited.

"I was already a vampire before my parents were killed. I'd been a vamp for a year before the attack." He glanced back at her. "You thought I was forced to turn?"

A nod.

His lips twisted. "No. I was one of the ones who chose to change."

"Why?" The word came out husky, rough. To choose to be a vamp, to drink blood, to *kill*?

He rose, gave her a fine view of his ass and stalked to the jeans they'd tossed aside at some point. He yanked them up. "I was working in the Middle East. The shittiest and hottest place the world ever forgot." Simon turned toward her. "One night, my men were ambushed. Cut down in the road by bullets and bombs."

Dee didn't move. Couldn't.

"They died around me, their screams in my ears." His fingers brushed over his stomach. "I bled out on the ground. My leg was shot to hell. My chest torn open. Every breath I took tasted of fire, and I knew, I *knew* I'd wouldn't make it off that road."

"But you did."

His eyes darkened to black. "A man came out of the rubble. He walked straight to me. Asked me if I wanted to live or die."

He'd chosen to live, as a vampire. Her lips parted.

"I heard the thump of a helicopter's blades then. Whirring in the air. They were coming to help us, but I was the only man still living."

So he could have made it without the change? He could have kept being human?

"I knew about the *Other*." He swallowed. "I'd been to so many places, seen things people wanted to pretend didn't exist. War brings out the monsters, Dee. It brings them out like you wouldn't believe."

"I'd believe almost anything." Sad and true.

"I knew looking up at him—I could see his fangs, see his eyes changing. I knew what he was, and I knew I wanted to be like him."

She sucked in a sharp breath.

"The medics could have tried patching me up. Could have saved my ass—and *maybe*, maybe I would have pulled through. But my job was to fight. I had to be strong. *He* could make me strong. Stronger than I'd ever been, and I'd never have to worry about choking on my own blood as bullets and hellfire took me down on a dirty road ever again."

No, he'd just have to worry about getting his head chopped off and having a wooden stake driven through his beating heart.

"You don't understand, do you?" His voice was grim. "Vampires are always young, always strong. That's a deal a man dying on a battlefield isn't gonna refuse. I wanted the bite. I would have done just about anything to keep living right then."

"But the helicopter—"

"I wanted the bite," he said again. "I wanted forever." His shoulders lifted, fell. "I'm not gonna lie to you. Not gonna say the change was forced on me. I chose."

"And would you choose the same thing now?"

His lips thinned. "Would you?"

"*I* didn't choose this, I didn't want—"

"Getting out is easy, Dee. Bleed out. Let the fire take you. Every single moment you live, you're choosing."

She knew he was right. She was choosing this life because for her, there was no alternative. "I'm not killing myself. That's not me." Too easy. Fight. Survive. Pak had taught her that. You survived, no matter what. You lived.

"It's not me, either." Soft. "I didn't know—didn't understand about the Borns when I was brought over. After the exchange, I woke up, strong, thirsty, so thirsty, and I didn't even feel the Born's power at first."

Ah, key phrase there. *At first.*

"Then the prick started trying to worm his way into my mind." His chin lifted. "That link gets weaker the farther you are from the Born, so my tactic was to stay as far away from Grim as I could."

Her fingers knotted around the sheets. "Guess that tactic didn't work so well, huh?"

"He knew what I was doing. Sometimes, it seems like Grim knows everything." He exhaled heavily. "To teach me a lesson, he went after my family. They didn't know. They had no idea what I'd become and when the vampires came for them . . ." He shuddered. "They suffered. Grim and Leo made sure of it. All so they could bring '*my ass in line.*'"

She flinched.

"I buried them, and I heard Grim's call in my head every fucking second." He unballed his fists, stared down at his palms. "He wanted me to come to him. Wanted me to kill. Wanted me to be part of his twisted vampire family."

"The alpha," she managed. "Controlling his pack." And sensing a challenge from within. "What did you do?"

He glanced at her. "Made a deal with the devil."

That didn't sound good. Dee rose, fumbled with her clothes, and managed to dress.

The silence in the room thickened.

She shoved on her shoes.

Simon just stood there, bare feet, bare chest. Watching her.

Dressed, armored, she finally asked, "What kind of deal?" *No, not for me. Don't tell me that you're—*

"I found a warlock in Vegas. Asshole named Skye. He has magic—dark magic—and he used it on me, for a price."

Dee licked her lips. His gaze darted to her mouth. "What price?"

"I bled for him. Thirty days straight. Skye drained me nearly to death before each sunrise."

"Simon!" Blood loss like that—

"In return, he put a spell shield in place for me. One strong enough to weaken Grim's call. Not block it completely, but to mute it so I could turn away from the Born." He stalked toward her. Lifted his hand and ran his fingers down her cheek. "And find you."

Her fingers lifted and curled around his wrist. "Why didn't you tell me all this at the beginning?"

"Because you would have run from me. No." A slow shake of his head. "You would have tried to kill me, and I needed you too much to have you turn away. You're my shot at freedom, Dee. Real freedom. This shield won't last forever. I'll be lucky if it lasts a few more months. Grim's too strong to keep out. I know it. Skye knows it. Grim knows it." His eyes blazed darkness as he told her, "I don't want to become what he'll make me."

Her fingers tightened around his. "You won't." He wasn't like the others. He'd fought too hard. Held on to his sanity by going right into the darkness.

"Over the years, there have been others who were changed and didn't become—" His lips flattened. "Vamps don't have to be killing machines. It's the Borns, they're in control. The Taken just dance like puppets on freaking strings. The Borns who have been tainted by the power—"

Or curse, depending on who you asked.

"—they're the ones who want the blood on the streets."

"Is that what Grim wants?"

A bitter laugh. "Grim wants the world. And if he can, he'll take it."

Not while she was around. "He'll keep coming for me, won't he?" Keep attacking those she cared for, just as he'd attacked Simon's family.

"It's his way. He separates his prey. Makes you suffer, tries to break you."

His flesh was warm against her. "I don't break easily." Never had. Never would.

"No, you don't." He leaned down, brushed his lips over hers. "That's one of the things I love about you."

Whoa, now, what was that—

"Dee, I know this thing between us—shit, I know I wasn't honest with you at the start, but you and me, what we've got between us, it's real."

"It's lust," she told him, fighting to keep her voice even. Couldn't be more.

"It's that." One brow rose. "But if it was just me wanting to fuck you, things wouldn't be so damn complicated."

Ah, okay.

"We want the same thing, Dee. We want to stop Grim."

A nod.

"Partners?"

She'd need him. No doubt. But when hell came calling, would she be able to trust him in those last minutes? Or would Grim take control?

His lips thinned at her hesitation. "When you drink from me, what happens?"

Pleasure. Need. Fire. Dee swallowed. "I get stronger." The revulsion wasn't there. Not with him. It had *never* been there with him.

"No." He stepped back from her, putting a few feet between their bodies. "What do you see?"

Her breath caught.

"I thought so. You see my life, don't you? Flashes?"

"Yes." She *knew* that wasn't supposed to happen. Sure,

vampires could use their power to look into the mind of prey, but she hadn't been focusing, hadn't been trying, hadn't even wanted to see—

"You saw with Leo, didn't you?"

"I saw him kill his wife."

Simon blinked.

"I saw that asshole Grim, standing over them, laughing." She'd seen Leo cry. If he'd been enjoying the kill, he wouldn't have shed a tear. Maybe, back then, he'd still had a conscience. A soul.

But no control.

"Borns don't have to focus their power to steal memories."

Steal memories. Not her plan.

"They have to focus *not* to do it. Their psychic power is so strong, the images come automatically."

Well, damn. She'd been afraid of that. "You don't have to try and convince me anymore." Time for her own honesty. She crossed her arms. "I know what I've become."

"Knowing and accepting are two different things, babe."

Hit. They were and she was a long way from accepting her new "life." "We'll hunt him together," she told him, straightening her spine. "But if I think you're turning on me . . ."

He marched to the bag she'd thrown to the floor last night. Pulled a stake out. "You'll shove this into my heart?"

Her gaze fell to the stake.

No. Not that easy. Not anymore.

Because the vampire had gotten to her. Made her care. Made her feel.

He tossed the stake into the air, then caught it easily with his left hand. "I'll prove that you can count on me. Trust me."

Maybe. If only she could.

She turned away from him, unnerved by his stare.

"Dee?"

She didn't glance back because she was too worried about what he'd see in her gaze.

"I'll take the lust. I'll take anything you can give me." His fingers brushed her shoulders. He'd moved fast and soundlessly. She should have heard him, with her enhanced hearing, she should have—

"And one day, I'll take everything." His breath blew over her nape. "Just like you'll take everything I have."

Dee shivered.

His mouth closed over her skin.

She leaned back against him, strength and power, surrounding her, seducing her.

Someone rapped against their door. Her nose twitched.

Timing, timing, timing. "Catalina, chill, all right? I'll be down in five." No way was she leaving right then. No, she wanted a moment, okay, more than a moment, to just stay in the quiet and pretend the big, bad eternal monster wasn't after her.

To pretend that she was just an ordinary woman wrapped in her lover's arms.

"That's not Catalina."

Dee's nostrils twitched. She smelled Catalina's scent. The light mix of incense and roses. She turned in his arms. "Yeah, it is—"

The door flew open and the light scent vanished. A spell? A trick? What—

"Oh, hell," she whispered.

Zane Wynter stood in the doorway, filling the frame, and his eyes glittered demon black.

Her time had run out. She knew he'd come for her. Come to keep the promise he'd given a year ago.

Zane had come to kill her.

Unfortunately for him, she wasn't ready to die yet.

Chapter 12

"Zane, no!" Dee's cry echoed in Simon's ears. Fear. Fury. So the demon had tracked them? Big damn deal. He'd never been afraid of a demon, and he sure wasn't about to start fearing one now.

Zane's gaze scanned over them. Froze on the stake that Simon still gripped in his hands. "Were you planning to take her out, too?"

What? His brow furrowed and then the words registered. No, one word. *Too.* "The fuck you say." He shoved Dee fully behind him. No way was a demon coming after *his* woman with death in his eyes.

"It's what she wants." The demon crossed the threshold. Strolled in and swung a blue bag from his shoulders. He shoved his hand inside the unzipped top and drew out a stake of his own. "What she's always wanted."

"You're not touching her." Killing the demon would be easy.

The only problem? He didn't want to rip the man's heart out, not in front of Dee. This demon had been her friend once.

A friend who was about to kill her.

"I won't hide from him," Dee said and her voice was clear. Strong. She stepped to Simon's side, her chin up, her head back. The charred ends of her hair had vanished while she slept. Her blond mane was tousled around her face. Her cheeks were flushed, her lips bright red.

Sexy. The woman always looked so sexy to him.

"Dee." The demon's eyes swept her body once more. "You're looking good for a dead woman."

She shrugged.

"I take it that this asshole is the one who changed you?" Rage slipped past the ice in Zane's voice. Cracked through.

"No." Her hand brushed over Simon's arm. "He's the one who saved my life. More than once."

A sad shake of Zane's head. "So you've already gone to his side, huh, Dee? Already forsaken—"

"I'm Born."

The guy's eyes bulged. "Bullshit."

"It's the reason my parents were killed. The reason the vamps came after me again and again. I'm Born and I'm going to take out the bastard—Grim—who is on my tail."

Damn. The woman sure had one hell of a bite.

Sexy. If there wasn't a demon standing there, glaring and threatening death, he'd lick that long column of her throat once more.

If.

"Sorry, Dee, that's not gonna happen." Zane glanced down at the floor, then back at her. "I got a promise to keep."

Then he lunged forward, the stake up, ready, moving faster than a human ever could and flying straight at Dee.

Simon tried to jump in front of her, but Dee shoved him to the side. Then her left hand shot out and she snatched the stake, ripped it right out of the demon's hand and snapped the wood in two.

The broken stake thudded onto the carpet.

She grabbed Zane, bunched his shirt in her fist, and jerked him close to her face.

He smiled at her. "I tried."

What?

"You gonna bite me now? Gonna sink those, um, really long and what looks like freakishly sharp teeth in my neck? Gonna drain me dry?"

The demon didn't seem particularly worried.

Dee rolled her eyes. "Don't tempt me, asshole. *Don't* tempt me."

The smile that had curled his lips faded. "You're still in there, aren't you, Dee? All this . . ." His hand lifted, traced her lips, and Simon had to bite back a growl. "It's just surface."

She blinked and her head cocked.

Surface.

Being a vampire was a hell of a lot more than that.

"Not a cold-blooded killer, are you?"

Dee freed him.

"If you were, you would have drained me by now." He straightened his shirt, then raised a brow. "Born, huh? Never saw that one coming."

She shoved a hand through her hair. "Me either."

Zane grunted and looked his way. "So what's your story?"

Simon just stared back at him.

"Man, you need to bring that down a notch. Dee and I weren't lovers. You want to get all territorial and kick-ass, save that crap for Tony."

Simon locked his jaw and gritted, "Why are you here?"

Another fleeting smile. "I'm here because if Dee really had become some soul-less bloodsucker, I would have kept my promise." His stare slanted to a watchful Dee. "Don't worry, sweet, I would have made it fast and as painless as possible." A shrug. "But the minute I saw you, I knew you were still my Dee—"

A woman screamed. Loud, high. Terrified.

The scent hit Simon then. Thick and cloying. Smoke.

Fire.

"Fuck!" Zane spun around and ran for the door. Dee and Simon raced after him.

Not another damn fire. Not again. Grim's pack, they just weren't going to stop, not until they killed Dee.

Not on his watch.

Zane shoved open the door at the bottom of the stairs and they walked into—

An inferno.

It should have been impossible. Fire couldn't spread this fast. With their senses, they would have known but—

But Delaney's burned. The flames crackled and licked at the ceiling, growing bigger, hungrier, and giving them a glimpse of sweet hell.

"Catalina!" Dee's scream.

The witch stood behind the bar, seemingly frozen. Her eyes were on the flames that surrounded her. Bright, dancing flames.

The demon swore and charged for her. He waved his hand and the flames dimmed around the witch.

He flew over the fire and grabbed her.

"Burn," she whispered, but Simon could hear her over the flames. "Burn so fast." She closed her eyes and turned her head against Zane's shoulder.

The flames shot higher. The smoke thickened, but the fire didn't race back toward the witch. Instead, it headed right for Dee.

"Wynter!" Simon yelled. The demon could control fire. He didn't know what kind of power scale the guy had, but right then, as long as the guy could stop the fire, he didn't care.

Zane hoisted the witch over his shoulder, then made a fast movement with his hand.

The flames flickered, faded.

Only to start rising once again.

"Magic!"

Yeah, he'd figured that out. Dee had a tablecloth in her hands and she was fighting the flames.

"No, forget it, Dee! Get out of here!" Zane ordered.

Good plan. Simon grabbed her arm.

The demon led the way, using his power to push back the fire that just kept rising, rising . . .

"*Her!*" The demon's snarl. He froze before the door. Simon barreled into him. So not the time for this—

But then Zane ran forward. The glass doors exploded around them. Smoke billowed up into the night. Simon sucked in sharp, clean air, choking as his lungs began to clear.

"Stop her!" He glanced up at the yell. He saw Zane struggling with the witch, and Simon glimpsed a woman with curly red hair running down the street.

He blinked and Dee took off. Fast, so fast, his little vampire. She caught the woman in two seconds and tackled her, sending her prey slamming into the pavement.

"*No!*" The woman's cry. Afraid. Furious. "*Why can't you die?*"

Oh, so not what she needed to be saying to Dee.

He bounded after them.

Dee flipped the woman over and pinned her wrists to the ground.

Simon saw the tears on the woman's cheeks. Long, thin trickles that slipped over her skin, fell into her hair.

"*Do it, Nina.*" The whisper was on the wind. He froze. "*Kill her or they die.*"

Dee's head snapped up. "What the hell? Hey, jerkoff—come out and face me!"

Another vamp. One of Grim's men. Had to be. But he was telling the woman to kill Dee? How was she supposed to do—

"*Ignitor!*" Zane's scream of fear.

No, *no*. Simon's gaze snapped back to the woman's, and he finally saw her eyes, the bleed of red.

Grim wasn't screwing around anymore. He'd pulled out the big guns.

"*Dee!*"

Ignitor—a human. A very, very rare human gifted with the power of fire. She'd burn Dee, burn her with just a thought and kill her in an instant. She'd—

"Hell, no," Dee growled when her T-shirt began to smoke. Then she slammed the woman's head back against the cement. Hard.

The Ignitor's eyes fell closed, hiding that deadly red, and she lay, limp, beneath Dee.

He could love that vampire.

Already did.

"I've got her," Dee called. "You get that other bastard!"

Done. Simon took off, legs pumping fast. He flew down the dark street, snaked into the alley. His nose twitched as he caught the scent of blood. A woman stood, weaving slightly, her hand on the grimy wall. Alcohol fumed off her but she'd been prey, too.

Close.

"Come out!"

The woman flinched. She looked over at him with bleary eyes. "Run," he told her quietly, flashing fangs.

She did.

That left him all alone in the alley with *his* prey. A Dumpster squeaked. A shoe scraped over the asphalt. Simon licked his lips. "Hiding with the garbage?"

The vamp came out, claws ready, a bit of blood still dripping down his mouth. "You picked the wrong side in this fight."

Simon lifted his brows. He caught the whisper of footsteps behind him. His backup. No way would he ever mistake Dee's rich scent. "I don't think so."

The vamp's eyes darted behind Simon, and for an instant, fear flashed on his thin face. Then he spun around, and leapt up, clearing the brick wall behind him in one bound.

Simon lunged after him. No way was this scum getting away from him.

The man knew how to leap over a wall. Really kinda sexy the way he could move so fast.

Dee exhaled, watched a bit longer, admiring her view, then she eyed the wall. Um, yeah, she could take that. She hoped.

Dee ran—*a running start never hurt anything*—then leapt. She cleared the wall, but slammed into the ground below. The impact jarred every bone in her body, but Dee rolled, and came back up on her feet and took off.

A park. A big, dark, yeah, things-could-be-hiding-here park. Overgrown grass. Too tall trees. Too thick brush. Great.

The vamp with the ferret face was fast; she'd give him that.

Her heart raced in her ears and her legs kicked beneath her as she charged after him and Simon. No way was this guy getting away, not after he'd set a freaking Ignitor on her.

An Ignitor. A vampire's nightmare. A being that could raise and control fire.

Not a good way for a vampire to die.

She'd watched vamps burn before. Dee just hadn't thought that would ever be the way she'd go out.

Of course, she hadn't thought she'd be a vamp, either.

Simon lunged forward and launched his body at the vampire. Even from the distance that separated them, she could hear the *thud* when their bodies crashed into the earth.

She pushed forward with a burst of speed.

Simon flipped the vampire over—and the ferret bastard started *laughing.*

That's when the hair rose on Dee's nape. When she realized that the shadows were too dark.

And that vampires didn't always rely on their first course of attack.

Backup plans. She wasn't the only one who had them. Dee let her claws out. *"Simon."*

His head jerked up.

"He's leading us by the balls. *It's a trap."* One they'd walked, no, ran, straight into. The Ignitor hadn't been the only threat.

Not by a long shot.

The vamps came from the shadows. Four. No, five. Oh, damn, six.

Simon rose slowly, no fear flickering in his eyes or showing on the hard planes of his face. His shoulders rolled and he smiled. "Guess you're all ready for an ass kicking, huh?"

The man might be insane. This many vamps? No, hell, no. Dee was very much afraid they would be the ones getting the ass kicking. She still didn't even understand all her Born powers. No way could she take on this many vamps at once.

Laughter. The wild, crazy kind you usually only heard in B-movies. Ferret-face rose to his feet. He spat at Simon. Blood hit the ground near his feet. "I-I knew they h-had a hole here."

More laughter. What was the deal with Mr. Giggles? "Can't take us all, c-can you?" His back straightened and that grin nearly split his face.

Simon's arm brushed hers.

Dee sighed and pulled out a stake. Some habits just couldn't be broken. Maybe they *shouldn't* be broken. She eyed the closing circle of vamps, looking for the head of the snake. Because there was always a head, one with dripping fangs. The alpha. The vamp who wielded the most power and who had to be taken down first, because otherwise, he'd take you down. Fast, hard, and dirty.

Just because she liked her sex that way, it didn't mean she wanted her second death to be like that.

There. The guy with the long, dreaded red hair. The one with green eyes that glinted and stared too hard at her. The one with his claws out and his hands up. He stood before the others, just by about a foot or two. Not toss-away prey.

Threat number one.

"Got him," Simon whispered.

Hey, if he wanted to go first. "Knock yourself out," she whispered and her gaze dipped to the woman on the alpha's right. Asian. Exotic eyes too dark and deadly, red, red lips, pale, smooth skin and—

The woman lunged forward.

What?

Dee snarled and brought her stake up. *Fight. Survive.* Her mantra. Always.

But the woman didn't come for her. Instead, her claws ripped into the still laughing vampire's back. Dug deep.

He screamed.

"Hold him tight, Jun."

The vamp screamed even louder when the woman dug her claws in deeper.

The alpha stalked toward him.

"What the hell?" Simon muttered.

Dee just shook her head and kept her stake up.

"You don't know us. You come down here, smelling of

fresh blood, bringing the risen Born, and you think we're gonna do your bidding?"

"Grim—" Spittle flew. "Grim's gonna—"

The alpha shook his head. "Grim's gonna die, and so are you."

A whimper now, not a scream.

The alpha vampire jerked his head. "Make it fast, Jun. But make it hurt."

"N-no, no, Grim—"

"Grim can rot. I'm not his bitch."

Wow. Now that wasn't a statement she'd expected.

Two other vampires rushed to Jun's side. They hauled the now begging vamp away and Big Red turned to face her.

A sliver of wood bit into her palm.

His nostrils widened, flaring a bit. "Going to kill me?"

"I was considering it," she told him honestly. "But I thought I might see your plans first."

A short, shrill cry burst from the darkness.

Make it fast, Jun. But make it hurt.

Looked like Jun had done both.

So killing was obviously on the agenda for him. Fair enough. It had been on hers, too, but she'd hoped to force answers out of the now dead vamp first.

"You going after Grim?"

If she survived the next five minutes, yes.

"And you . . ." Big Red turned his green stare—green, when it should have been black, definitely a time for a vamp to switch to the hunting mode—on Simon. "That spell still working for you?"

Simon tensed. "How do you know about—"

A hard laugh. "I know about a hell of a lot." His gaze trekked back to Dee and he smiled.

Okay, that smile had goose bumps rising on her arms. Because while his eyes hadn't so much as flickered in color, his fangs were out and Dee could *feel* his power in the air. Pressing around her. No, surrounding her. He hadn't gotten his little gang of vamps to attack them, yet, but Dee had the very distinct impression that the order could come at any moment.

Jun came back to his side, her steps sure and steady. Her hands reached for the lead vampire, her hold possessive.

"I felt you—" he murmured, "the moment you rose."

Jun's nails lengthened into claws. Blood trickled down the male vamp's arm when those claws slashed his skin.

Dee braced her legs and got ready for the attack that had to be coming. As far as she knew, there was no way this guy should be feeling anything about her. "Did you now?"

"Um. Been waiting a long time on you."

If Jun's glare got any hotter, Dee figured she might start to burn a second time that night. "Just how long have you been in this game, Red?"

"Name's Tore," he said, "and baby, I've been in this game longer than you can imagine."

Born.

"Oh, I don't know. I can imagine an awful lot." She caught the slight hitch in Simon's breath and knew he'd just realized they were dealing with a Born. Out of one fire, into another. "So are you some screwed-up prick like Grim? And what the hell are you doing in *my* town?" Cause no way, *no way* had this guy been in the city long. Word traveled too fast about the Borns, and Pak hadn't said anything about two of the super vamps being around.

Pak wouldn't have kept that Intel from her, would he?

The faint smile wiped from Tore's face.

"He's *nothing* like Grim," Jun rasped and Dee knew the chick was walking a pretty short anger leash. *"Nothing."*

"Good to know." Simon's body was in the same false relaxed stance as hers, and she knew if she so much as inched forward, he'd jump to attack.

"But we still don't know why the hell he's here, and yeah, *Tore,* I do know exactly who you are." Banked fury rumbled in Simon's voice.

Someone let me in on the party. Dee darted a quick glance at Simon.

His black eyes burned. "He's Grim's brother."

What? Damn, talk about one powerful bloodline. Two Borns?

"An unfortunate circumstance of birth," Tore murmured. "Can't really choose family now, can we?"

Her heart slammed into her chest. "No, we can't." You couldn't always save them either.

But you could avenge them.

"I thought death would finally let me escape the bastard." Tore shook his head. His dreads brushed over his shoulders. "Should have known things wouldn't be that easy." His eyes raked over her. "I really thought you'd be . . . bigger."

Dee shook her head, fed up. "Look, are we gonna stand around here pissing and moaning all night, or are we gonna fight?"

"Not so fast," Simon growled. "We need to—"

"I can't kill him," Tore told her, patting Jun's hand with a soft, "Easy, love." One red brow rose. "But according to the seer—"

"Uh, *you* want to kill Grim?" But, then, didn't everybody?

"He killed me once. Payback should be . . . acceptable."

"Right." Dee shook her head. "I don't get it, why can't you—"

"Kill him?" Simon fired at the same time.

"Because we're linked. Grim can't control me, but he can *feel* me. He can slip into my thoughts, no matter how hard I try to shield my mind, and he knows when I'm coming for him. He runs, always runs, and leaves a bloodbath for me to clean up." His teeth snapped together. "Blood bonds, you know? There was no bite between us, but we shared a mother and the bond linking us has always held."

This guy didn't sound like a raving lunatic. He didn't act like a power mad vamp, either.

He'd come into town, without raising a stir, without leaving a river of blood in her streets.

"Can't get it, can you?" Jun asked, voice sharp. "Even now that you're one of us—"

Uh, no. Not quite.

"—you still think we all deserve to rot, don't you?"

No. Her eyes went to Simon again. No, all vampires weren't evil. Some fought like mad to keep their souls. Their spirits. Some of them, well, they just got stuck in a curse or a war they didn't understand. "I've never gone after every vampire," Dee said slowly and she kept her focus on Simon. He glanced at her. Their eyes held. "Only those with bounties on their heads." The killers. Those who loved to torture and raise hell.

"Like the bounty that's on *your* head?" Jun pressed.

Simon's jaw locked. "Don't push me," he growled at the chatty chick.

Her hero. So sweet. Her fingers lifted and brushed against his cheek. His head turned, just a bit, and his lips pressed against her palm.

"You're making a mistake," Tore said. "You shouldn't trust him. Take him, screw him all you like, but don't let your feelings blind you. You'll die if you do."

Simon attacked. He lunged at the other vampire, wrapped his left hand around Tore's throat and lifted the stake he'd snatched from Dee—

Jun raked her claws down Simon's side.

The vampires closed in.

"Stop!" Dee screamed. No, Simon wasn't going out in front of her. No. Way.

At her cry, every vampire froze. Some of them—wait, did a few of those guys just lower their heads?

A vampire celebrity. That's what she was now. Hell. "Let. Him. Go." But nobody moved. "Jun, chick—I'm talking to you." She could take that vampiress down, no doubt about it.

"He *won't* kill my chosen mate!" Jun didn't ease her hold, but she didn't go in for another attack, either.

"Yeah, well, he won't insult mi—" *Whoa.* What was that? No way she'd been about to say *mine.* "He won't insult the guy that's had my back this whole time. I know Simon's linked to Grim. I know the spell won't hold forever." Her shoulders squared. "It's a chance I'm willing to take."

Tore whistled, or well, kinda gurgled.

"Simon . . ."

His hand fell away from Tore's neck, but the stake remained pressed right over the other vampire's heart. "I'd die to protect her."

"You'll probably have to do just that." Tore's gaze dropped to the stake. "Lesson for you, little vampiress. When you get to be as old as I am—as old as Grim—killing us is hard." His fingers rose, curled around the stake. "It'll take more than a stake through the heart to keep Grim down."

She'd heard a rumor like that years before. Talk of another Born who'd been staked and nearly decapitated, but the guy had gone to ground and risen again. "So what's your killing tip?"

"Burn him. Burn him until there's nothing left."

Easier said than done.

Simon swore and stepped back, yanking the stake with him. "Why don't you just tell us where to find the asshole?"

"Go back for your charred witch. She knows."

The vamps began to retreat into the shadows.

"And where are you going?" Dee demanded.

"I just wanted to see you and to figure out if you were up to the task before you." A somewhat sad shake of his head. "You're not."

Now he was going to insult her? "I could've had you dead on this ground in the first minute."

"And I could have taken your heart in the first thirty seconds." A taunt. One that had her hands clenching. "Don't hesitate on your kills. Stop thinking like a human."

Impossible. Inside, she still was human.

Deep inside, and she always would be.

Surface. Maybe Zane had been right about that. Maybe rage had been blinding her for too long.

"When you face Grim, strike fast and strike first. Because you won't get a second shot." He turned away.

So did Jun. Protecting his back. Good girl. She could admire that.

"Oh . . ." He stopped, looked back. "Tell the Ignitor they're dead."

Then he was gone.

But the knot in Dee's gut had just gotten bigger.

Spells were powerful things. A few words, charms, a wisp of magic, and the world could change.

Dee and Simon rushed back to Delaney's. Simon half-expected to find the street swarming with fire trucks and neck-craning bystanders, eager for a glimpse of tragedy or heroism.

But Catalina's spell held, and though smoke curled lightly from the shattered windows, no humans were near the bar. If a human came by and glanced at Delaney's, they'd see no damage. No wreckage. Not while the spell was in place.

But Simon saw it all.

Catalina stood in front of the broken doors, her shoulders slumped, her clothes stained with soot.

The demon wasn't near her. He'd positioned himself next to a parked truck. A beat-up, older, gray pickup. When he caught sight of them, his head jerked. "You get the bastard?"

"He's dead." Not by his hand. *Tore.* Who would have thought that vamp would come calling? Simon had known he was looking at the Viking, even before Tore had opened his mouth and started talking about Grim.

The guy's reputation definitely proceeded him.

He jerked his thumb toward the truck. Even with the tinted windows, he could see the slumped figure of the woman. "She still out?"

"Yeah, Dee hits hard."

Dee grunted at that. "When someone is trying to fry me, I do." She stalked toward the bar. "Catalina?"

The witch didn't turn.

Dee touched her shoulder. She flinched. "Catalina, I-I need your help."

Finally, the woman turned. Her face had bleached of color, and her lips quivered when she asked, "Do I get to kill her?"

From the corner of his eye, Simon saw the sudden stiffness of Zane's body. "Cat . . ."

"She would have killed me."

"No." Dee's hand fell away. "She was looking for me. This wasn't a hunt, Cat. She wasn't here to bind or destroy you."

A hunt. Simon's brows rose. Witch hunts were supposed to be nightmares from the past. Burning and screaming and hell.

From the past.

Then why did they keep happening so often in the present?

"Doesn't matter why." Catalina's chin lifted. "She would have burned us all."

Simon remembered the tears he'd seen streaking down the woman's cheeks. And she was right. The fire could have destroyed the building in one fast fury. But, lucky for them, they'd all had time to leave before the fire burned their flesh away.

With an Ignitor, they could have been destroyed in seconds. An Ignitor always had perfect control over the fire.

The woman had hesitated with her flames. Why? Slowly, he said, "I think there's more going on here than we know." *Tell the Ignitor they're dead.* His gut knotted. Couldn't be good. "Let her talk. Let's find out what she knows."

"I want her *dead*." Fury and fear talking from Cat.

He knew 'em both when he heard 'em.

"Stand down, Cat. Stand. Down." A demand from Zane. One that came just as—

The Ignitor blew out the back window of the truck. She hurled herself through the flames, crashed into the cement. Stumbled, but managed to get to her feet.

Zane took her down. Hard. "And don't even *think* of burning me because, baby, I control the—"

"They're dead," Simon said, the words ripping from him. Probably the wrong time. Should have used some tact, but the witch was looking twitchy and with her magic—no way could they take chances. They needed someone left *alive* to question, and he didn't want to lose another link to Grim.

"Simon!" Dee's soft and shocked voice.

The Ignitor stopped thrashing beneath the demon. "Wh-what did you say?"

"They're dead." Who was he talking about? Didn't know. Had to be someone close to her. "A vamp told us."

A sob broke from her. Not one of those soft sniffles that some women could do, but a hard, chest-shaking eruption of agony. Pain.

Her face reddened and the tears leaked from her eyes. She tried to curl into herself, but Zane held her fast. "What the hell?"

Then Dee was there. Staring down at the other woman with recognition. Understanding. One who'd been there, and seen the darkness. "Her family. It's . . . Christ. *They're gone.*" She swallowed. "I-I cried like that, too. Zane, l-let her go."

He stared down at the woman, the struggle on his face.

"She won't hurt us," Dee said.

The woman's breath gasped out. She shuddered and cried as if the world were ending.

For her, maybe it was.

Simon's hands clenched. *What if the vampire was wrong? Lying wouldn't be something new for his kind.*

For any kind.

How many times had he lied? Tricked? To further his own plans—too many times to count. "We haven't seen the bodies," Simon said. The words slipped out, an effort to comfort. That agony—no, he couldn't see it. Couldn't hear it. Because when he looked at her, he saw Dee's hell too easily.

And remembered his own.

No, Mom! Mom! Dad! So much blood.

Her watery eyes turned to him. Hope, faint, flickering, shined through the pain.

He locked his jaw and Simon gritted, "A Born vampire named Tore wanted us to deliver a message to you. He's the one who said they were dead. We have no proof and—"

"Wh-what about Greg?"

Greg? "The vampire who brought you here to kill us?"

Zane's hands were tight around her wrists. Too tight. When the demon suddenly freed her, Simon saw the red imprints on her flesh. Zane swore when he caught sight of the marks.

"Y-yes, h-he's the one—" She pushed herself up.

"Greg's dead." Dee put her hands on her hips. "Very dead."

Hope again, brighter this time. "Then there might be a-a chance. I-if we can get to the house before anyone else ch-checks in, I can get them out—"

They're dead.

Simon shook his head. False hope, that's all he'd given her. Freaking false—

"The vampires drained the man first. The one with streaks of silver in his hair." Catalina's voice. Calm and cool. Simon's gaze found her huddled on the ground, leaning over a thick shard of broken glass.

Her eyes were fixed on that glass. No, on what she could see *in* the glass.

Scrying. A witch's talent.

The human's heartbeat raced in his ears. Pounding, fast, too fast. Dangerous that.

"They held the woman, made her watch. Then it was her turn." Catalina picked up the glass and blood dripped from her fingertips when the sharp edges cut her. "Death waits in that house near the water. Only death."

The Ignitor didn't cry out again. The tears came silently, long, pouring streams, and Dee snarled.

Her fangs were out, her claws glinting, and when she rounded on the witch, her eyes were perfect midnight black. "See *him*." Grim.

The blood drops splattered onto the ground. The scent drew him and power pulsed in the air.

Simon crossed to the witch.

Catalina's eyes had been glassy with her magic. A dazed blink seemed to bring her back to them. "I-I didn't mean—I haven't even cast my circle—"

No time. The bodies were piling up. The evil closing in.

No more attacks.

Our turn.

Simon swiped his claws over his forearm. He lifted his hand and let the blood drop onto the darkened glass. "See him through me."

A glow lit her eyes, then she stared down at the glass once more. He couldn't see a damn thing. Soot. Ash. The red smear of his blood. Darkness. But Catalina stared and stared, and the silence thickened around them.

"*Where.*" A demand from Dee. He should have known her patience would break first.

"Texas." Soft, tired. "Waiting, in a place called *Heuco,* near the Mexican border."

Hueco. Hollow.

Excitement burned through him. "Cut the link." She couldn't look too long. With Grim, there was no telling who he'd forced onto his side. An Ignitor was just the start. He could have a witch or even a warlock. Probably a warlock. When choosing his weapons, Grim would go right for someone who'd stepped onto the dark side of magic. A warlock would be able to sense Catalina's power if she stayed tuned in too long.

The glass shattered in her hands. "Can't find me now," she whispered. "But I found you."

Hot damn. They'd done it. His gaze met Dee's. Her lips began to curl, just a bit.

He hurried to her. Kissed her hard and deep. Tasted her.

The end was coming.

Not for them, oh, no. For them, it would be a beginning. They'd have forever.

But for Grim, hell waited.

Simon would get his freedom. Dee would have her revenge, then they'd have each other.

Pretty fucking perfect.

*   *   *

"Is the trap set?" Grim asked, his eyes on the woman who danced before him. Human. He liked the human dancers best. This one—her eyes smiled, flirted. Her heart raced and all that sweet blood pumped with every sway of her body.

"Greg didn't report in."

At that, Grim pulled his stare away from the woman. Music beat, a sensual rhythm, and he knew the woman kept on slithering. "How long has he been missing?" He didn't worry about guarding his words with the dancer. No need with her.

"An hour." Malik, a vampire who'd been with him since the guy's first Taken breath five hundred years before, met Grim's gaze directly.

An hour was plenty of time to die. Grim rubbed his hand over his chin. "The parents are dead?" His Ignitor was such a useful tool. Weak package, but an incredible power inside.

"Their bodies should be found tomorrow."

A quick tip to the cops, yes, that would do just fine. "And my brother?" Like he didn't know the asshole was around. The instant Tore had crossed the ocean, he'd felt the fool. He'd taken steps to prepare for him. Tore wouldn't have an advantage in this hunt.

"No word yet."

There wouldn't be. "He won't come for me." Tore had learned his lesson the last time when Grim had left the dead children for him to find.

His brother had always had a soft spot for the kiddies.

When you knew someone so well, it was easy to work their weak spots. He knew just how to make Tore suffer.

His brother had begged him for death over twelve hundred years ago. When he'd seen what Grim had become. When he'd found the bodies and known that he'd be the next to feel Grim's fangs on his throat.

There'd been no controlling the bloodlust. No stopping the vicious thirst. But he hadn't wanted to stop it. He'd just wanted to kill.

He'd granted his little brother's wish. Too bad Tore hadn't stayed down.

"He'll be our next project," Grim said, giving a nod. "It's time we freed him from his torment." A gift.

The music ended. He glanced over at the woman. Heaving chest. Glistening lips.

He'd screw her first.

Then kill her.

"It's a pity. I always loved my brother."

Malik didn't speak. Didn't call him a liar. Or a fool.

And Grim was both. After all, he'd let Tore survive for this long. He should have taken his head long ago.

But when his brother had woken—*just like me.*

Sentiment. Attachment. So yes, he had a soft spot for the man he'd known as his brother. Tore had tried to save him once, right before his father's bitch of a new wife had betrayed them all.

Tore had come to him, worked to free him from the chains, but there hadn't been enough time.

Too many warriors around them. Too much rage.

Blood eagle.

He squeezed his eyes shut but the memory of agony seared his flesh. His hands reached behind him automatically, touching his back.

No wings.

But he'd never forget, *never.* The snap of his ribs, the jerk backward—

Death had not come fast enough as his blood spilled onto the ground.

The silence hit him then. Thick and complete. His arms still behind him, he looked up at the dancer. Dark skin. Long, supple limbs. Her eyes were on him. Studying. Watching.

Watching like all those others. Watching and laughing as he fell to the ground.

No one had helped him then. No one.

"We'll kill the Born bitch." Grim's voice came out hoarse. He'd screamed that long ago night. Screamed until they took his breath and ripped his lungs out.

Blood eagle. No myth of Viking torture. Real. *Real.*

He would not die again. The vampiress coming would know the agony. Not him. Not again.

She'd die. He stepped forward. The dancer lifted her chin and asked, "Kill me . . . or change me?"

Humans were always wanting to live forever. He reached for her and didn't answer.

Because he'd never wanted to be a liar.

Or a killer.

Such a pity he was both.

Chapter 13

That day Simon dreamed of agony. Of a snow-covered battlefield that turned from white to red beneath him. Simon twisted on the bed, jerking and shuddering, but he couldn't make his eyes open. Couldn't escape.

Hands caught his body. Held too tight. Two men. One on each side. Long braids surrounded their faces. Thick helmets sat on top of their heads and some kind of cape or cloak billowed behind them.

A scream burst from him as fiery pain pierced his back. Simon choked, struggling for breath. He heard a snap, as if a bone were breaking. Again—

What the hell?

Pain, so much pain. Death would come. Death had to come. *I will die with honor, I will not—*

"Wake up, vampire."

His eyes flew open at the soft voice and he sprang up, breath heaving. His hands flew to his back. He expected to find the flesh torn open, his ribs ripped out and broken, to look like—

"You dream of him." Catalina eyed him and shook her head. "His link to you is growing once again."

Fuck, no. Simon ran a trembling hand over his face.

She glanced toward the door. A cheap motel room door. They were on the Louisiana/Texas border. She'd come with him and Dee. Come with the demon and the Ignitor—the woman who could only sit and cry.

"If you don't kill him soon, he'll start to control you again." No censure there. Catalina just seemed to be stating a fact.

Okay, she *was* stating a fact.

Simon climbed from the bed. When had the witch come in? "Where's Dee?" He reached for his shirt. Good thing he still had his jeans on or Catalina would've gotten a show.

"With Zane. She wants him to take the human away." Catalina blew out a hard breath. "He wants to stay by Dee's side."

He yanked the shirt over his head. "Do you know what's going to happen?" He'd first gone to Catalina weeks before. He'd known she was close to the hunters at Night Watch. He'd told her about Grim and asked if she understood what would be coming.

"I've been waiting for you." Her first response. *"You're the one who's come for Dee."*

Her shoulders rolled and she glanced back at him. "I know if I go with you, I die."

He blinked at that. "You been looking into the future?" There was a price for that. A heavy one. And looking forward took dark magic.

She gave him a weak nod and rubbed her right hand over her forehead. "It was the fire. I had to make sure I wasn't going to—"

The door swung open. *"Well, that guy is a pure asshole."* Dee stormed inside. "Won't listen to a thing I say, and the woman—Nina—she's doesn't even seem to know where she is." She stopped, blinked. "Uh, what's going on?"

Catalina's spine straightened. "I'm leaving."

Dee gave a fast smile. "Good. I knew you'd see reason, at least. I mean, you could have stayed in the city, you didn't even have to come this far."

"Everyone is going to die, Dee."

Her lips parted. She hesitated. "Wh-what's that?"

"I looked." Catalina shook her head. "I saw death. Zane was surrounded by flames. I burned. Nina—her throat was cut." She swallowed. "And you . . ."

"What about me?"

Catalina's eyes darted to Simon.

Shit. Not good.

"You die, Dee." Said again, softly. Sadly.

"I've already died once."

"You won't come back this time." Catalina looked back at her. "You can't win against Grim. I saw—"

"You're afraid." Dee's arms crossed over her chest. "I know you are. Hell, I'm scared, too, okay?"

Had Dee just admitted that? No way. Simon stepped toward her but she threw up a quick hand. "Just . . . hold on. When you touch me, it's hard to think."

Well, damn.

She turned that hand and pointed at Catalina. "You can't look into the future when you have fear in your heart. Even I know that."

Catalina didn't speak.

"You mess with the Dark, and it'll show you the things that scare you the most, not what will be." Dee gave a hard sigh. "I've been playing these games for a while, and I know about witches. And what you can and can't see."

"I saw death." Catalina's hands clenched. "I'm not going to a slaughter for a fight that can't be won."

"He killed my family. Simon's family. Nina's family. He won't stop." Dee paused, then said, "We have to stop him."

"You'd kill us all for vengeance?"

"Watch it, witch," Simon warned. The fear in Catalina was new. The fire had ignited the terror and the strong woman he'd met now seemed to have vanished. Fear could do that. Twist you. Change you. "Walk away if you want. This fight isn't yours." It was his. There'd be no stopping for him. No choice.

Her gaze held his. Sadness there. "You'll kill her," Catalina whispered.

Simon's heart shuddered in his chest. No, no, he wouldn't.

He'll start to control you once again.

His vision dimmed. Fear, his own, licked at his gut and rose to his throat as—

"If you send her after him, you're as good as killing her," the witch finished and Simon's breath came back.

"No, I'll stand by her. Grim's afraid of her. He knows she can kill him." Or else he wouldn't want her dead so badly.

"*Can.*" Catalina's eyes closed. "Just because she can doesn't mean she will."

"I will." Absolute certainty in Dee's voice.

He'd back her any day.

Catalina's lashes lifted. "You're always so sure of yourself. From the first moment I met you, you were so strong—"

"You mean when that idiot warlock came and tried to bind you?"

A warlock like Skye. A former wizard who'd turned to the dark.

"We kicked his ass, didn't we?" Dee murmured and Simon wished he could have seen that.

Wished he could have known Dee, before hell came calling at both of their doors.

The witch licked her lips. "We did." A pause. "And I thought—I thought we'd be able to kick ass again. When he"— a weak flutter of her hand toward Simon—"came to me, asking me for the promised Born, I thought we could make everything all right. Thought we'd be strong enough to face what's coming."

"*We will be,*" Dee said. Her voice was sure and confident but Simon happened to glance down, and he saw that her fingers shook.

"I'm not." Simple and as certain as Dee sounded. "I'm leaving tonight. I don't even know where I'm heading," Catalina said, lips curving down, "I just have to get away from here. The fire—"

Fire. The one thing that could scare a strong witch. Grim had known exactly what he was doing. *Separate.* Yank Dee away from the friends who could help her.

Grim could have gotten the Ignitor to attack Dee at any time. But, no, he'd waited until Dee sought shelter with Catalina.

He'd sent his other goons with fire the first time. But the second time, he hadn't been playing. Grim had brought out the big guns. *Ignitor.*

Burned around her.

One down. Grim was working his twisted magic.

Dee stepped away from him and crept close to Catalina. She pushed a hand through her short hair and stared in silence for a moment. "I understand."

No pleas to stay. No guilt trips that they could use the witch's magic.

Dee's arms wrapped around the other woman. "Just be safe."

He caught a glimpse of Catalina's face. Simon saw the tear that leaked down her cheek. Her arms clamped tight around Dee. "You, too."

Friends.

But Catalina was still walking away.

And Dee was trying to force the demon to leave her side. *Friends.*

She wanted them safe and being safe meant that she didn't want them anywhere near Grim.

Catalina eased back and swiped her hand over her cheek.

Then she walked away. The door shut behind her with the softest of clicks.

Dee's shoulders straightened. "You want to tell me..." she began slowly, then glanced back at him, "why I had a vision of you, *dying,* in some freaking blizzard right before I stormed in here?"

He blinked. How had she—

She rubbed her eyes. "Damn, Simon, that was bad. One minute, I was talking to Zane—idiot won't listen to me. The next, all I could see was you and you were—"

"It wasn't me." He could give her that much, at least. It had to be their blood link. Grim was trying to tune back to him, but Dee was slipping inside his mind, without even trying.

Her body turned fully toward him. Her gaze dipped over his chest and she crossed to him. "Uh, yeah, it was." She walked behind him. Her fingers trailed down his back and Simon stiffened at the light touch. "What they did to you—"

"Not to me," he said again, his breath sucking in. Her scent always got to him. Sensual and rich.

"I *saw* you."

Because she'd been in his mind, and the images had taken hold of his consciousness and hadn't let go. "Grim." Her palms pressed into his back, seeming to burn his flesh even through the T-shirt. "What you saw—it was him."

Her breath feathered over his flesh. Warm. His eyes closed. She lifted the back of the shirt and her lips pressed into his skin.

Simon swallowed. "They called it the blood eagle."

Her fingers slipped down the skin of his back and he knew she'd remember the image from the dream. Vision. Whatever the hell it had been.

Torn, broken, ribs spread to look like an eagle's wings. "An old Viking torture." One he knew had been used on Grim. Their link had shown him that before.

Her lips rose and he missed the touch of her mouth. "Why?"

Glancing over his shoulder, he met her stare. "Not all monsters are born, Dee, some are made." Once upon a time, a very long-ass time ago, Grim hadn't been the sick twisted bastard of today. He'd just been a man. One who'd been broken. Savaged.

"If the stories are true," Simon said, watching her carefully, "the first thing he did on rising was to find every man who'd participated in his torture, and he ripped them apart."

Her gaze held his. "Revenge." The same thing she sought.

He gave a nod. "There's a price, you know." Why hadn't he realized how heavy the price would be for her? Why had he only thought of himself? Of the way he wanted his life to be?

He'd pulled Dee into this war, yanked her into the blood.

"I've always known there was a price." A mirthless smile tilted her lips. "Why do you think I put a kill order on myself?"

His hands knotted at that. No way. No damn way would that demon Zane ever come at her with death in his eyes.

"I've seen death for the last sixteen years," Dee said. "I've always known I was living on borrowed time."

Not borrowed.

"What I don't understand is why me?" Pain there, breaking beneath the surface. "Why the hell am I one of the Born? I'm nobody. *Nobody*. I was a freaking clueless kid when the vamps came after my family. I wasn't special. I'm *not* special."

He caught her hands. Held her tight. "You're the strongest woman I've ever met." True. He'd never seen her back down. A fighter, straight to the soul.

Her gaze fell. "When I was a kid, my family used to go to church together every Sunday."

He waited. Dee's life, before the nightmares.

Her stare didn't meet his. "A lot of people think God cursed vampires. Cursed the Borns and they spread the virus—"

Was that what people were calling it these days? A virus?

"—like a plague. That's why the holy water works on vampires."

Yeah, he'd been burned by that once. Holy water and vamps didn't mix—that one wasn't a myth.

"So what did I do, Simon, that would have condemned me at fifteen?" Her eyes rose. "What did I do that was so bad, I was cursed, too? I lost my whole family—*what did I do?*"

Nothing. His fingers tightened around hers. "I don't know why you're a Born." He'd chosen this path. For her, fate had chosen. "I know the stories, too. That the first Born committed a betrayal, that all vamps were punished for his crimes." He shook his head. "You didn't do anything wrong. Nothing, got me?"

Her face was as blank as a doll's. "But I'll still wind up like Grim, won't I?"

"*No!* You'll never be like him."

She flashed a bitter smile. "I think I already am." A pause. Then, quietly, "And deep down, so do you."

No. "Dee, I—"

"Fuck!" A snarl from outside. "Dee!" Zane's voice. His fist thudded against the door. Half a second later, the door came crashing open. "She's gone." His chest heaved and his eyes glinted back.

Dee nodded. "I know. I told Catalina that—"

"Not her!" He shook his head and snarled, "We both knew the witch would cut and run. Cat can't handle fire. That shit just brought up too many bad memories for her and she's too afraid of burning." He slammed a hand against the door frame. "Nina's bolted."

A curse erupted from Simon's lips. Her family killed—yeah, they'd had that confirmed by a quick call to Dee's friendly cop contact.

A massacred family.

An Ignitor who knew the location of the Born vampire behind the slaughter.

"She's gone after him," Dee said, and it was what they all knew. "How long of a head start?"

His jaw clenched, Zane gritted, "At least three hours. I thought she was sleeping in her room. She'd been crying so much, I didn't even think to go in there and check."

Shit. Three hours.

Hell of a lead she had on them. With that much time, she'd definitely get to Grim first.

Ignitors were so strong psychically. Strong enough to create and control fire with their minds. But nature was a sly bitch. For all their psychic strength, Ignitors were so very weak physically.

A careless touch could bruise them, like when Zane had wrapped his fingers around the Ignitor's wrists.

And killing them would only take one blow.

If Grim saw her coming, if he *felt* her, Nina would be dead. But if he didn't . . .

Burn, bastard.

"Simon." Dee's voice, vibrating with tension. "Let's get on the road, now."

He was already moving. He grabbed his bag. This was it. Final match.

Should have never brought Dee in on this.

He'd thought they would make the perfect team. Same enemy. Same goal.

But if anything happened to Dee . . .

Can't lose her.

Won't lose her.

How had his master plan gotten so screwed up?

Zane braced his legs apart. "He's gonna kill her. We have to get there before—"

Dee marched up to him, that weird, faint smile on her face. Her hand pressed against his chest. "I told you before, this fight's not yours. Not yours. Not Cat's."

Zane's eyes narrowed as he stared down at her. "You think I'm walking away from you? You're not going out on a death fight. I've had your back before, I'll have it again. I'm not—"

"You don't have a choice." Her right hand snaked up his neck. "Sorry." Her left hand came up, and delivered a hard, fast hit to his chin. The demon went down. "After all the times with Tony, you should have seen that coming." She stared down at him, her body taut.

Simon approached her slowly and very, very cautiously. "Wanna tell me what that was about?"

She glanced up. The demon lay sprawled across the threshold. "In case Cat's vision wasn't pure shit, no way am I gonna risk him." Emotion there. Affection. Love.

The fist that slugged his gut told Simon that he was jealous. Had been jealous of the demon from the very first. A bond existed between Dee and Zane. One born from time and struggle. Trust.

What he wouldn't give for Dee to care enough to punch the crap out of him.

Trust.

Love.

Her shoulders sagged. "I pulled the punch, you know. I used my left hand." Still, she had vampire strength now, so the punch wouldn't have been anywhere near soft. She bent, ran her fingers over Zane's jaw. "But demons are strong and he won't be out long."

No, he wouldn't be. And when he woke, Simon knew Zane would come after them. Because the demon cared for Dee, too. Cared enough to come on his own with a kill-order.

If you cared enough to kill . . .

Simon lifted his gaze. "Let's get the hell out of here." Not lovers. Dee and the demon had never been together sexually, so he shouldn't even think about attacking the guy while he was out.

But he'll be there for Dee when this hell is over. When she doesn't have to fight the nightmares of her past any longer, the demon will be there.

And where will I be?

Would Dee even want him in her life once Grim's threat was gone?

He hadn't thought that far ahead.

Dee dragged Zane inside the room. Simon grabbed Zane's legs, and they hoisted the demon onto the bed. Dee shoved a pillow under his head. "Don't come after me," she whispered.

Zane wouldn't be able to hear her.

She reached for his hand. Turned his wrist over. "I-I have to know where you'll be. I can't risk you. *Won't.* Not for my revenge."

You'd kill us all for vengeance? The witch's question.

No, Dee wouldn't.

She stared at the demon, swallowed, and bit him.

Simon froze. No, no—he didn't like to see her mouth on the demon. Not one bit. *Taking his blood.* A growl rumbled in Simon's throat. Not her. Not him. No—

Dee wrenched her mouth away. Her eyes met Simon's.

"Not . . . another." His snarl was a guttural demand.

"Simon?"

He grabbed her arms and hauled her away from the bed. *No time.* His jaw locked. "Get in the car."

And away from the demon.

A demon now forever linked to her. Just what he needed. More competition.

As if he didn't have enough shit going on.

Simon hauled her out, left the demon, and didn't look back. As far as he was concerned, there had never been any use in looking back.

They climbed into Dee's SUV. Zane's motorcycle was gone. Either courtesy of Nina or the witch. Either way, he knew the demon wouldn't be slowed down for long.

Backup would come, whether they wanted it to or not.

"Uh, it's my vehicle, you know, I should be the one to—"

He floored the accelerator and they shot out of the parking lot, leaving a trail of spewing gravel behind them.

The black SUV fishtailed out of the lot. The two in the vehicle were so intent on their prey that they didn't glance around. Didn't take notice of the one watching.

Pity.

Another mistake.

The key turned and the ignition kicked to life. Trailing them would be too easy.

Killing them—harder. But not impossible. Nothing was impossible.

The slow twang of country music filled the car's interior, and the vehicle pulled from the concealing shadows.

"How long until we reach Hueco?" Dee's voice was steady. The words were the first she'd spoken in the last hour.

Simon kept his foot stomped all the way onto the accelerator. Even burning up the black interstate road, it would still be "after dawn." A piss-poor time to go riding into the town. He'd be weak. All the vamps would be.

He and Dee would be outnumbered. Grim would have a guard force. Lots of vamps and who knew what else.

"Then if we've got nothing to do for the next six hours—"

Probably longer.

"Why don't you tell me what's got your butt in such a twist?"

His knuckles whitened around the wheel. "You didn't have to drink from him," he bit out. *Your butt in such a twist.* Nice.

"I wanted to know if he was coming after me. Us."

He could still see her mouth on the other man's wrist. Her lips so red against his dark flesh. Tasting him. Taking him.

The SUV swerved onto the median and Simon yanked the wheel so the vehicle slipped back into the right lane. "You took his blood. You linked with him." Wasn't it enough that the two of them already had some kind of bond he didn't understand?

Trust. Yeah, Dee trusted her demon.

"I linked with you, too. I didn't hear you complaining about it."

No, that was the problem. He'd all but begged for more. The feel of her lips. That tongue—

Good fucking thing the demon had been knocked out.

"I-I thought I had to do it. After what Cat said, I didn't want him following us." Quiet, subdued.

Since when was she subdued? What the hell? He slanted her a quick glance and tried to get the crazy bat-shit jealousy under control.

Fear. That's what it really was. Fear about facing Grim. Because what if the bastard was too strong? And then . . . cold-eat-your-soul fear that when the battle was over, he'd lose Dee.

One way or another.

When did she become more important than freedom? He cleared his throat and tried to unclench his fingers before he broke the steering wheel. "I thought you didn't believe the witch."

A sound, could have been a strained laugh or just a long sigh, came from her lips. "Sometimes, I'm not sure what I believe anymore. I shouldn't have let them leave the city with us. I knew the whole time that was a mistake."

But the demon had been adamant, and he'd herded the shattered Ignitor and the still-dazed witch with him.

"I tried to sleep at the motel, but I just—I just kept seeing Catalina, surrounded by the fire."

But the fire surrounded you, too. Why wasn't Dee scared for herself? Didn't she care?

"I couldn't make her face the flames again. And Zane—oh, hell, after what I saw—"

His gaze snapped to her. "What you saw?"

Her hand lifted, then fell limply back in her lap. "Every time I bite someone, I'm going to see the person's life, right?"

Unfortunately, that was the way of the Born. Most saw that as a strength. A way to get into the minds of prey and control them.

Not Dee. He could tell she saw it as some kind of punishment. Another one, for her.

"He's already been through enough. I'm not going to have him dying for my fight."

He reached for her hand and linked his fingers through hers. "*Our* fight." She wasn't in this alone. She wasn't going to ditch him the way she'd done the others.

He wouldn't leave her side. No matter what. "I'm not gonna turn on you, babe. I don't care what the witch saw, *I won't turn.*" The spell might be weakening. Grim might be starting to find a link again, but it wouldn't matter. Grim would be dead long before the spell wore off completely.

Her fingers tightened around his. "I know."

Simple. Certain.

Trust?

His breath expelled in a hard rush and his heart thundered against his chest.

"There's something you should know." The leather groaned beneath her as she shifted to stare at him. "I didn't want to bite Zane. Didn't want to bite that freak vamp Leo. Since turning, I've *needed* to bite. The bloodlust has been there, no denying it. When I first opened my eyes and saw Jude . . ." He heard the click of her swallow. "I thought I might even lose control."

The first cravings were the strongest. The most dangerous. That was why he'd taken her to Pak. Pak knew how to care for vampires. He'd guarded dozens of Taken over the years. Guarded them, and had to put some down.

Simon knew if he'd stayed with Dee, her bloodlust would have flared and instead of calming her, his own control would have broken.

They would have broken.

But now they were stronger. Together, they were stronger. Not. Gonna. Break.

"You are different. I wanted you. I wanted to bite, and I wanted you to bite me."

A confession like that, from a hunter . . . from *her*.

His gums burned as his teeth grew and the crotch of his pants got way too tight around his expanding cock.

"You're the one I want, Simon. Only you."

Their joined hands rested on her soft, jean-clad thigh. "When this is over," he managed to say, the words coming out hoarse and hard, "you're not getting away from me." He'd have to explain, have to tell her everything—

But she wouldn't escape him.

"Good." He caught her faint smile. "Because you'd better not even think that you're getting away from me."

Ah, damn.

She'd done it to him again. A sucker punch. Tony would never let him hear the end of this one. Zane jerked up in bed. His gaze flew around the room. Gone. Of course. What else?

He jumped up, automatically checking the clock. How long had he been out? An hour? Two? Judging by the faint light trickling through the blinds, a hell of a lot longer.

Dee had used that vamp strength on him.

He almost smiled. Almost.

Then he caught sight of the marks on his wrist. Faint. Small. Two circles.

Sonofabitch.

She'd taken his blood. Gotten a lock on him.

"Fine, princess—so you know I'm coming. What else did you expect me to do?"

He stormed to the door. *Car.* He'd steal one from the lot, get on the road, and call for backup. Pak might even have some other hunters in Texas that he could send in for them. Easy deal.

Dee wouldn't get rid of him this easily.

He wrenched open the door and caught the scents too late.

Three vampires. Tall, thick, with teeth ready and claws out. They stood just past his door, smiling.

"Knew we'd find someone waiting," the one in the middle said, and his fanged smile widened. "Let's see how long it takes to make the demon scream."

A really, really long time.

Zane lifted his hands and tossed out a smile of his own. "Who's first?"

They all attacked at once. Figured.

Dee sucked in a sharp breath and lunged forward. The seat belt cut into her chest. In the distance, the faint purple light of dawn streaked across the horizon.

Weakness.

"Dee? What's wrong?"

She licked her lips. "Zane. For a minute there, I thought—" She'd thought he called her name.

"You should try to get some sleep," Simon told her. "Save your strength."

What strength? She could already feel the pull of the sun. The tiredness, the weakness. "*You* should sleep." He'd been driving all night. Even outrun two troopers. Impressive. "Let me take the wheel for a while."

He glanced her way. "I'm all right."

She wasn't gonna get into a pissing match with him. "Slow down and let me take the wheel." The guy was sexy as hell, but bossy.

Good thing she liked him. Okay, more than liked him. *Don't go there, not now.*

Later there would be plenty of time to sort out the sick, tangled mess of her emotions. To see if there was anything between her and the vampire other than the thick, hot need.

A need she felt even now. Had felt since his fingers pressed against the top of her thigh hours before.

She knew he had to smell her arousal. Just as she'd caught his thickening scent.

And the big bulge in his jeans—yeah, another dead giveaway. But he'd ignored it. She was trying to do the same. *Trying.*

The car slowed. Finally. The speedometer eased back down, down . . . eighty, seventy . . .

They'd turned off the Interstate an hour ago. The SUV snaked down some lonely, twisting road that seemed to head nowhere.

But to death.

To Hueco.

The flash of headlights filled the SUV's interior. Ah, after all this time on empty roads, they had company.

A motor roared and Dee tensed.

The lights behind them burned brighter, filling the SUV's interior with a hot glow. The motor roared louder—*coming for us.* Not the friendly kind of company. "What the hell?" Dee jerked around. Someone was coming, all right, bearing down on them fast. Too fast. "Simon!"

The SUV raced forward, but, too late—

Never noticed the other car. Should have looked back sooner. Too worried about what waited ahead.

The car hit them. A jarring, brutal hit. Once. Twice.

The SUV flipped. Metal screamed. Glass shattered. The vehicle rolled across the road.

The air bags exploded. The world in front of Dee became a cloudy white.

Her claws ripped into the bags, cut them out of her way.

She shoved the broken glass aside, managed to peer out the window—

And saw that another car had come from the waning darkness. No, not a car this time. A truck—coming right at them. At her.

Ambush. Fucking ambush.

Dee shoved against the metal, but the sun had already weakened her. *Trapped.* Pinned by the twisted door. "Simon!"

No answer. She turned to look at him. Not moving, slumped over the seat. "Simon?" A whisper now, not a scream.

No, no, this couldn't happen to him.

Blood loss, the easiest way to kill a vamp.

The car slammed into them again. Then the truck hit.

Metal tore into her flesh, cutting past the skin, driving into the muscle and all the way down to the bone.

Simon.

This time, before the darkness came, *this time,* he was her last thought.

And her regret.

Chapter 14

It was the pain that woke him. The sharp stabs of agony and the nauseating throbs that shuddered through his body. Simon forced his eyelids to lift.

Bright.

Too fucking bright.

His eyes closed. What the hell had happened? He and Dee had been driving down one long, lonely ass stretch of road. They'd long since abandoned the Interstate. He'd had her sweet scent in his nose. He'd wondered when he'd have *her* again, then—

Lights.

The crunch of metal.

A scream.

Silence.

His eyes flew open. *"Dee!"* Should have been a roar, but it came out more like a weak growl.

The SUV twisted around him. Bent, broken. Metal dug into his side, cut into his legs and held him pinned in the seat. The steering wheel—shit, it felt like the thing was trying to go through his chest.

He couldn't see Dee. The way he was trapped, Simon couldn't even turn enough to see her.

And he couldn't hear her. Not the rasp of her breath. Not the thud of her heart.

But he could smell—gasoline, rubber, and blood.

So much blood.

His. Hers.

Not Dee. No, not her.

The rays from the sun poured through the shattered windshield. He could feel the sun's powerful drain on his strength. Human. That's what he was right then.

And a human couldn't get out of this metal trap.

"Dee!" His cry was louder now, but there was still no sound from her side of the car.

A long sliver of glass had shot through his right arm and embedded in the seat. Gritting his teeth, tasting blood, Simon wrenched his arm up.

Fire.

"Dee? Babe?" He barely glanced at the mess he'd made of his arm. He grabbed what looked like part of the hood and heaved it back toward the broken windshield. He managed to shove it about four inches. *I hate the damn sun.* But those inches were enough for him to see. "Dee?"

Blood matted her blond hair. Her head hung limply from her neck, and blood dripped slowly, slowly, down her face and onto her lap.

"Babe?"

He should be able to hear her heartbeat. Yeah, damn it, his strength was low, but he should be able to hear—

Thud.

Weak. So very weak. His breath caught, and he waited for another beat. Waited. Waited.

Nothing.

"Look at me!" A scream. Fury, fear.

Thud.

But her eyes didn't open and he could see why. There was so much blood around her. So many wounds. So much pain. Shit—it looked like someone had ran right into her. But they'd been hit from behind, not from the side, hadn't they?

He shoved the broken metal again, freeing up more desperate inches. He could reach her now. Simon slid his fingers through that precious space and managed to brush her cheek.

Ice cold.

No throb from her heart.

Dying.

Dead?

The easiest way to kill a vampire . . . Everyone knew—make 'em bleed.

The bastard that had come after them, no doubt one of Grim's Taken, had known just what he was doing.

He'd struck at dawn, when the sun would keep them weak. He'd left them trapped. Bleeding.

Not an easy death.

Slow.

Painful.

Grim would want them to die like this.

Sick fuck.

"Not the way for you," Simon whispered and his fingers trembled as they feathered over Dee's bloodstained cheek. He took a breath, tried to catch her sweet scent, just once more.

But he only scented blood now.

A soft tremble reached his ears, a small vibration. Her heart? Please, it had to be.

He caught the nape of Dee's neck and managed to tip back her head.

No moan came from her lips. No whisper of life.

Too late.

No, no—he *wouldn't* be too late. If she was gone—

Stay, Dee. Stay.

He wrenched his shoulder but managed to position his wrist over her mouth. He wouldn't have much longer. He could feel the lick of cold in his own body. *Not much longer.*

But he'd give her all that he had.

His wrist pushed between her lips. "Bite me."

She didn't. Her fangs weren't out. Her lips didn't move.

"Bite me!" A snarl of fury. She wouldn't die while he watched.

Thud.

The slightest press from her teeth.

Dee. Do it, babe. Bite me.

"Live," he whispered.

Vampire instinct took over. He'd seen it happen before. Seen a vampire on the brink of death. His teeth had shot out and he'd latched onto his food without conscious thought.

Dee's teeth sank into his flesh. His blood trickled into her mouth.

Take. "Take." Everything.

Her mouth tightened around him and she began to feed in earnest, greedy gulps as the bloodlust rose.

He would *not* watch her die.

Her lashes began to flutter.

But fate would make her watch him.

"It's done?" Grim asked as his hunter stalked into the room.

A smile stretched the hunter's lips. Slow. Satisfied. "Both of them are bleeding out now. With the sun up, they'll never get out of that damn metal."

He nodded. "Good." Fire had never been the best way to go. He saw that now. Blood, the slow drain, the agony of knowing what would come and being helpless to stop it—

As I had been helpless.

—that was the end for his enemies.

Grim turned away and stalked to his bed. The dancer lay there. Still alive, but low on blood. He'd let her keep living a while longer. He'd rather enjoyed her. "Which one do you think will die first?" Not that it mattered. But the one left behind would have the greater torment. *If* there was an attachment there, and his vamps had told him the woman and Chase were close.

Lovers.

The body's needs and desires could make the soul weak.

"The bitch will go first."

Anger there. His brows drew together. "Did something to piss you off, did she?" Not surprising. Dee had earned her reputation for a reason.

In another life, he might have admired her.

In this life, he just needed her dead.

"She took the hardest hits. She'll die long before dusk. They *both* will."

They'd better.

"Do you still feel him?" his perfect hunter asked.

Him. Chase. The guy Leo had turned years before. Grim closed his eyes, tried to focus and find the ungrateful bastard but—

Nothing. "Maybe he's already dead." Maybe. But the truth was that he hadn't felt a connection to Chase since the Taken had traded with the warlock.

So Chase could still be alive, or he could be dead. Again.

He glanced over at the bed. The dancer was awake. She'd been awake the whole time they talked, but she'd kept her eyes closed. Like a good little girl, pretending to sleep.

Maybe because she didn't want to see. Maybe she wanted to pretend she wasn't involved in this.

Wrong.

His tongue slipped over the edge of his sharp teeth.

The dancer wasn't getting out of his den alive, but maybe he'd Take her. Maybe.

She drank greedily, desperate, hungry, *needing* the blood that spilled onto her tongue. More. More.

Dee felt the ice rising in her body. The numbing cold, and she fought it, drinking as much of the warm liquid as she could.

Drinking.

Her eyes opened when the blood flow began to ease, and she squinted, staring at the bright light. The broken glass.

Attack. Two vehicles. One from behind, one from the side. *Right at dawn, when we were the weakest.*

Smart bastards, she'd give them that, she'd give them—

Simon's hand dropped.

Dee sucked in a sharp breath. *What*— "Simon!" The blood on her tongue, the warmth in her veins.

His.

All his.

She turned her head to the left, craning to see him. "Simon!"

A weak smile curved his lips. Such pale lips. Such tired eyes. "What did you do?" she whispered. Stupid to ask, she knew. She fumbled, managed to grab his hand and hold tight.

"You . . . had to live."

So did he. Dammit, *so did he*.

His eyes began to close. "Don't . . . watch me . . ."

Her fingers clenched around his. "We're gonna get out of here." They were trapped in a damn tin can, but she'd get them out.

Crushed. Smashed in by the two vehicles and left trapped. The bastards would pay.

"Promise . . . don't watch . . . me—"

His eyes were closed as he finished, "Die."

No. "Simon?" The chill was back, raising the hairs on her arms and numbing her flesh. "Simon?" She squeezed his hand and realized what he'd done.

His life, for her. Bastard.

Dee dropped his hand and shoved against the metal. Shoved and pushed and jerked and twisted and—

Tears trekked down her cheeks as the sunlight poured onto her. "You're not leaving me!" A scream.

Not like her father.

Her sister.

Her mother.

No one else would die for her. No one.

Dee screamed her fury into the light and kicked up with her knees. Bones snapped, flesh tore, but she fought through the pain and tried to tear her way out of the hell that held them in its hungry grasp.

When he saw the SUV, saw the metal tossed away on the side of the road, Zane's heart seemed to stop.

"*Holy fuck.*" From Jude. The shifter had found him at the motel and helped him to kick the shit out of those vampires.

You won't find her. The bitch'll be dead before you even get close. Last words from one of the vamps.

Zane slammed on the brakes.

"She could still be alive!" The fierce whisper came from Erin Jerome, Jude's lover. Of course, the woman had been at Jude's side when he'd stormed up to the motel. Not like she was ever going to miss a good fight.

Zane jumped from the car, ran as fast as he could, and heard the thunder of Jude and Erin's footsteps behind them. *Be alive.* She had to be. Dee couldn't—

"Fuck! Fuck! Fuck!" Her scream. *Dee.*

His heart started beating again. He hurried around the side of the beaten metal pile, ready to rip and fight his way to her.

The passenger door flew at him.

Zane hit the ground. *What the hell?*

"*Simon!* You open those eyes, you understand me? Open them!" Then he saw Dee, crawling out of the car and dragging her vampire with her. Blood covered her, him, and the woman was snarling and swearing as she jerked out her man.

She stumbled, slipping, and Simon's weight hit her, knocking her flat.

Zane shoved up to his knees. "Dee!" He should have known the woman wasn't dead. The ambush the vamps had set on her—yeah, he'd gotten the full details on that one, courtesy of some threats and the skillful use of Jude's claws—hadn't succeeded. She was still alive, still fighting and—

She rolled her vampire until he lay on the ground. Her hand smoothed over his cheek. "Simon?"

And Zane realized she didn't know he was there.

Didn't know any of them were there.

"We're out," she whispered and her fingers left a bloody trail on Simon's cheek. "Everything's okay now, *we're out.*"

"Oh, sweet hell." Erin tried to shove past him, but Jude caught her arms and held tight.

"No," he told her softly, "not when she's like this. The bloodlust—"

Dee's head snapped toward them. Zane expected to see the black stare of a vampire driven to desperation, instead, he saw Dee's warm brown eyes, swimming with tears. "Help him." A demand, a plea. *"Help him."*

Zane reached a hand out to her.

She grabbed him. Damn, but the woman was *fast,* even with the sun out.

And strong.

Stronger than she should have been.

Her fingers clamped around his wrist. "He needs blood."

Clenching his jaw, Zane gave a nod. Not what he'd ever do for anyone but her.

Dee used her claws to cut a thin line on his wrist. He held his hand over Simon's mouth.

"You need blood, too," Erin said, her voice steady and strong. Zane's stare jumped to her and he saw that she had her wrist up. "Take what you need."

Shifters didn't normally offer up their blood to vamps, but Zane knew there was a friendship between the two women. More than that.

Dee had risked death for Erin on one of the Night Watch cases. When you went to the line for someone like that, a bond formed.

Dee hesitated, but her fangs were already out.

Too much blood loss for both of them.

Chase's fangs weren't out yet, a bad sign. With the blood at his mouth, he should have responded by now.

"You saved my life," Erin reminded her. "It's my turn."

Dee took Erin's wrist. Bit.

Another link. Zane's attention moved to Jude. He already had his wrist up. The first time that the shifter had ever offered blood to a vamp.

But Dee wasn't just any vamp. She was one of their own.

After this day, they'd be tied to one another, through Dee, forever.

His breath hissed out as a hot pain sliced his wrist. A quick glance showed that Simon's fangs were out now.

He just had to make sure the guy didn't take too much. After all, they had one hell of a fight waiting on them all.

A real bloodbath.

Simon awoke to darkness. Quiet, total darkness. No pain wracked his body. No cold chilled his soul.

Alive.

Or as alive as he could be.

"You scared the hell out of me." Dee's voice. Soft, shaking, and coming from right next to him.

His nostrils flared and he inhaled her scent. Rich, sensual. His Dee.

When he concentrated, he heard the drum of her heart. Strong and steady.

He rolled and realized he was in a bed. *In a bed with Dee. Don't need anything else.* Simon reached for her and touched warm flesh.

Her lips crushed down on his. A hard, angry kiss. Fury and passion. "Don't ever do that to me again," she ordered and kissed him again. Harder.

His mouth opened beneath hers and her tongue swiped inside. *Yes.* His arms rose and locked around her body.

Her nipples stabbed into his chest. Naked. He felt every inch of her sweet flesh against him. Every single inch.

She shifted against him, straddling his thighs, and she rose above him. "You nearly died."

His eyes had adjusted perfectly to the darkness so that he could see that fierce tilt of her jaw. "You were going to live." The choice had been easy for him.

"Bastard." Her nails raked down his chest. He didn't know how they'd both gotten naked, but he sure wasn't going to complain about it right then. "What the hell gives you the right to make that kind of choice?" she demanded.

He caught her hand. Brought it to his mouth and pressed a kiss to her palm. *Because I love you.*

Monsters could love. Vampires who stalked the night could feel.

They weren't soul-less devils. They yearned. They wanted. They loved.

The woman had worked her way right under his skin and into his soul. He hadn't even seen the threat coming until it was too late.

But then her heart had trembled and he'd known she was slipping away—*my life for hers, in an instant.*

Love.

Hell, he knew he'd really fallen for her long before. When he'd first started to watch her. To see how bravely she fought. How fiercely she protected the ones she thought were Innocents.

He blew lightly against her fingers and saw the shiver that worked the length of her body. "I wasn't going to let you die, not when I could save you." And she would have died. One look at her injuries and he'd known they were much, much worse than his.

"You do that again . . ." She lifted onto her knees and glared at him, but had to swallow before she could mumble, "I-I'll kill you."

Sweet. He almost smiled. Almost. "Why don't you fuck me instead?" His cock was up, so stiff it hurt, and the memory of her cold flesh seared his mind.

Warmth.

Life.

Sex.

He wanted it, *her*—and he wanted to claim her right then. Where they were, what the hell had happened to them, how they'd both survived—those details could come later.

Now, he just needed her.

Her fingers wrapped around his cock. Her grip, warm and strong, tightened around him. Simon's breath hissed out as she guided him to her sex.

Wet—warmer. Hot.

Flesh to flesh. Sex to sex.

His cock pushed past the quivering lips that guarded her core. He felt the brief resistance of her inner muscles, the strain to accommodate his length. With a flex of his hips, he drove deep in a long, steady glide.

Her eyes held his. The brown bled away until only darkness remained.

A darkness to match his own.

She rose above him, slowly at first, letting him feel the wet retreat of her sex, the soft silk of her body. His fingers clenched around her hips and he pushed her back, arching up with a hard thrust.

Still her eyes stayed on his.

He could see the edge of her fangs, but she made no move to drink from him.

Her sex squeezed him, and she rose again. A long-torture-him move. Sweat beaded his brow as he watched her. The heat and fury of their previous lovemaking was gone. This was different.

He pushed up and his mouth closed over her nipple. He sucked her, licked, laving with his tongue. Such tender flesh.

Her fingers sank into his hair and she held him close as she rose again, then sank back down, taking his cock balls-deep in her slick heat.

The need to thrust, to shove deep and take control, pounded through him, but he yanked the lust back on its leash.

She needed this. So did he.

Softness, restraint. Control.

For once.

Because death had been too close.

Her fingers tugged at his hair and his mouth freed her breast. He looked up at her.

"Kiss me," she whispered.

Like he had to be asked.

Her head lowered and her mouth took his. No fury this time. Only need.

Only need.

Her hips rocked against him, the slow motions driving him out of his mind.

Not yet. Can't come yet.

Her tongue licked across his lips. "You scared me."

Rise. Fall.

The hot fist of her sex milking his cock.

His thighs clenched beneath her and his spine stiffened.

"I thought . . ." She drove down on him, a bit harder now, a little more desperate. "Th-that you'd die on me."

That had been the plan.

Her fingers slipped down his neck. Caught his shoulder and her nails dug into the skin. *"Why?"*

She'd stilled on him. Her sex was so tight and hot and she'd stilled.

His breath heaved out. All he could smell was her. All he could taste was her. Feel—*her.* "Don't you know?" he gritted, his cock ready to burst. One more glide, just one.

Her nails dug deeper and her slender hips didn't move. "Tell me."

He looked up at her. Nowhere to hide. "Because I *would* fucking die for you. I nearly did."

The bloodlust, no the lust for *her,* only her, broke free. He grabbed her hips and shoved up, deep and hard, and she came around him, choking out a cry as her eyes widened and the ripples of her release contracted around his cock.

He climaxed on a long, hot wave of pleasure and he held her, as tight as he could, and knew that no way, no fucking way, was he gonna let Sandra Dee go.

He'd die for her, and, hell, yeah, he'd kill for her. In a heartbeat.

Because the truth was the woman held his heart in her hand. In the same hand that she usually held her beloved stakes.

When her heartbeat slowed down and the tremors finally left her body, Dee sucked in a deep breath. *Probably shouldn't have jumped him right away.*

But she'd needed him. *Too close to death.*

Her nails raked down his chest. Paused over the heart that

raced beneath her touch. He watched her, with eyes gone smoky again.

"We were out for two days," she told him, aware that her voice was too husky. A good orgasm did that to her, though, and with Simon, the orgasms were always good.

Her sex clenched with a little aftershock of pleasure and she saw his pupils flare.

Move. Before she took him again. No, before he took her. His cock was swelling again, growing and stretching and pressing just where she needed him to—

Dee pushed up on her knees and carefully separated their bodies. They'd have company soon, and as much as she'd like another ride, the pleasure would have to wait.

Dealing with the psychotic undead came first.

Simon's gaze dropped to her sex and he licked his lips.

Dee swallowed and rolled away from him. "We're at a motel, about three hours away from Hueco." They'd retreated. Well, not them so much as Zane and Jude had retreated for them. Because when the hunters had first found her and Simon, she hadn't exactly been in a frame of mind to help out and plan much.

But Jude and Zane had been right. Retreat was the only option. They'd been too weak for anything else.

"Why do I feel so good?"

She glanced over her shoulder and saw him staring down at his unmarred chest. No wounds. The horrible gashes were gone now. Grabbing her shirt, she told him quietly, "Shifter blood." Plus a helping of demon blood.

But it was the shifter blood given freely by Erin and Jude that had really healed them. There was power in a shifter's blood. Shifters were beings that some believed carried two spirits and with two spirits, the strength influx was double.

Without that shifter blood, they'd both still be unconscious, their bodies struggling to heal from their wounds.

"It was a fucking ambush, wasn't it?"

Dee found a pair of panties and shimmied into them before yanking up her—

"I love your ass."

She glanced back at him. Yep, his gaze was on her butt. She hiked up the jeans.

His gaze rose to her face. "Your Night Watch hunters got us out?"

"Yes."

"I figured the demon would be coming. I knew he'd get you out of that metal hell. Just had to make sure you survived long enough."

The rage stirred then, and she'd tried so hard to keep the fury in check. "It didn't matter how long you survived, huh?"

He blinked.

"You left me in that trap, alone, and I could hear you dying—" Her voice broke at the end. Weak. Hell.

A muscle flexed in his jaw. "And before I forced you to drink, I *saw* you dying. My choice, Dee. Mine. You can bet that I'll do anything to save you. *Anything.*"

The emotion was there, swimming in his eyes.

She wanted him again. Wanted his arms around her and his flesh against hers. Clearing her throat, she managed to say, "When this is over . . ."

"I'll fucking love you forever." Bald. Flat. No hesitancy. Just stating a fact.

Her lips parted.

"Remember that, okay? When the shit comes down on us again, or when you learn that my past isn't nearly as pretty as it should be, just remember. You come first for me, and you always will." A hard shake of his head. "It just took me a while to realize it. What can I say? Sometimes, my priorities are shit."

I'll fucking love you forever.

No one had ever said that to her before. No one and she—

She didn't know how she felt. There was no ready response on her tongue. She could only stare at him and realize that the curve of his lips looked sad.

Because he understood. He knew her better than any of the others ever had.

A rap sounded at their door. "Playtime's over," Zane called out.

But Simon's stare didn't waver.

She should say something. Anything. Her hands shook as she pressed the snap of her jeans. Her sex—inside, she could still feel him. "The plan . . ." she cleared her throat and tried again. "The plan's to attack tonight. We go in under the darkness and we hit them fast and hard. They—they won't expect us." Thanks to Erin and some magic strings she'd pulled, the story of their "death" had made the local headlines. "If luck's on our side, they won't even know we're attacking until it's too late."

"Grim will know." Certain.

Her jaw locked. "And he'll die." Because this madness was ending. Revenge—hell, why did it seem so empty now? Why, when she looked at Simon, did she just want to run to him and—

To run *away* with him.

No. Grim wouldn't stop if they fled. If he found out they were alive, he wouldn't stop until they were dust.

She couldn't walk away with a monster like him out there. Because there would be other families. Like hers. Like Nina's.

Nina.

Was she still alive? Where was she? Dee had thought of her when the pain eased and the bloodlust lessened. Zane had gone out scouting, but he'd found no sign of the woman.

Maybe she hadn't gone after Grim. Maybe she'd just run.

Couldn't blame her. Not a bit.

A harder knock shook the door. "If we're taking Grim out, we need to move."

Yet Simon stood, as still as a statue before her.

Because he was waiting on her to say something.

I'll fucking love you forever.

But she didn't know what to say. Her throat was tight. Her heart nearly ripping through her chest.

And she was afraid.

When she loved, people got hurt.

So Dee swallowed back the words that wanted to rise up and she held his stare, so scared of what he made her feel.

Simon finally turned away, and grabbed the clothes she'd lain out for him.

Her shoulders fell. Emotion. She'd never been good with feelings. Never understood them, not the good ones, anyway.

Rage. Hate. Vengeance. Her life. Those she understood.

Love? That scared her. Love led to pain. She'd had enough pain.

But when Simon had said he loved her . . .

Her heart had stopped. Her breath had died.

Dee didn't know what she felt for him. She wanted him, needed him, and if anyone tried to hurt him, she'd kick some ass.

Love—what was it, really?

Spending forever with someone? She glanced at Simon. All she could see was his strong, stiff back.

Her hands still trembled so she balled them into fists. Not now. This wasn't the time.

But things weren't going to end like this.

Forever? Dee exhaled. Marriage and a picket fence had never been for her, she knew that, even before her change. Her life was too hard. She was too hard for someone to love.

No, Simon said he loves me.

She turned away and gave him a few minutes to dress. And she gave herself some time to get herself together. Seriously, she had to get a grip.

When he was done, she schooled her features, and they marched to the door. With a jerk of her wrist, she opened the door. Zane waited for her, his hands crossed over his chest. The paleness that had drawn his features before—because of the blood he'd lost—was gone.

His hooded gaze raked her. "You sure you're up for this?"

Of course not. But there were only two options: Kill or die. Dee cleared her throat, then asked, "Are you?" She'd tried to ditch him once, and, in typical Zane style, he'd come through to save her butt.

She didn't want to risk him, but knew there was no way he'd let her get in another sucker punch.

"I'm your backup, baby."

A snarl sounded behind her and one black brow rose. "Guess lover boy's awake, huh?" Zane asked.

The floor creaked. "Yeah, he is." Simon came to her side. She glanced back and forth between the two men. Simon's jaw worked and then he managed, "Thank you."

A crooked smile twisted Zane's lips. "Hard, wasn't it?"

"Fuck yeah."

"You sound just like Dee." The smile vanished. "Giving you my blood was harder."

A grim nod. "I won't forget."

"I won't let you." A pause. "And believe me, I call in my debts."

Yes, he did.

Zane's gaze turned back to Dee. "What are our odds?"

She forced a shrug. "I figure about forty-sixty."

A low whistle. "That sucks."

Dead right. Dee squared her shoulders. "Let's do this." Before more vamps came hunting for her. She didn't want to be caught off-guard again. Three recent, brutal attacks. When Grim wanted you dead, the guy just didn't stop. Now that she was Born, he was desperate to stop that "prophecy" from coming true.

Grim didn't fuck around.

He was about to learn that neither did she.

Chapter 15

He'd pay his debt to the demon, one way or another. Simon stalked across the barren earth, keeping his head low as he followed the male shifter to Grim's lair.

Jude Donovan moved easily over the rough terrain, never taking a misstep, and his woman, the deceptively delicate ADA Erin Jerome, kept perfect pace with him. Another shifter. The guy's mate.

Simon didn't know much about her, other than that she worked in the Baton Rouge prosecutor's office and that the tiger was very, very possessive of her.

She hadn't given him blood, something else he knew. Probably because the tiger wouldn't allow her to link with a male vampire.

"This is it," Jude's nearly soundless voice had the group pausing.

Simon glanced over at Dee. Heavily armed, eyes shining in the darkness, she was one fine sight to behold.

"You sure about this?" Erin asked, casting a quick glance at the ramshackle buildings that waited in the distance. They couldn't get much closer or the vamps would catch the distinct scent of the shifters. They'd have to hang back for now, with the demon. "Just walking right up to him, um, that doesn't seem like the best plan."

"No, it's not the best plan. But it's all we've got now."

Dee's eyes narrowed on the line of buildings. "How many, Jude?"

His head cocked. "Ten vamps. Two humans, but—" His nose twitched. "Somebody's dying in there."

Simon stiffened. Of course, Grim would be having one of his parties.

"Nina?" Dee whispered.

"Who?" Erin asked.

"The Ignitor I told you about," Zane said, his voice emotionless.

Erin shook her head. "Ignitors make me nervous. Anyone who can burn the flesh from me with just a look . . ." She shuddered.

Simon tossed her a long, level stare. "Trust me, the vamps in there are a hell of lot scarier than she is." They could be killing her while they stood outside, shooting the damn shit. He stepped forward and heard Erin's mocking laugh.

Her claws flashed before his eyes. Wickedly sharp and very, very long. "The day I'm afraid of a vamp is the day, well, hell, it's the day that'll never come."

He could only shake his head. "It'll come, trust me."

"No." She jerked her thumb toward a watchful Dee. "It's her I trust."

His eyes narrowed. Did he have to worry about an attack from her, too?

"Who's hurt, Jude?" Dee demanded, seeming to ignore the byplay.

Jude's lips thinned. "Human. That's all I know. So much blood in the air." He shook his head. "It's hard to say for certain."

Dee inhaled deeply. "Yeah, I can smell it."

So could Simon. A scent that had once repelled him but now slipped inside and tempted him closer. "Let's go join the party," Simon muttered. Before the party joined them. Every second they stood out there, they risked exposure.

If they were slipping in, now was the time.

Dee gave a curt nod. "Stay back," she told the others. "If this goes to hell—"

"Then we'll be there to pull you out," Zane finished quietly.

Her eyes shifted, became black to match the darkness. "No, if I die, you get out of here, fast, because, Zane, you might be a badass, but no way can a demon take down a Born. Especially not one who's been around for so long."

At least a thousand years. Plenty of time to amass power. A whole freaking army.

One that he hadn't called to his side. Why not?

"You guys should go now," Dee said, voice rising a bit. Her hands balled to rest on her hips. "I can feel—there's really not much time left."

What? Not much time, she—

Jude's head jerked. "Shit. They're coming."

A faint, sad smile from Dee. "Not they. *He.*" Her gaze tracked to Simon. "I really thought he'd find us sooner."

Simon blinked. Grim? The bastard knew—

Jude swore and grabbed his mate's hand.

"Go," Dee said again. "Come dawn, this will be over."

One way or another.

The shifters vanished into the shadows. They had to move fast or the vampires would find them. Then they'd drain all that powerful blood.

Zane held his ground.

"I need you as backup," she told him, but didn't look the demon's way. No, her eyes were on the shadows that crept ever closer. So close now. *"Zane, go."*

The demon left. Disappeared into the darkness.

Grim is coming.

Simon gave his head a hard shake. "How does he know—"

Her broken laugh carried on the wind. "Oh, Simon, did you really think he wouldn't be able to feel you? This close?"

He tested the spell. No, it was still there, still—

"He knows, Simon, and he's coming." Calm. He realized he was part of her plan. The lure to draw out Grim.

She stepped toward him and reached for his hand. "This is what we've been waiting for. We'll end this tonight."

They had the weapons. She had the promised strength. And he *wouldn't* turn on her.

A streak of fire lit up the night. "What the hell?"

"Nina!" Dee spun away. "No! She's here and she's going after Grim!"

His vampiress ran toward the flames.

And he went after her. Walking into the fire. No, running into it.

As his legs thundered across that barren Texas soil, he felt a brush in his mind, then the soft echo of a voice.

"Welcome home, bastard."

Fuck.

Zane's head jerked up when he saw the flash of flames. Oh, shit. Not good.

The human—Nina—she'd get her ass killed.

Maybe that's what she wanted. To die so she could join her family.

He'd wondered about Dee once. Wondered if she didn't take the toughest cases because she wanted out, too.

Humans didn't understand. Getting out was the easy part.

He slid a stake out of his bag. One of Dee's, of course. A tiger's roar echoed in the distance and he knew that Jude and Erin were scouting the area, eliminating guards and doing their best to make sure the coming bloodbath didn't take out the good guys.

Not that any of them were really that good.

He watched the flames a moment. They were racing across the roof of the building on the far left. The building that looked like some old stable.

The fury of an Ignitor. Something to see.

His fingers clenched around the stake.

A scream pierced the air. A long, tortured scream—a cry that was ripped from a woman's throat.

The flames flickered. Began to die.

Because Nina was dying?

No. Not another death on her hands. Dee raced forward with a fierce burst of speed. Two vamps came out at her, but she knocked them back, swiping her claws over one's throat and burying a stake in another's flesh. She missed his heart, but he hit the ground, shrieking loud enough to make a girl think he was dying.

So much for a quiet entry.

But being quiet didn't really matter now. Grim knew they were out there.

She turned, following the woman's scream and the thickening scent of blood. A house, ranch-style, waited. Dee didn't bother with the door. She hurtled through the big picture window, Simon's curse following her.

Rolling, she jumped to her feet, claws up, ready for anything, ready for—

Death. A woman, with long, dark hair twisted over her face, lay on the bed. The white sheets beneath her were stained red.

More glass shattered behind her as Simon fought his way into the room.

Her gaze searched over the area. The odors of sex and blood were everywhere. But that woman wasn't Nina.

The hair on her nape rose and Dee spun around.

He stood in the doorway. The bastard who had haunted her nightmares. Tall and lean, his hair streaked with gold and his eyes pitch black. "Been a long time, little Sandra Dee." Grim paused. "I knew the fools hadn't managed to take you out." His dark stare swept over her body, slowly. Not sexually. No interest there. Just an assessment. Thorough. He shrugged. "I thought you'd be easier to kill."

"Yeah, you're not the first person to make that mistake." She'd never forgotten his face and his soul-less eyes.

Beside her, Simon stood as still as freaking stone. *The bastard was trying to get back in his head.* She didn't have to be a mind-reader to know that was coming.

Even though she *was* a mind reader now.

Deliberately, Dee stepped in front of Simon. Her turn.

Grim's lips quirked, but he made no move to attack. "You're too late to save her."

Dee's gaze darted to the bed.

A cold laugh. "Not her. She doesn't matter." He smirked. "The witch."

Her blood iced. No, no, he was just screwing with her. Catalina was long gone. She'd run so she wouldn't face the fire.

"She had her uses, I'll give you that." He lifted his hand, then pointed right over Dee's shoulder. Straight at Simon. "After all, with just a little fire, she gave me . . . you."

Her gut knotted. Why had the fire been in that old stable? If Nina were attacking, why hadn't she set her fire here in the main house?

"Can you feel me, asshole?" Grim snarled at Simon, and the smile left his face. "Because I can damn well feel you."

Dee glanced back. Sweat coated Simon's face and his eyes flickered back and forth, back and forth, from black to gray. Torment etched deep lines onto his face. "Get . . . out," he growled.

He'll turn on you.

Screw this.

"Witches can burn so fast," Grim murmured, "but your witch, I made sure she—"

Dee leapt forward.

"Do you want me to kill them all?" Grim shook his head and lunged to meet her. One hand ripped the stake from her fingers and her wrist cracked beneath his hold. His right hand grabbed her neck, held tight, and he lifted her off the ground. "*Do you?* Because I can kill every one of those bastards you brought to *my* land. Your demon, your stinking animals—"

Zane. Jude. Hell, *Erin.*

"The witch let me back in." He brought his face close to

hers. "She didn't want to touch the dark magic, not at first, but when the fire started, she was all too eager."

Dee couldn't breathe. If he snapped her neck, she'd be helpless. Paralyzed, but still living, until her body could heal. He wouldn't give her the time to heal. He'd stake her. Behead her. Burn her—

Like he'd burned Catalina?

Why wasn't Simon helping her? *Attack. Get the bastard!* Her mental cry blasted out, and she tried to reach him desperately on their blood link.

And she slammed into a brick wall. A wall that hadn't been between their minds before.

Grim.

He yanked her close to his face. "I had him first, and I have him again." He threw her against the wall. Dee hit, hard, and her body shuddered at the impact.

She glanced up to see Grim studying Simon with raised brows. "You're the one who caused all this trouble for me."

A fine tremble worked down Simon's stiff length.

Grim shook his head. "Usually, the willing are the easiest to control. And you were willing, weren't you, Chase? So ready to live forever."

His choice. Dee shoved up to her knees. *Simon?*

Damn brick wall. She couldn't see it, but she knew it was there and she wanted to smash her fist right through it.

Simon's eyes jerked toward her. A flash of smoky gray. He lifted his leg, as if he were going to take a step.

"A puppet on a string."

He froze.

Grim laughed again. "Too damn easy." He turned his head toward her. "I can make him do anything, you know. *Anything.*"

Dee's fingers brushed against her ankle holster. Not packing a gun. Old faithful.

"I wonder . . ." His gaze rose to the broken window. "Do you think she's still alive? The flames should have taken the stable by now."

But the flames had flickered. She'd seen them waver right before she'd heard the scream. The scream had brought her here, instead of to the fire.

"You're a fucking liar." Dee rose to her feet, keeping her hands close to her sides. "Catalina is nowhere near here."

"My men caught her right after she left the motel." He shrugged. "I knew where you were, every minute. *I knew.*"

And he'd gotten his vamps to follow and attack her and Simon. Then to attack Zane. Yeah, he'd told her all about his run-in with the vamp crew.

Had Grim gotten to Catalina, too? Her heart kicked up in her chest. *If I go with you, I'll burn.*

Maybe Cat had been seeing her future after all.

Dee's gaze jerked to the flames she could see in the distance. Was Cat still alive?

The flames danced.

Sweat began to slick her palms. Couldn't afford that, not now. "Simon." She said his name deliberately, injecting fury into the word.

His head jerked.

Grim's brows pulled together. "You know, I was going to kill you . . . but it'll be more fun if he does the deed for me."

Her eyes narrowed to slits. "I'm all about fun." *Time's running out. The fire.*

Grim's attention shifted totally to Simon. "Kill the bitch."

Simon's lips peeled back, revealing his fangs. "Fuck . . . off." He shuddered, shaking so hard it looked like he was convulsing.

Or fighting one very strong compulsion.

Fighting for me.

Just like she'd fight for him.

When Grim's jaw dropped, Dee attacked. She jumped at him, ready for his attack this time, and when he went to grab her, she drove her right hand into his side. Her claws dug deep, and the broken bones throbbed in a sickening wave. She rammed her head into him and her left hand came up, the stake ready.

She drove it right at his heart. It plunged into his flesh, but he twisted and she knew she'd missed her mark. Dee wrenched the stake, jerking it to the left, and Grim snarled.

Then she took him down. Her right leg hooked under his and she tripped him, knocking him flat like Pak had taught her so long ago.

She kept that stake in him, because she *would* finish him, one way or another.

Hold on, Catalina.

"No!"

Dee's gaze jerked up just as Nina came barreling through the door. Blood covered her shirt, reddened her hands and face.

"No! You can't! He's *mine!*" Nina yelled.

It was a fury Dee understood, but, really, dead was dead. It didn't matter to her who made the kill. They'd all have their vengeance.

Fire raced across the carpet, coming straight at Dee. "*Mine!*" Nina screamed again.

Dee sprang back, slipped, and fell to the floor. If the Ignitor wanted her justice, fine, then she could have it.

Nina's hands dug into the door frame and her breath shuddered out. "Had to . . . leave . . . witch alive . . . couldn't let . . ."

What?

The fire drifted into smoke.

Grim sat up. His fingers curled around the stake, and he yanked it out. Blood spattered onto the floor, the wall. "Nice try." His teeth snapped together. "Last try."

Nina sobbed behind him.

And color her fucking stupid. Dee's jaw dropped. What had he told her just moments before? "*I knew where you were, every minute. I knew.*" Not because he'd linked with Simon. No, that link hadn't kicked in until—*until he'd broken Catalina.*

That meant—hell. Her eyes lifted to meet Nina's glittering and teary stare.

So blind.

"It's past time for you to die," the Ignitor said, not to Grim, but to Dee. Nina's skin was so pale. The blood looked like bright red clown makeup on her flesh.

"He killed your family!" Dee snarled.

The Ignitor smiled. "That was the price."

Dee didn't dare look Simon's way. If she could keep their focus, he might be able to break free of Grim. Maybe. "The price of what?"

"My services." She waved her hand and fire snaked out to circle Dee.

Shit.

"For my fire, he had to kill my family."

Dee surged to her feet. "Why didn't you just do it yourself?"

"Because they knew what I was." Spoken with sadness.

Dee stared into her eyes and *knew,* too. It wasn't that Nina was an Ignitor.

She was a monster. Down to the soul.

"They wouldn't let me get close enough to kill them. They left me—I was sixteen and they left me." Nina's lips flattened. "It took me so long to track them."

And longer to find a vamp willing to take them out.

Grim's hard laugh filled the room. "Tore didn't know. For once, the bastard didn't know the game."

Dee swallowed back the sick rage that boiled in her throat. "You're one fine actress, Nina." She'd known just how to act. Just what to do. From the corner of her eye, Dee saw that Grim had risen to his feet. He had her stake gripped in his hand. The only thing that separated the two of them was Nina's small line of flames.

"Thanks. I owe you for that bit," Nina said.

Dee's breath caught. What?

"I saw you. That night, when your family burned . . ."

They'd been dead long before the fire.

"I was there, watching." A cold smile. "And making those flames dance. Grim wanted a sample of my power, and I gave it to him."

But she would have been—

Around sixteen. Close to Dee's own age.

Guess it hadn't taken her that long to find her vamp. He'd just taken his sweet time killing for her.

The better to control his weapon.

"I had a sister, too," Nina murmured. "I wonder—Grim, did she beg like hers?"

Dee snapped. She raced right through the fire, barely feeling the lick of the flames as she went after that burning bitch.

She punched Nina. A hard hit right in the jaw and down, down she went, those eyes closing, the flames dying and—

"Kill her. Fucking *kill* her," Grim ordered.

Arms grabbed her, held tight. Her claws raked against flesh that was warm and strong and familiar.

Her heart stopped as his scent filled her nostrils. Simon.

"S-sorry . . ." His gasped whisper, right in her ear.

Then his fangs sank into her throat.

The flames drew him closer. Zane moved easily, keeping low to the ground and staying in the shadows. He'd expected to see more vamps around the place. He'd taken out two, had found the signs to indicate Dee and Simon had eliminated at least two others.

The fire flared higher and he caught the faintest of sounds beneath the crackle. A whimper.

His blood seemed to ice. He rushed through the open stable doors, heading through the thick curtain of smoke.

A broken, twisted doll lay on the ground. She'd curled into a ball and the flames were closing in on her. He'd know that long mane of white-blond hair any place. Hell, no.

He ripped off his shirt and began beating at the fire. Trying to shove it back as best he could.

Too big. Too strong.

Zane sucked in a sharp breath and tried to focus his energy. He was strong enough for this. He had to be.

The whisper of wind blew across his face. Wind he'd stirred. With a push, he sent the wind against the fire and the flames shifted, chasing to the left with the force of the wind.

There, just enough. He jumped through the flames. Zane grabbed Catalina and threw her over his shoulder. She was so stiff, so still.

He covered his mouth with her shirt and ran back through the fire. *Can't keep it down. Can't stop it.*

The smoke, a thick wall of gray, blocked his vision but he shoved forward. If he couldn't find the doors, he'd just tear down a wall. He'd—

"Going somewhere?" A vamp loomed from the smoke, teeth bared, claws out.

No time for this shit.

He hadn't heard Catalina draw a breath. Hadn't heard a sound from her since that faint whimper.

Keeping one arm secured around Catalina, he grabbed the vamp and heaved him back into the fire.

Then he took out a wall and got his witch to safety.

It's all right, Cat. I won't let the flames get you.

Her worst fear. One that had come true too many times for her.

And for him.

The fresh air slapped him in the face and a shout broke from the line of houses. More vampires, coming fast.

He ran for the woods and really hoped Jude would appear to cover his ass.

In the distance, a tiger roared.

About fucking time. Jude had better have his sexy little lady by his side, because they were going to need her to take out these bloodsuckers.

Chapter 16

Dee's body trembled against his and Simon tightened his hold around her slender form.

Her blood flowed onto his tongue and with it, their link strengthened. The voice that had been shouting in his mind since he'd followed Dee inside this hell finally quieted, and his focus shifted back to—

Her.

Kill Dee?

No fucking way.

His eyes closed for just a moment and his teeth eased from her neck. His tongue swept over her flesh. The sensual caress was the only reassurance he could offer her then.

"I said to kill the bitch!" Grim's fierce shout.

Simon's head lifted and he stared at the Born he'd fought to keep out of his head for so long. The man who'd ordered the hit on his family. On Dee's.

The Ignitor lay on the floor. Still unconscious because his Dee didn't screw around.

Neither did he.

Dee laughed. "The man might die for me, nearly has, but no way would he ever kill me."

Damn but he loved her.

He met Grim's dark gaze. The bastard's hold had all but vanished now. Whether from Dee's touch, her blood, or just her, he didn't know.

But the end had come. Not for them, but for Grim. "Your brother sends his greetings, Grim. I think he really hopes you enjoy hell."

The Born's face changed then, went slack with surprise and a flash of pain. Grim's gaze leapt to the bed. To the still form of the woman. "I'm not . . ." He shook his head. "Tore can't kill me, he's not here, I'd know—"

"He's not killing you." Dee's body vibrated in his grasp. "We are."

Grim's stare snapped to them and his lips rose. "Still on that, are we?"

"Yeah, we are." So fierce, his Dee.

"A fresh vamp and a fool who couldn't appreciate the new life he'd been given?"

Enough talk. Time to end—

"Your knight, is he?" Grim sneered at that. "Don't you know, dear Dee, he's been luring you in—*for me*—from the beginning?"

Simon's hands dug into her shoulders.

"That attack in the alley. The near hit with the gunshot. Your lover arranged that. He almost got you killed."

Dee glanced up at him.

"And that woman, the one who died so well for my men. Grace, wasn't it, Simon?"

Grace. Dee's friend. The one he'd used to manipulate her.

"She gave you all that wonderfully wrong Intel on Simon, didn't she? I wonder . . . how could she have made a mistake like that?"

Fuck. Fuck. Fuck. He should have explained all of this to her before. Should have made her understand—

"I know." Soft. "I know everything he did," she said.

His jaw dropped. She knew and she was letting him touch her? Not screaming? Not staking him?

"And I know he wasn't doing it for you, asshole." Her dark stare turned back to Grim. "He was working to kill you, not to set me up."

She knew? How—

"I knew from the first bite. I'm Born, remember? *I knew.*"

Well, shit.

Hate twisted Grim's face. "You should have run while you had the chance."

A ripple of her shoulders. "Not really the running type. More the kick-your-ass type."

Flames raced across the floor.

Grim's laughter filled his ears. And Nina—dammit, she jumped up.

"Burn, bitch!" Her scream of fury, directed right at Dee.

Grim slipped through the doorway, his laughter following him.

The flames rose too high, too fast. Nina's eyes flashed red, the vessels near bursting as she pumped all her power right at them.

Dee stumbled back against him. "Run!"

They charged toward the window. The fire chased after them.

"Burn, burn, burn." A chant from Nina. Fucking insane. The flames caught Simon's back and legs, biting at the flesh, and he clenched his teeth at the agony. He fell, the fire rising around him as—

"No! Not without you!" Dee grabbed his arms and yanked him out the window with her. The broken glass cut his stomach and chest and then Dee was hitting him, pounding on his body. No—striking at the flames and putting out the fire.

Burning her flesh, to save him.

A shriek echoed from the house. The flames came at them again.

"Grim has himself one hell of a guard dog," Dee growled, breath heaving out.

Simon's gaze scanned the yard. Three vamps came out, claws and teeth ready, but they didn't attack. They just watched.

Ready to watch us die.

"This is the way it ends for you." Grim's taunting voice. He walked from the shadows of the house. Blood dripped down his chest. "For both of you."

Simon caught Dee's hand, held tight. Surrounded by fire and vampires.

He looked at Dee. Shoulders back, chin up. Eyes blazing black. Not afraid. Not his Dee. Never afraid.

No, not her and she was—

Smiling?

"I know what happens next," Dee said, and her soft voice carried easily over the crackle of flames.

"Me, too," Grim snapped. "You burn. And you scream. Then you die. Right in your lover's arms."

"You believe in prophets, don't you, Grim?" The flames were so close that the heat seemed to graze his flesh, but Nina was holding back now, watching Dee. Why?

Because Grim had his hand up, and like the good lapdog that she was, Nina wouldn't strike without his order.

"After all, you set all this into motion." Dee's right hand— which looked broken—lifted to indicate the flames and vampires. "Because a demon had a vision and told you that I would be your killer."

Grim's lips thinned.

"You killed my family," she continued. "Everyone I ever loved because you *thought* a fifteen-year-old human girl would one day kill an all-powerful Born."

"The demon was right! You would have come for me!"

"I came now for vengeance. Because of you. *You* are the one who set this in motion. *You.*"

He shook his head. "No, no, I wasn't dying again. Those bastards, they betrayed me before. I wasn't going to die like that again!"

His eyes darted to the vampires who stood so still and silent. "My men won't turn this time. They'll stand by me."

"This isn't about them." Simon had no idea where she was going with this, but he caught movement from the corner of his eye. Slow, careful movement. His nostrils flared, just a bit, but he couldn't smell anything but the smoke and blood.

"I won't stand by you," Simon called out. "I won't be your fucking puppet anymore."

A muscle jerked in Grim's jaw.

Simon turned his stare on the line of vamps. "Sure you're on the right team?"

One of the vamps cut his eyes toward Grim. Hesitation there. And anger in the man's eyes.

He hates that control, just as much as I did. "What did he make you do?" Simon demanded, aware of that shadow slipping ever closer. "Kill your lovers? Your family? How did you prove your loyalty to him?"

Because that was Grim's way. Loyalty could only be shown in blood.

"And if you didn't kill them, he did, right?" Like the bastard had taken out his family. "None of us signed on for this shit, but we can get out. He just has to die!"

Grim took a step back. His hand rose again to trace the side of his back. Always checking for the wounds he'd had so long ago. Now, Simon understood.

"I know what's going to happen," Dee said and she was so close to the flames. He wanted to haul her back, to force her behind him, but this time, this moment was hers. And he'd follow wherever she took him.

"You believe in your prophets." She lifted her hands high. "I believe in my witch."

Unease flickered over Grim's face and the vampires began to move in closer. Not closer to the fire, but closer to Grim. For his protection? Or—

"She scryed to see how this fight would end."

Uh, yeah, and that shit hadn't been so positive. Simon swallowed and ignored the fierce throbbing in the back of his legs. The blisters would heal, eventually, *if* they survived this night.

"Catalina knew she would die in the fire. That's why she was running when your men caught her."

Grim's eyes widened, just a bit.

"Grim!" Nina's voice screeched. "Let's just kill them, now, let's—"

"She saw you die." Dee's finger lifted and pointed at the Ignitor.

"The hell you say! *You* die, you—"

The shadows seemed to grab her. Nina's words choked off and a thin line of red appeared on her neck.

"Your throat gets cut," Dee said, just as Nina's body fell to the ground.

The flames sputtered away.

The shadow—it was Zane. Standing there, body trembling as he stared down at the woman.

"I saw death. Zane was surrounded by flames. I burned. Nina—her throat was cut." Catalina's sad voice drifted through his mind.

But no, after that, she'd said—

"You die, Dee." The whisper of her words filled his head even as Dee sprang forward and said—

"You die, Grim. You. Die!"

Grim came at her with fury, meeting her armed with the stake she'd used on him.

He drove that stake right at her chest.

"No!"

But Dee was ready. She spun away from the vamp, and the stake grazed her side, not her heart.

Simon grabbed Grim and wrestled the bastard to the ground. He ignored the claws and teeth and fought to hold the Born when he buckled, struggling to keep him pinned as—

"You die," Dee whispered again and she had a stake in her hands. The stake she'd taken from Simon when his arms were locked around her and no one could see. The stake had been hidden near his waist, just waiting for her.

Grim lurched up.

She shoved the stake into his chest.

Grim's eyes flared wide and he sucked in a sharp breath.

Then he smiled. "True," he whispered, and blood spilled from his lips. "Both . . . right . . ."

The bastard smiled, and died.

Grim's vampires inched forward.

Simon glared at them. "Your choice. Die with him or get the hell out of here."

They stared back at him.

"My mother . . ." One whispered. "He made me . . ."

"My wife . . ." From another.

"My son." Grief. Fury. "I begged him, but I couldn't stop him!"

Not born monsters. We are what we become.

Simon stared back down at Grim's still face. Once, Grim had just been a man, too. A man betrayed who'd woken to the power of a near god.

Dee's fingers slowly loosened their death grip on the stake. Her breath exhaled on a hard sigh. She trembled.

Grim's lashes were closed. His lips unmoving. No heartbeat. No breath.

Death.

Simon took Dee's shoulders and pulled her away from the vampire. Over. Finally.

"Dee?"

He caught a scent then. A wild, fierce scent in the night. *Animal.*

No, shifter. Jude had to be close. More of the cavalry, but coming too late this time.

The vampires stilled, and he saw their eyes dart to the shadows. They knew when they were being hunted. Fear trickled into their dark gazes.

Then they bolted.

Not as dumb as he'd thought. Just lost, like he'd been.

"Is he dead?" Zane wasn't looking at them. His eyes stayed on Nina's body and his shoulders hunched.

The stake was buried in Grim's heart. The bastard wasn't so much as twitching. Yep, looked dead.

He pulled Dee toward him. "Sonofabitch, woman, you scared me! Catalina didn't tell us Grim would die, she said you—"

Her knees buckled and Simon saw her chest—saw the blood that covered her. "Dee?"

A stake. A fucking stake. She'd gotten the Born, but he'd taken his death blow.

Both . . . right.

Because they were both dying.

Her lashes fell closed. No, no, screw that. Simon grabbed the stake and yanked it from her chest. She was still breathing. Her heart still beating. The stake had missed its mark, it had missed! She wasn't going to die, no, she wasn't going to—

"Easy." Zane's hoarse voice ordered and Simon realized he'd been screaming. Begging.

"*Live,*" Simon whispered now.

Grim had missed her heart. He could hear Dee's heart beating. She'd be all right. She just needed blood. She just needed—

Her lashes lifted. Such dark eyes. Weak, but, still Dee.

"I will," she promised. "I will."

He crushed his lips onto hers and kissed the woman as hard and deep as he could.

Surrounded by death, but she was alive.

He leaned his forehead against hers and just held her.

"Missed . . . heart . . . barely . . ." she breathed the words.

"You just scared the hell out of me," Zane snapped.

And she'd nearly killed him.

"Over," she said, whisper soft. "He can't hurt us anymore."

The voice was gone from his mind. The link cut. "Let's get out of here." Away from the death and back to the life that waited for them.

But Dee shook her head and glanced toward Grim. "Always come back . . ." Her hand lifted to her shoulder. Pressed hard. "They always . . . come back."

"Not this time." Catalina's certain voice.

She came from the darkness. Soot and blood covered her clothes. Jude walked at her side, clad in a pair of jeans, and his woman held the witch's arm, helping her to walk. "This time," Catalina said again, "he'll stay down."

She stopped near his body. Catalina stepped away from the shifters and lifted her arms. Her chant came, quick but soft, and the wind stirred.

Power. Licking in the air. So much power.

And not all of it was from the positive source a witch should use. Simon felt the taint of darkness, saw it reflected in Catalina's eyes.

Changed.

Grim had left his mark on another victim.

A ball of fire exploded—no, *Grim's* body exploded into flames. Burned and burned until nothing was left.

Not even ash.

"Guess he won't be coming back from . . . that," Dee managed and they watched the fire sputter.

No, he damn well wouldn't.

A reminder never to piss off a witch.

Bye, asshole. Have fun in hell.

"I didn't die." Dee felt like she'd been hit by a bus or a stake. But then, she had. She winced as she lowered her body onto the chair that Simon had pulled out from who the hell knew where.

Catalina stood a few feet away, rocking back and forth, her eyes on the ashes that fluttered up into the sky.

A cleanup team was en route. Pak's teams always moved fast. Soon, nothing would be left of this place.

Just the memories of what had been.

"Did you hear me, Cat?" Yeah, good, her voice was getting stronger because the blood flow had finally stopped. "Your future was wrong. I didn't die. I'm sitting right here, I'm—"

Catalina finally looked her way. "The night's not over."

Well, shit. Wasn't she a ball of sunshine? Not that Cat really liked sunshine these days. Dee blinked. "Uh, you're still alive, too."

A shiver worked over Cat's body. "Doesn't feel that way."

"No." Softer now as she thought about exactly what Catalina might have gone through. How long she'd been with Grim and his little fire-loving friend. "I guess it doesn't."

Catalina's shoulders squared. "I'm not going back to Baton Rouge."

Not what she'd expected. "Where are you going?"

Her gaze slanted over to the stable. Smoke drifted from the roof. "Somewhere I can forget."

Forgetting wasn't always the answer.

"I shouldn't have left you," Catalina said. "You needed me. I-I shouldn't have run."

"It wasn't your fight."

A steady stare. "Wasn't it?"

Dee swallowed. "How long—" She had to ask.

"I'd just left the parking lot. They got me—" She cleared her throat. "It was fast."

"And the spells? What all did Grim want?"

Catalina's eyes darted to the men. Zane and Simon were standing in front of the house. Simon's gaze kept coming back to Dee. Checking her. Watching.

He'd forced her to drink from him. A good thing because without the blood, she'd have fallen on her face.

"He wanted Simon to kill you."

Dee met Simon's gaze.

"Grim wanted me to send out a command spell. One that would force Simon to act."

"And you didn't." Catalina might not have stayed to fight, but the woman had guts. She'd held out against Grim and she'd—

"And I did." Dee's stare came back to her just as Catalina's head sank.

Wow. Hadn't expected that. "Then why am I still breathing?"

"Because he loves you."

It felt like another stake had been plunged into her chest. Only this time, it found its mark in her heart. "You don't—"

"He should have killed you. He should have turned on you and joined Grim. You would have died. I would have died. Everything I saw would have come true." A hard rasp of breath. "But he fought my spell and he fought Grim."

"He wanted his vengeance. His freedom." That was why he'd fought so hard. Not for—

I'll fucking love you forever. The words she'd never forget.

"He wanted you."

She glanced back at him.

His gaze bored into her. So much heat. Need.

Was her own stare like that?

"For you, he'd fight magic and monsters."

He had.

Catalina turned away. "I-I'm going . . . tell Zane."

"You tell him." Those two had some complicated crap going on.

"I'm not what he needs. Or what he wants." Sadness there. An ache. "I saw his future. She's not me."

"You've been wrong once already," Dee reminded her, and she tore her gaze from Simon. Catalina couldn't just leave. She belonged with them.

But Catalina didn't look back and her head shook once, slowly. "Didn't you hear me, Dee? The night's not over yet."

Her lips parted, but Dee had no idea what to say. *What more could happen?*

"I saw you." Catalina's voice drifted back to her. "Surrounded by vampires. No way out. *No. Way. Out.*"

Understanding finally hit. Catalina had never said that Grim took her out.

The others—they were the ones she needed to fear.

They went back to the same seedy motel. They could have stayed at the scene, made sure Pak's team arrived, but screw that. Dee was about to fall on her face and taking care of her was Simon's priority.

She'd taken blood from him at the scene. Not too much. Just enough to kick-start her healing, and then she'd stared around at the darkness, worry in her eyes.

The big, bad bastard was dead. What did she have to worry about?

She shuffled into the room before him, wrinkling her nose. "I smell like death." Common, for many vampires, but not for her.

Never her.

She stripped, right there, even before he'd slammed the motel room door shut, and Simon just took a minute to enjoy the view. World class, really.

Then she headed for the bathroom and his gaze followed her ass. Dimples. Nice, lick-me dimples right at the top of that curve.

He took a step to follow her.

The lady kicked the door closed.

Okay.

The shower blasted on, the roar of the water easily penetrating through the thin door.

Simon hesitated, his eyes on that door. She'd shut him out, so that clearly said she didn't want him stripping and joining her for some water fun.

But there'd been something in her eyes since Grim's death. Not fear. Yeah, worry, but—

Pain. More than just the physical wounds.

He locked the motel room door and strode toward the bathroom. His knuckles rapped against the door. "Dee?"

No answer.

His hand dropped to the doorknob. If she told him to fuck off, he'd leave her in peace. But if she was in there, hurting, he wasn't going to walk away.

He turned the knob and stepped inside. Steam had begun to rise and to drift lazily in the air, but Dee hadn't entered the shower yet. She stood near the tub, head bowed, shoulders hunched.

"Dee?" He said her name again, softer.

She glanced back at him and the sight of tears on her face was a punch right in his gut. "It didn't make any difference."

What? Fuck, but now he *hurt*. He grabbed her arms and yanked her against his chest. "Babe, what's—"

"I thought killing him would make some of the pain stop. That it would give me some peace." A hard swallow. "But when I close my eyes, I still see them."

Them. Her family. Simon blew out a breath and held her even tighter. "I know." He did. Because there was still a hole in his heart for his family. A hole that vengeance hadn't healed.

"My fault." A whisper. Stark.

The water fell in a hard stream.

"Nothing that happened was your fault. Not then. Not now."

She tilted her face up to look at him. "They died because of what I am."

"*No.*" Absolutely certain. "They died because some sick freak believed he was going to change the future."

She paled a bit at that. "You really think the future's set? That the prophets out there aren't bullshitting?"

Careful now, because he'd heard Catalina's last words to her. Not that he'd let that come to pass. "I think Grim sealed his fate a long time ago."

Her hand pressed against his chest. "And what about your parents? Did killing Grim bring you peace?"

"Not peace." Never that. "But justice."

She gave a slow nod. "Justice. It still feels empty." Her lip began to tremble then. Tough Dee, who could face down a Born and send him to the devil with a grin. "I'd rather have just had . . . them."

The woman was breaking his heart. He tucked her head against his chest and held her as the water poured. "I know."

He let her cry. The tears she'd kept inside over the years. The tears she'd stopped shedding once she began fighting.

When the tears finally stopped, he lifted her and carried her to the shower. It was time to wash away the pain and the past.

Maybe, just maybe, it was time for them to begin again.

They didn't talk in the shower. Simon stripped and joined her. The water beat on them and washed away the blood and the battle.

And they didn't talk.

He carried her to the bedroom, put her in the middle of the bed.

The water glistened on her skin and her eyes, so very dark, met his.

Then she parted her legs.

He came down beside her, putting a stranglehold on his need. This time wouldn't be about heat and desperation.

This time, he'd give her something more.

Because that's what she'd given him.

His lips touched hers. A light, fleeting kiss. Simple. Soft.

His fingers trailed over her body. Caressed her breasts, the nipples that hardened beneath his fingers.

"I want to forget." Her whisper.

The first thing she'd said.

His cock, fully swollen and thick with need, pressed against her leg. Forgetting—fleeting. The memories would come back. They always did. But he'd give her this.

Hell, he'd give her anything she wanted.

He wouldn't rush. Because he needed, too. Her taste . . .

He kissed his way down her neck. Licked the scars from her past battle. Tasted her nipples and sucked her flesh into his mouth. She twisted beneath him, rising and pulling in a quick breath.

And, finally, *finally,* the scent of her arousal began to fill the air.

Because he'd never take her when she didn't want him.

His fingers slipped between her parted thighs, found the hot flesh, and eased into her.

This was what he wanted.

Her eyes turned to black.

He licked a path down her stomach. Blew lightly over the blond curls that hid her pink flesh.

"Simon . . ."

He'd always liked the way she said his name, especially when she wanted him. That hitch, the way the end of his name sounded like a moan on her lips.

He put his mouth against her. Took her cream on his tongue and tasted her flesh.

Her hips arched against him, a helpless jerk of her body. His tongue slipped over her clit. Her gasp filled his ears.

When her fingers sank into his hair, he knew she wanted more. Wanted harder. Faster.

Wanted to come.

"Not yet." He said the words against her sex and she shuddered. The pleasure wouldn't be fleeting. Not for either of them. It was time she learned that.

His lips closed around the swollen button of her desire, and he sucked, using lips and tongue to give and to take.

Her moan broke.

He gave to her, slowly. Learning every curve. Exploring her flesh. His tongue drove into her and her legs shook. He licked her. Lapped at her and wanted more.

Everything.

"Simon, I'm going to come!"

No. Not yet.

He eased back and his fingers worked her flesh. Drawing out the release, making the desire build with soft strokes and deep plunges of his fingers.

His cock twitched. The need for her was so fierce he burned.

Bite.

The bloodlust was there, as it always was, because he didn't just want her body. He wanted her blood. Her heart.

Everything.

And he would have it.

She twisted against the sheets. The water had dried from her skin and her breasts thrust up against him.

So pretty. So perfect.

He caught her nipple with his mouth. Sucked deep and hard.

She squirmed beneath him.

Not about forgetting any longer. About them.

She'd remember that.

One last lick, and he lifted his head. Her eyes had gone blind with need and black with desire.

He positioned his cock against her slick heat. Pushed the head inside, just a few inches.

Waited.

Her gaze met his.

Simon caught her hands. He threaded his fingers through hers and pinned her against the mattress.

He took her then. Thrust deep and sure and felt the sensual heat of her sex around him.

His teeth clenched and he reined in the beast—tried to, anyway.

Her legs wrapped around him, and her ankles dug into his ass.

More. There, in her eyes. What she wanted—

He withdrew. Thrust deep. Again and again. The bed rocked. Their bodies trembled, but he took his time and he took his pleasure.

And made damn sure she took hers.

Bite.

He didn't look at her neck. Didn't take his gaze from hers. This time would be different. It had to be.

Her sex squeezed him and the telltale ripple had his spine tingling.

He thrust harder. Faster. The control began to disappear, and the need, that blind, consuming need, had his breath heaving and his hips surging.

She came, the contractions of her sex making his own climax erupt as he pumped into her. The long, hot wave blasted through him, into her, and the pleasure stole his breath.

Still he thrust. Even as his cock jerked and he climaxed inside her, he thrust.

Harder, but slower. Deeper.

His fingers tightened around hers.

She whispered his name.

And came again.

Sweet fucking hell.

Yeah, he'd die for this woman. In a heartbeat.

They began to gather in the darkness. First, just a few. Two. Then three. They came together silently as they felt the psychic snap of the old connection.

The bond was gone. The Born dead.

One there knew his killer. A vampire who'd seen the woman kill Grim.

Vengeance?

A life for a life?

Slowly, the others came. Humans once. Killers, monsters now.

They waited.

More would come.

Chapter 17

"Why didn't you ask me about the asshole in the alley?" Dee forced her head to lift at Simon's question. Really, she just wanted to lay there, her head pillowed on his chest, and listen to the steady beat of his heart. But maybe they needed to go ahead and have this, um, little talk.

She met his stare and her shoulders tensed a bit as she asked, "Why didn't you tell *me*?"

"Because I thought you'd run from me or try to stake me if you knew the truth."

"The truth?" One eyebrow rose. "You mean the fact that you paid a killer to shoot me—"

"I paid him to *miss*."

She knew that, but . . . "Can't really trust guys like that, you know. Sometimes, they'll take your money and shoot whoever they want."

His fingers trailed down her back and rested at the base of her spine. "That's why I made sure I was between you and the gun, every single moment." His jaw hardened. "You know what happened to him."

Actually, no, she didn't know that part. She wasn't some kind of all seeing, walking, talking crystal ball. All she'd had were glimpses. Snatches of conversation. His memories. The few that had filtered through the blood link. What became of Mr. Trigger Happy, she had no idea. So she just stared back at Simon and waited.

"There wasn't a choice, Dee. He forced my hand."

Ah, one of those stories that wasn't going to end well.

"Frankie came after me, okay? He shot me in the back and would have killed me—"

"Wait." Her eyes narrowed. "Frankie?" The guy's face flashed before her eyes. Broad features. Balding hair. "Frankie Lee?" She should have put those pieces together sooner.

"Yeah."

She whistled and drummed her fingers on his chest. "Went big-time slumming, huh?" Word on the street was that Frankie would shoot his own mother—and, actually, had—for a quick grand.

"He came after me," Simon repeated, his face tense. "There wasn't a choice."

Silence for a moment, then Dee ventured, "I'm guessing old Frankie won't be taking any more hits."

His palm pressed harder against her back. "I swear I didn't pay him to kill you. I wouldn't have done that!"

"But you didn't even know me then. I was just a hunter to you, another—"

"You were everything." Rasped. His eyes blazed at her. "You still are."

What did a woman say to that? Dee pulled away from him and reached for the sheet. She just needed to cover up, to take a second to think.

He grabbed her wrist. "You don't want to hear about how I feel, do you? Too damn bad, babe." His thumb rubbed over her pulse point. "You know I came after you because I thought you'd take down Grim."

And she had. A point for the good guys. Well, semi–good guys, anyway. "I know you wanted to be free, you've already—"

"I wanted you. Want you." Simon shook his head. "From the moment I saw you, I wanted you."

Fair enough. She'd wanted to jump him, too. He'd tackled her; she'd wanted to return the favor.

"I thought it was just lust, Dee. That I could take you, enjoy you, and walk away."

Kind of hard not to flinch at that one. With her left hand, she jerked the sheet up to her chin. Simon held tight to her right wrist. "So you were using me for sex and death?" Grim's death. No getting around she'd been a means to an end there. But she'd thought there might be more. *He'd* made her think that.

I'll fucking love you forever.

Say it again.

But now the guy wasn't talking rose petals and sunsets.

"I knew I was lost." He brought her hand to his mouth and kissed the flesh of her palm. "When you died in my arms."

Okay, she definitely flinched. Not her best memory.

"I wanted to change you. You were dying in front of me, and I *knew* you were supposed to be a Born. Catalina had told me about you."

Had she really thanked the witch properly for that? Nah. She hadn't let Cat know how much she appreciated the woman's secrecy. Payback, um, gratitude would come eventually.

"You weren't going to stay dead."

Who did these days?

"You weren't supposed to stay dead," he amended. "But I was shit-scared and when your eyes closed, I wanted to change you."

Her heart stilled at that.

"I wanted it so fucking much." Another hot kiss against her palm.

"But you didn't try." No bite. No exchange of blood.

"No." His breath blew against her flesh. "Because if I was wrong about you, if the witch and that damn seer were wrong, I wasn't about to make you into the thing you hated."

And she had hated the idea of vampirism. Becoming a vampire had once been her worst nightmare. Strange, because now, things all seemed so different.

"If you were dying, I wasn't going to make you come back

to me. That was the hardest thing I ever did." His lips thinned. "Watching you die and not knowing if you'd ever open your eyes again."

The last thing she'd seen had been him. "You left me." The words came out as an accusation and she realized that, yeah, that had bothered her. No matter what was going on between them, no matter what secrets he'd kept—and she'd known there were secrets even then—she'd expected him to stay with her.

"I thought I was the last person you'd want to see."

He'd been the one she wanted the most.

"I knew you needed time to adjust. Seeing me . . . I was afraid it would push you too much." His gaze held hers. "But then you came to me."

Sex.

Blood.

So much hunger.

"You weren't afraid of me," he said.

"I was afraid of myself." A stark confession, one she should have given sooner. "I didn't want to become—"

Like Grim.

Like Leo.

Like so many of the others she'd taken down over the years.

Not a monster. She hadn't wanted to be a woman ruled by the bloodlust and lost to humanity.

"You have the control, Dee. You're not going to turn and start killing innocents." He freed her hand and rose, moving slowly away from her. "That's not going to happen with you. There's no Born to take over your mind. No one to force you. There's just . . . you."

It had been just her for years. Maybe she was tired of that. She wrapped the sheet around her body. "So what happens now?" Did she go back to Night Watch? Keep hunting? While he—what? Got the hell out of town as fast as he could?

Just . . . you.

She'd be left alone? Again?

Only this time, she wouldn't be looking at a few empty years before her. She'd be looking at forever.

Without him.

Shit. When had the vampire started to mean so much? Because she couldn't breathe without tasting him. She wanted his touch, his mouth, his blood. Him. Always him.

"Pity we didn't meet before," she whispered. *What would life have been like?*

She glanced over, saw him hauling on a pair of jeans. He froze at her words, then gritted, "I wish to hell we had."

So did she. "Simon . . ." What could she say? Her eyes drifted over him. Broad, strong shoulders. Muscled chest. Slim hips. So sexy. So—

Simon.

Vampire. Man.

Hers.

Dee's breath caught. "You—you came to me because you thought I'd stop Grim."

A nod.

"But if you just wanted to be free of him, why did you keep putting yourself between me and—" Everything. Everyone. "I can take care of myself, you know. You don't have to jump in front of me every time things get a little dicey." A very bad habit he seemed to have there.

He snapped the button on the jeans. Yanked up the zipper. Denied her the too pleasing sight of his still aroused flesh. "I was protecting you because you're mine to protect."

Okay, now she was nearly cutting the sheet with her death grip.

His eyes narrowed and he stalked around the edge of the bed. "You want to clear the air about what's happening here? Okay. Fine."

Uh, maybe she should yank on some clothes, too. She reached for her shirt. He grabbed her arms and pulled her against him. "This is a fuck-off talk, isn't it? One dressed up in some kind of nice, polite chitchat."

His eyes turned to black.

"I never told you to fuck off," she managed, voice quiet.

"*Yet.*" His fingers tightened around her. "I protected you because you were mine to protect, got it? I knew I wanted you from the beginning." He kissed her, hard, deep, and had her nipples tightening, her sex clenching, and her toes curling. *Oh, yeah.* "Mine," he gritted again. "I wasn't going to let anyone—Grim, your demon friend, or even your witch—stand between us."

No one was between them now. Only the thin sheet.

"The start was screwed-up." His chin lifted. "I'm not denying that. Yeah, I lied. Yeah, I tricked you. But I'm also the man who was ready to die for you. I'm the—"

"You said you loved me." She threw out the words.

His eyes glittered down at her.

Dee took a deep breath and tasted him. *I'll fucking love you forever.*

Until Simon, no man had ever said that to her and meant it. Sure, guys would claim love all the time if they thought a quick lay was coming.

He licked his lips. "I did."

"You meant it?" And she meant for her words to come out as a statement, not a question.

His hand rose, the strong fingers curling around her jaw. "I meant it."

Not a lie. Not some trick to get her help. The pressure on her chest eased and warmth spilled inside her. "I want to hear you say the words again." Because she could be stubborn, too. Neither one of them was perfect. Far, far from it.

"I. Love. You." Almost angry.

Her heart slammed into her ribs. Standing so close, having his vamp powers, he had to feel the sudden kick. She swallowed. "Th-that's good—"

"No, it's not." Definitely angry. "It's shit. It's me, thinking about you, all the time. Me, wanting you, every damn minute. Me, not being able to even breathe without tasting you."

"I feel the—"

"I want to make you smile. Want to make you laugh. Because you know what, Dee? You don't laugh. *You don't.* And you should, babe. Cause you're beautiful when you smile and when you laugh, I bet you'd take my breath away."

He'd just taken hers.

"I want you naked, yeah. *Hell yeah.* But I want to hold you in the morning. Want to talk to you in the darkness. I want to look at all the days that are coming and know I'll be spending them with you. Because if I know that, then forever sure doesn't seem like such a bad deal."

Not bad at all.

He glared down at her. "I want all that. I want you. Right now, I'm scared because I think you're about to tell me to get out because from the moment that I came into your life, I've just brought you trouble, while you've brought me . . . everything."

Oh.

He sucked in a breath, and stepped back, releasing her. "I'm not going to force you to stay with me. I couldn't, even if you weren't strong enough to kick my ass."

Her lips wanted to curl. No, she wanted to laugh. For him.

"You want to walk out that door and go back to the life you had before me, then do it." Simon moved aside. "But know this—you won't find another man who loves you like I do. And if you do, I might just have to show up and kick *his* ass." He yanked a hand through his hair. "If you wind up with that demon bastard, ah, Dee—just *don't.*"

Zane.

"We almost slept together once." The admission came out, probably at the wrong time. She always said the wrong thing.

His eyes closed in a slow blink and his face hardened.

"We're friends. Thought maybe we could be more."

His fangs were coming out. A jealous vampire was a dangerous one.

"But we were better friends than anything else. Zane understood me, the anger and pain inside." Because he had the same brew stirring in him.

"Why didn't you sleep with the prick?"

"Because I wanted a friend. Needed one, and I never let my lovers get close." Not even Tony. "Until you."

That had his eyes widening. "What are you saying?"

So hard. Dee inhaled and took a risk. About time for one. "I'm saying I didn't count on falling for you, vampire. I knew you were using me. I thought I'd use you, too." Brutal truth time. They should have that, now. "I couldn't hurt you physically. You could handle my strength and my bloodlust and me."

He just watched her. Dark gaze so steady.

"I never counted on falling for you," she said again, softer now. "That wasn't part of my plan." But she'd gone and fallen anyway. "I taste you, too. I want you, always. I want to protect you. Fight for you. I want you in the dark. Even in the light." Though it seemed like she'd had little light in her life. Maybe that would change now. Who would have thought? It might have taken becoming a vampire to see the sunlight.

And to see that sometimes, the best things could be hiding in the darkness.

Not just monsters.

Men.

"I don't want to go back to the way things were before." Cold. Hollow. Pain shadowing her. "I want to try living this time. Really living, and I don't want to be alone."

His lips parted. "Don't tease, babe, just don't fuckin—"

"You're not perfect, Simon Chase. We both know you're a liar and a dirty fighter." She smiled now. A big, wide smile. For her. For him. "Good thing for you, I am, too."

Hope lit his face.

When was the last time she'd felt hope? *Right now.* "I think I love you, vampire." Loving what she'd feared most.

Had Catalina seen this one coming?

No, she'd just seen death.

Dee shoved that thought from her mind. The sun would rise in less than an hour's time. The witch had been wrong.

Life. Love—that was what waited for her. Not death.

Not again.

It was time for her to be happy. With her vampire.

Dee let the sheet fall. "You want forever?"

His gaze slipped over her body. Heated.

"Let's start with right here, this moment, and we'll let forever come later." Right now, she wanted him.

Love.

Scary. But she could handle scary. She'd proven that, and she could handle him.

She lifted her hand and offered her palm. "Stay with me?" *Love me?*

His fingers curled around hers, warm and strong. "Always."

She had to blink because her eyes were tearing. Silly. "Kiss me."

His lips brushed hers. A tender caress. She knew he could be tender, with her.

When the knock came at the door, she didn't turn from him. Dee pulled him closer.

But Simon tensed against her. His tongue slipped over her lips and his head lifted. "Is that . . ."

She stared up at him. Dawn hadn't come.

She knew the instant he caught the scent. The same scent that already filled her nose.

Catalina is wrong. Wrong.

But Simon was already spinning away from her. Grabbing her jeans and a shirt and tossing them to her before he turned to the door, fangs bared.

"Since when does evil knock?" She asked him, only half-kidding because a knot was tightening in her belly. *This close.* She'd come so close to being happy.

Should have known fate would screw her over again.

Dee pulled the shirt over her head and shimmied into the jeans. "Why aren't they kicking the door down?" And it was them. She could smell 'em. At least five vampires. Six?

You were surrounded. Catalina's stupid words wouldn't stop playing in her mind.

Simon shook his head. "I don't know."

Not like vampires were into playing nice.

He grabbed their weapons, tossed her a stake, then reached for the door knob.

"Simon!"

A pause, then he glanced back at her. Dee wet her lips and said, "I really do love you." That regret wouldn't be with her, no matter what was waiting out there. She'd tell him how she felt.

Like she hadn't been able to tell her family.

"Why do I still feel like you're saying good-bye?" His fingers hesitated over the knob.

Because I could be.

No, no, Catalina was wrong. "Do you think our futures are set? That what witches and demons see, those images are the only future we can have?"

"Hell, no," Simon said immediately. "I don't give a shit what they see. I know my future." His stare could have burned a lesser woman. It just made her blood heat. "I'm looking right at her." He jerked his thumb toward the door. "Once these assholes out here are gone, I'll be taking her again, too."

That sounded like one fine plan. Now if the fear in her belly would just go away.

"Forever, Dee. Forever starts now."

He yanked open the door.

No one waited outside. Just the odor of the vamps, drifting on the wind. A warning? Had they been trying to scare her?

She stalked to Simon's side. In the distance, she could just make out the faint pink rays of dawn.

I'm not going to die tonight. "What's happening?"

Simon crept out of the room. The parking lot waited to the right. It looked deserted.

Like she didn't know how very deceiving looks could be.

"Grim's men?" she asked. He'd know. He had a better lock on them than she did. Sure, the link to the master was severed, but there was still a connection between his Taken.

And the guy had grown a whole freaking army.

Will they all come after me? Is this just the beginning?

The men stepped from the waning shadows. Two. Three.

A woman rose from the darkness. Another stalked to her side.

Or is this the end?

A hot wind blew against Dee's face as she stood in the doorway. These weren't Born vampires. All were Taken. She was stronger, even if she was newer to the Undead world. She could handle them.

Simon's shoulder brushed hers. No, *they* could handle them.

Her fingers tightened around the stake.

Two more vampires appeared.

What the hell was this? Some kind of vamp convention? A human was going to look out one of those dirty windows and see them, and the local deputies would swarm this place.

It wasn't so easy to keep things quiet when the sirens started blaring.

"You came after the wrong woman," Dee told them, letting her voice ring out. *I was so close to being happy.*

Stupid. She couldn't even have a minute's worth of happiness. They were always going to hunt her, just as she'd hunted them. Always.

The vampires bowed their heads and turned their hands out, showing her their empty palms. Right, like vamps needed weapons to kill.

"We're not here to fight you," one of the women called out, not lifting her head.

"Of course. You're just here to wish me a good freaking morning." Hurry up, sun, rise. Stupid prediction.

"Born."

"Slayed Grim."

The whispers drifted to her.

Dee inched forward. Simon stayed right beside her.

"Your good old leader Grim deserved the death he got." Actually, he'd probably deserved a much more painful death, but she didn't exactly have the do-over option. "He was a sick freak and he needed to be put down." Probably not what these vamps were looking to hear.

Tough. She wasn't going to sugarcoat. Her eyes scanned the lot. Okay, that made seven total. She and Simon could take them.

"We're not here to kill you." The vampire still didn't look up. Dee realized the vamps had formed a semicircle around her room. She tensed.

Simon has my back. And he did. He stood with her, strong and steady.

"Good," she told them, determination firing her blood. "Because I'm not dying today." No, she wouldn't. She'd just found something to live for and she wasn't about to give it up.

Screw off, Catalina.

"Are we?" The quiet question floated in the air.

Her brows snapped together and Dee glanced at Simon. A quick, fast glance.

Surrounded. It hit her then. Vampires surrounded her.

But Simon was one of those vamps, and she trusted him. With her life and her heart.

"Are you going to kill us?" the woman asked, still not looking Dee's way. Her long blond hair covered her face. Dee stared at her, a chill skating its way down her spine.

"That depends." *Let's try for some honesty.* "If you're twisted like Grim and you get off on hurting humans, then, yeah, I'll come after you. It's what I do." That wouldn't change. She'd seen too many innocents die. No way would she let a killer walk.

"And you think some vampires can live . . . without hurting others?"

Before, she hadn't. But she'd been blinded by her own rage then. She was finally starting to see straight now; it had just taken dying to open her eyes. "Yeah, I do." Her fingers were wrapped so tightly around the stake that the wood bit into her flesh.

She stared at the line of bodies and wondered who would move first. Who would attack.

Dee wouldn't draw first blood, but she would make sure she drew the last drops.

"We waited for you." The woman looked at her then. A long scar cut across her cheek. A scar she must have gotten long ago. In another life. "Waiting was so hard . . ."

"We've been waiting for you, Sandra Dee . . ." Words from that terrible night. Grim's men. Waiting for her death.

But these vampires had been waiting, too—for what? Her eyes narrowed as she watched them.

Born.

They'd been waiting for her to free them.

The vampires began to drift away.

Simon's hands settled on her shoulders. "I told you, Dee. Sometimes, monsters are made."

And sometimes they were Taken.

A tear tracked down the woman's cheek. "My son . . ."

That was all she had to say. Dee understood. Grim had played his twisted games with everyone.

"You won't see me again," the vampiress told her. "Not any of us." Her chin lifted. Pride there. Strength. "We're more than the evil that people think."

But people had been fearing vampires for centuries.

And forgetting that once upon a time, vampires were people, too. She'd forgotten that. No, she hadn't wanted to remember.

The vampires faded as the sun rose. Dee watched them, silent.

Simon stood with her as the sun inched across the sky. Dawn was such a beautiful thing. Pity she hadn't enjoyed the sunrises more.

"We should go inside. Get some rest."

Because another night would come. Another. Always another.

With more darkness to fight.

Dee reached for him and rubbed her fingers over the hard line of his jaw. She wouldn't be fighting alone anymore. No, her vamp would be at her side.

She'd be at his.

The darkness could come. They'd be ready.

They'd kick ass.

Make love.

And live for-damn-ever.

Death hadn't come for her. Catalina had been wrong.

No, maybe she'd been right. As she stared at Simon in the growing morning light, Dee knew her old life had ended. But a new life . . .

It waited for her.

All she had to do was reach out and take it.

She kept the stake in her right hand and curled her arm around Simon's neck.

Then she kissed him in the sunlight. Just as she'd kiss him in the moonlight.

Sometimes, a woman had to make her own happy ending.

And, sometimes, she had to leave room for a little bit of hunting on the side.

Because you had to keep life interesting, and after all, someone had to stop the bad guys.

She'd slay them all, soon enough.

But first, she'd take her vampire and, as he'd promised, he'd take her.

For-damn-ever.

If you liked this book, go out and get Emma Lang's
RUTHLESS HEART, out now . . .

Grady had never met a woman like Eliza, if that was even really her name. She talked like a professor, rode around with twenty pounds of books, and could build a campfire like nobody's business. Yet she was as innocent as a child, had a sad story about a dead husband he didn't believe for a second, and seemed to be waiting for him to invite her along for his hunt.

He snorted at the thought. Grady worked alone, always and for good. There sure as hell was no room for anyone, much less a woman like Eliza.

He had damn well tried his best to shake the woman, but the blue-eyed raven-haired fool wouldn't budge. Truth be told, he was impressed by her bravado, but disgusted by his inability to shake her off his tail the night before. Rather than risk having her do the same thing again, he decided to ride like hell and leave her behind. He should have felt guilty, but he'd left that emotion behind, along with most every other, a long time go. Grady had a job to complete and that was all that mattered to him.

The only thing he was concerned about was finding the two wayward wives he'd been hired to hunt and making sure they regretted leaving their husband, at least for the five seconds they lived after he found them.

Grady learned as a young man just how much he couldn't trust the fairer sex. His mother had been his teacher, and he'd been a very astute pupil. No doubt if she hadn't drunk herself to death, she'd still be out there somewhere taking advantage of and using men as she saw fit.

The cool morning air gave way to warm sunshine within a few hours. He refused to think about what the schoolmarm was doing, or if anything had been done to her. If she could take care of her horse and build a fire, she could take care of herself. Food could be gotten at any small town, but then again maybe she could hunt and fish too.

Somehow it wouldn't surprise him if she did. The woman seemed to have a library in her head. Against his will, the sight of her unbound black hair popped into his head. It had been long, past her waist to brush against the nicely curved backside. Grady preferred his women with some meat on their bones, better to hang onto when he had one beneath him, or riding him. He shifted in the saddle as his dick woke up at the thought of Eliza's dark curtain of hair brushing his bare skin.

Jesus Christ, he sure didn't need to be thinking about fucking the wayward Miss Eliza. If she was a widow, no doubt she'd had experience in bed with a man. It wasn't Grady's business of course, so he needed to stop his brain from getting into her bloomers, or any parts of her anatomy.

As the morning wore on, Grady's mind returned to the contents of her bags. The woman didn't have a lick of common sense and fell asleep, vulnerable and unprotected. Good thing he didn't have any bad thoughts on his mind or she wouldn't have been sleeping. She even snored a little, something he found highly amusing as he'd rifled through her things.

Her smaller bag had contained a hodgepodge of clothes, each uglier and frumpier than the last, a hairbrush, half a dozen biscuits in a tattered napkin and some hairpins. A measly collection of a woman's life, and quite pitiful if that was all she had. Perhaps she'd been at least partially truthful about taking everything she owned and hitting the trail. Her husband must have been a poor excuse for a provider if this collection of tags was all she had.

The bag of books was just that, a bag stuffed full of scientific texts ranging from medical topics to some titles he couldn't even pronounce. In the bottom of the bag was a battered copy of *Wuthering Heights*. He didn't know what it was but it was much smaller than the other books, likely a novel. She obviously put the spectacles to good use judging by the two dozen tomes she had in her bag. He wondered how she'd gotten it up on the saddle in the first place.

"Fool." He had to stop thinking about Eliza and what she was doing and why. Grady would never see her again.

As a child, Grady learned very early not to care or ask questions. It only bought him a cuff on the ear or a boot in the ass. A boy could only take so much of that before he kept his mouth shut and simply snuck around to find out what he needed to know.

As a young man, it served him well and garnered the attention of the man who taught him how to hunt and kill people in the quickest, most efficient way. Grady had learned his lesson well, even better than his mentor expected. When the job was put before him to hunt and kill the very man who had taught him those very skills, Grady hesitated only a minute before he said yes.

The devil rode on his back, a constant companion he'd come to accept. He didn't need a woman riding there too.

Try THE PIRATE, the latest in Katherine Garbera's Savage Seven series, available now from Brava!

"Excited about your trip?" he asked, stepping out of the shadows.

He was a rough looking man but still attractive. A light beard shadowed his strong, square jaw. His dark hair was shorn close to his head, revealing a scar twisting up the left side of his neck.

As a surgeon, she could tell that whoever had stitched up what she guessed to be a knife wound hadn't been to medical school. As a woman she guessed that Laz hadn't minded, since if the wound hadn't been stitched up he probably would have died.

She'd been single for almost two years now, but this man wasn't like any of the men she'd dated. An aura of danger hovered about him. It might be due to the fact that he captained a crew of men who looked like they'd be better suited to crew Johnny Depp's *Black Pearl* in Disney's *Pirates of the Caribbean*. Or maybe it was due to the fact that when he looked at her, she had the feeling that he looked past the confines of her profession and saw the woman underneath.

"A little nervous, actually."

He laughed, a rough sound that carried on the wind. "Somalia—hell, all of Africa—has that effect on people."

The sea around the tanker seemed calm, and on this moonlit night with no one else on deck, she felt like . . . like they were alone in the world.

"On you?" she asked. She couldn't imagine this man being nervous in any situation, she thought. He radiated the calmness she always experienced when she was in the operating room. It was a calmness born of the fact that he knew what he was doing.

"Nah. I've been around this part of the world for a long time."

"Why is that? You're American, right?"

"Yes I am. But I was never one for staying put. I wanted to see the world." There was a note in his voice that she easily recognized. It said that he was searching for something that he hadn't found. Something that he might never find. She understood that now.

It was funny, but before her divorce she would have thought he was unfocused or didn't know himself well. But now she understood that sometimes life threw a curve and dreams changed and your way was lost. Hers had been. She'd been drifting without a focus and she hoped this summer in Africa would help her to find her way back to who she had been.

Did this rough looking man have dreams? Dreams that she'd be able to relate to? At one point in her not so distant past she would have seen Laz as a man she had nothing in common with. A man whose dreams would make absolutely no sense to her. She no longer looked at the world in the black and white terms as she used to and she guessed she had to thank Paul and his philandering ways for that.

"Well, you are certainly seeing parts of it that are off the beaten path," Daphne said.

She'd spent all of her life taking the safe route. College followed by medical school. Marriage to an up-and-coming lawyer who morphed his successful career into a successful Senate bid. She'd had two children with Paul Maxwell and raised them to be very successful teenagers before Paul decided that it was time to trade her in for a newer model. A microbiologist named Cyndy who didn't have stretch marks.

She shook her head. She wasn't bitter.

Really.

It was just that when Paul had walked away from their marriage he'd broken something that she'd always claimed was her destiny. He'd broken her dreams of a fifty-year wedding anniversary party. Her dreams of being married to the same man for her entire life. And she was still trying to figure out who she was if she wasn't going to be Mrs. Paul Maxwell.

She realized she'd let the conversation lag while she'd been lost in thoughts of her ruined marriage. She looked over at Laz.

"Our group goes to the places that really need aid," she said.

He gave her a half-smile that showed her the dangerous looking man could also be sexy in a rough-hewn sort of way.

"Good for you."

She glanced over at him; it was hard to see much of his features in the dim lighting. "Are you being sarcastic?"

He shrugged. "Not really. I admire people who walk the walk."

She had no idea if he was sincere or not. But she'd always tried to be honest about who she was and what she wanted. She heard the sound of another engine. "Did you hear that?"

"Yes, ma'am. I think you should go below," Laz said, standing up straighter. He tossed his cigarette over the railing.

"Why?"

"Pirates operate in these waters, and Americans are some of their favorite targets. Go below where I know you'll be safe."

She hesitated for a moment but then saw him draw out a handgun. Moonlight glinted off the well-polished steel of his weapon. His entire demeanor changed. He no longer wore an aura of danger. He was danger. She'd think twice about talking to this man if she saw him on the street back home. In fact she'd do her best to avoid him.

Keep an eye out for BEDDING THE ENEMY
by Mary Wine, coming next month . . .

He was staring at her.

Helena looked through her lowered eyelashes at him. He was a Scot and no mistake about it. Held in place around his waist was a great kilt. Folded into pleats that fell longer in the back, his plaid was made up in heather, tan and green. She knew little of the different clans and their tartans but she could see how proud he was. The nobles she passed among scoffed at him but she didn't think he would even cringe if he were to hear their mutters. She didn't think the gossip would make an impact. He looked impenetrable. Strength radiating from him. There was nothing pompous about him, only pure brawn.

Her attention was captivated by him. She had seen other Scots wearing their kilts but there was something more about him. A warm ripple moved across her skin. His doublet had sleeves that were closed, making him look formal, in truth more formal than the brocade-clad men standing near her brother. There wasn't a single gold or silver bead sewn to that doublet but he looked ready to meet his king. It was the slant of his chin, the way he stood.

"You appear to have an admirer, Helena."

Edmund sounded conceited and his friends chuckled. Her brother's words surfaced in her mind and she shifted her gaze to the men standing near her brother. They were poised in perfect poses that showed off their new clothing. One even had a lace-edged handkerchief dangling from one hand.

She suddenly noticed how much of a fiction it was. Edmund didn't believe them to be his friends but he stood jesting with them. Each one of them would sell the other out for the right amount. It was so very sad. Like a sickness you knew would claim their lives but could do nothing about.

"A Scots, no less."

Edmund eyed her. She stared back, unwilling to allow him to see into her thoughts. Annoyance flickered in his eyes when she remained calm. He waved his hands, dismissing her.

She turned quickly before he heard the soft sound of a gasp. She hadn't realized she was holding her breath. It was such a curious reaction. Peeking back across the hall she found the man responsible for invading her thoughts completely. He had a rugged look to him, his cheekbones high and defined. No paint decorated his face. His skin was a healthy tone she hadn't realized she missed so much. He was clean-shaven in contrast to the rumors she'd heard of Scotland's men. Of course, many Englishmen wore beards. But his hair was longer, touching his shoulders and full of curl. It was dark as midnight and she found it quite rakish.

He caught her staring at him. She froze, her heartbeat accelerating. His dark eyes seemed alive even from across the room. His lips twitched up, flashing her a glimpse of strong teeth. He reached up to lightly tug on the corner of his knitted bonnet. She felt connected to him. Her body strangely aware of his, even from so great a distance. Sensations rippled down her spine and into her belly. She sank into a tiny curtsy without thought or consideration. It was a response, pure and simple. Her heart was thumping against her chest and she felt every beat as if time had slowed down.

A woman crossed between them, interrupting her staring. It was enough time for her mind to begin questioning what she was doing. Fluttering her eyelashes, she lowered her gaze, forcing herself to move through the court on slow steps. She ordered herself to not look back. She was warm, warmer than the day warranted. The reaction fascinated her but it also struck a warning bell inside her mind. She should not look back.

But a part of her didn't care for that. It clamored for her to turn and find him again. His eyes were as dark as his hair but lit with some manner of flame. She wanted to know if he was still watching her, wanted to know if she glimpsed the same flames in his eyes that she felt in her cheeks.

Ah yes, but fire burns . . .

Helena smiled. She enjoyed the way she felt, a silly little sort of enjoyment that made her want to giggle. The reason was actually quite simple. The way he looked at her made her feel pretty. Court was full of poetry and lavish compliments, but none of it had touched her. His eyes did. The flicker of appreciation was genuine.

She had never felt such before.

"Good day to ye."

She froze. The man must be half specter to move so quickly. But she wasn't afraid of him. Quite the opposite. Her gaze sought his, curious to see if his eyes continued to fascinate her up close.

She was not disappointed. Her breath froze in her lungs, excitement twisting her belly. His gaze roamed over her face and a pleased expression entered his eyes. In fact it looked a bit like relief.

She was suddenly grateful to Raelin all over again for having freed her of the heavy makeup. The way he looked at her made her feel pretty for the first time in her life.